BOTTLE BORN BLUES

VOLUME 1: THE SPOILS OF WAR TRILOGY

CONOR H. CARTON

For Helene and Hannah

AUTHOR BIO

Conor Carton has a lifelong ambition: to be the greatest space pirate cowboy outlaw wizard in the universe!

Writing is part of the rigorous mental and physical preparation he is undergoing to achieve this goal. In the meanwhile, he's an Irish middle-aged suburbanite who has been married to the same wonderfully understanding woman for decades and has a daughter he adores.

PROLOGUE

THE WAR WAS FINALLY OVER. No one had actually won, and no one had actually lost. It had simply stopped when the woman who had surfed a tsunami of blood across the Systems was swamped by an even bigger wave of blood created by those who opposed her. She had made a desperate dash to the place where her doomsday weapon was held only to die on the threshold. Everyone was so exhausted from the conflict they simply stopped when she was no longer leading the charge.

There were no winners, no triumph, there were clear losers. The bottle born had lost long before the war and continued to lose long after the fighting had stopped. They had lost their freedom, then their energy and finally their natural physical bodies. Developed in vast farms, harvested for their inherent energy, they were the most important and valuable commodity in the inhabited systems situated on the fringes of deep space. Finally, they were realizing their own strength and were ready to get off their knees.

A war that is not lost nor won never ends, it just moves to the shadows and continues without the flash and clash of military battles. Those who had not lost developed new plans that would finally bring them victory. They knew what others had forgotten; to the victor goes *the spoils of war*. The time to leave the shadows and stand in the blazing light of final, absolute victory had arrived.

"WELCOME to the Mengchi Centre for the Promotion of Histor-ical Knowledge. My name's Shakbout and I'll be your guide today."

I always paused after this introduction to gauge the group of visitors and to get ready for another cycle of the winner's history recited by one of the losers. My somewhat slim self never stood out in a crowd—not at a height of two metres, pale skin and dark-red hair, sage-green eyes, and *extraordinarily* ordinary features.

The group I was about to lead on a short tour through the carefully edited and constructed narrative that the Centre preferred to broadcast was the usual spread of off-world tourists and local school students. We were all standing in the entrance hall of the CPHK the place where all tours started. It was a beautiful space, a kilometre long and 750 meters wide, paved with off white slabs that were comfortable to walk on with the main entrance at one end and the gift shop at the other. No visitor ever walked the length directly, they were carefully guided, either by visible guides like me or by more subtle means, to take one of the numerous moving spiral stairways up to the exhibition galleries.

The walls rose for two kilometres up to a ceiling that was a wide spiral up for another two kilometres. The distance did not prevent the details of the decoration of the spiral being easily visible from the floor. Magnifying charms were used to make the distance appear much less than it was. The spiral was decorated with an instantly recognisable and understandable map of the systems. Your eye was gently led around the inhabited system up to where Thiegler itself was right at the edge deep of deep space. It looked as if Thiegler might fall into the dark void which was funny since Thiegler had tried very hard to drag the inhabited systems into a different void.

Every tour started from the same point and followed the same route across the hall. After that they could follows different trails depending on the tour. The Standing Committee was very careful to ensure that the historical narrative that was served up matched the profile of the group. The differences were not obvious unless you went on each tour and heard the shifting emphasis and had the interest in comparing them all to see what was being included and excluded. I had followed each tour and recorded them and spent many hours watching and listening. In the event I was ever asked I would have said it was a training exercise for myself to ensure I could be deployed on any tour. The truth was that I was looking for something and the CPHK was as good a place to search for it as anywhere.

Since everyone looked ready, I started by leading the group over to the imposing—in fact, absolutely astounding—image on the west wall of the lobby. The image was huge, over two meters tall and three meters long, hovered close to but not touching the wall, it was 1.5 metered off the ground and as we assembled in front of it, we all looked up at the exactly the angle that the maker of the image had wanted. Standing at that point it appeared that we all stepped into the image and became an active audience for the event taking placing in front of us. We stood in the doorway of a long rectangular room with rows of columns down each side, each viewer saw different patterns on the columns, I saw something different each time I stepped into the room. I sometimes saw flowers and sometimes I saw blood, once I saw bodies trapped in the columns writhing in pain.

Directly in front of us a handsome woman, no one ever described her a beautiful, dressed in a clearly high-ranking military uniform, was driving a double-headed war axe into the skull of a somewhat fishy-looking lifeform standing before her. She did not look upset or furious or murderous, simply determined. This was a woman clearly doing something that needed to be done.

There was no blood which always disturbed me. There should have been blood, oceans of blood spilling out on the floor of the CPHK. Blood should have been gushing over us as we stood in front of the image. Instead we stood safe and clean in front of it. I started my information fog machine and spoke.

"The creator of this image is unknown. No record has ever been found of who created it, when it was created, where it was displayed, or if it was in fact displayed anywhere before its discovery in a submerged warehouse in Lake Zan following restoration work carried out on the outer banks 150 years ago."

I took the scripted pause before continuing,

"There's some debate about the subject of this image. The most likely suggestion is that it is a scene from the Ranger Cycle, the stories of the gods first told by Oxlus of the Thakaan System. In the centuries that followed more details and stories have been added. It is estimated that at the present time there a fifteen different Ranger Cycles that cover the actions and deeds of over a thousand gods. As you may imagine there has been considerable debate since this image was first discovered which event from the variety of Ranger Cyclers this is. While there is no firm agreement the current majority opinion is that it shows the triumph of Hardleigh, a god from the Olean Ranger Cycle, over the assassin sent by her jealous cousin"

Gazes were riveted. So far, so good. "The image is woven from trapped light, fractured air, and some unidentified crystal dust with an unknown process. This level of magical mastery has arguably not been demonstrated again. The Standing Committee wishes to preserve this image as a unique viewing experience: it should *only* be seen and appreciated in its original form."

I paused, allowing them to study the picture while I waited for *the* question. This time it came from one of the students.

"Can I get a copy of the image?" he asked with that acquisitive tone the question always rests on.

"I'm afraid not, but there's a range of very attractive items available in the gift shop, which we'll visit at the end of the tour." I waited for the regulation two seconds, turned and headed for the stairs; confident the group would follow.

My shadow stayed behind, staring at the image. My shadow was a dangerous mental necessity for me to survive intact in the job. It provided an alternative script, saying words I longed to say but dared not—they had to be voiced somehow or the pressure inside would become so great, I might do something extremely stupid.

My shadow turned to address his group, the shadows of everyone I had every guided through the maze of "almost information" during my time at the Centre. "It's true that the creator of that extraordinary work is unknown, but there's no question as to what this image is—this image of Empress Ingea driving an axe into the unsuspecting head the leader of the Wrexen Federation who had arrived to sign a trade agreement. This action marked the start of the longest, most devastating conflict in the history of the systems. It was the signal to the Imperial Fleet to launch a overwhelming attack on the Wrexen Federation. The Wrexen Federation is better known today as the Sickle Quadrant. When you look at the Empress, you have to admire her— the creator demands it—she's confidently and calmly taking decisive action. A leader in fact, as well as name. The Wrexen Chief has a subtly malicious air about him; clearly, he intended to harm the Empress and she responded with decisive action. That one of the most extraordinary creations in history celebrates one of the most stupidly malicious events in history has to be one of the effective jokes ever played. Best of all the unknown maker makes us all complicit in this action, we are the approving audience for the action." My shadow surveyed the crowd, and all stared back dumbly.

My shadow swallowed a bittersweet smile. "The Standing Committee had a collective *shit fit* upon discovery. It clearly celebrates the moment as a triumph; the image is woven with the most explicit sense of justified pride at the Empress' decisive strength and wisdom. Thiegler was Ingea's home planet, the location for the action. Despite a genuine regret at the unimageable misery and destruction caused by the bottomless greed of the Empress, there is an unavoidable and sneaking pride at the scale of her achievement."

Dramatic pause. My shadow, incidentally, was a total ham when it came to public performances. "The Sickle Quadrant is holding with who knows what creatures—brewed in Ingea's own farms as a last-ditch effort to defeat the Quill Alliance forces—creatures which are still a threat to all lifeforms in the systems to this day. Displaying the image is a dangerously balanced risk, only achievable by the mystery that surrounds it. Allowing the image wider circulation would be a reminder of things best left undisturbed. Ambiguity is a good tactic as it creates breathing space, which allows for utterly breath-taking artistry to emerge and overshadow content." My shadow didn't take questions.

I led the tour group into the Hall of the First Instance. In the short tour this was the first stop, a look at the most development of the most important industry in the combined systems. There was no way to avoid this place on any tour, it was one of the most significant reasons that visitors came to the CPHK. It was also one of the most truthful exhibits in the centre. I led the group to the first exhibit, a large cabinet containing models of strange looking creatures. Some were cut in half to display internal arrangements, others appeared to be wrapped or bound in an assortment of cages. I could feel the prickles of curiosity among the crowd, each one was a barbed needle stabbed into my gut.

"This exhibit is a unique Cabinet of Curiosities, the result of the work of a dedicated collector who, over the course of his lifetime, sought to gather specimens of original Pre-Shoshone artefacts. What you see are ornamental versions of functional artefacts; they survived as they were designed simply for display purposes. There's also evidence that they were used as teaching aids. On the top row, three in from the left, you can see that the StoneBeater has been carefully arranged to show internal lines of energy, and each highlighted in a different colour. This energy is sometimes referred to as magic due to the complete lack of convincing alternative explanations for the source and nature of the energy and its properties. There are some lifeforms here which have never been identified, they became extinct and no records have been found to identify them. It has been suggested that these lifeforms were used exclusively for the production of Ornamentals and as such fell out of mainstream production and have been lost to history. "

My shadow had slunk into the room while I'd been talking and was hovering by the first exhibit. It took a minute for the crowd to join him. He spoke without facing them, staring at the contents of the exhibit.

"Someone realized that some of the small native Thiegler lifeforms were capable of manipulating their surroundings subatomically to support themselves in an extremely hostile environment. Someone else realized that if a human picked up one of these lifeforms, they could channel and focus that process quite usefully. Due to the completely mysterious nature of this power, it was called magic and that essential mystery is the only thing that has stayed the same since the start. Of course, magic is a horribly unscientific word, so it was quickly replaced with the much more suitable energy.

"All it took was the bottomless greed and limitless imagination of humans to realize that this magic was a road to dominance and power ... if it could be reliably harvested. They had to find a more convenient way to carry the lifeforms, so they invented frames. It was then discovered that these frames increased the quantity of energy each lifeform produced and they channelled it more efficiently ... and also killed lifeforms a lot faster. This is when commercial farming of the lifeforms began—factories that twisted, broke, and carved lifeforms to fit into frames, which killed them even faster when they forced power at a greater rate. These relics date from before the Shoshone developments."

Carefully ignoring my shadow, I moved my tour group over to a large display, cut in half to show various layers and interactions. A marvel of precision and detail, it delivered an astonishing amount of complex information at a glance. The model was one of the early pre-Shoshone super-farms. There were 15 levels on display—from breeding bottles on the bottom to final saturation and production stations at the top. To the far left, you could see recycling chutes where depleted product was directed to the furnaces as high-grade fuel.

I waited as three group members ambled around to peer at the model from various angles. They seemed quite intrigued. "This is a scale model of the largest of the pre-Shoshone super-farms that we had here on Thiegler. Frames were linked together to create greater levels of power output. These frames became bigger and bigger, producing more power and requiring a greater supply of lifeforms to fill them. The farming process had developed very quickly as innovations lead to greater production, and finally the development of bottle breeding which vastly increased the supply of power rich lifeforms. It was bottle breeding that lead to the development of super farms and allowed for the production of power on scale sufficient to alter the lives of everyone in Thiegler. Power was distributed across a grid which drove industrial development and expansion. Thiegler quickly became the manufacturing hub for the systems. The power from the farms allowed for production processes that could not be achieved anywhere else. To support increasing demand for power, depleted product from the bottle breeding process was used as fuel to provide for the requirements of the farm. This provided for nearly 70% of the power requirement and enabled the economics of the super farms to be profitable. Still the whole process was reaching the limit of development when the Shoshone process was established, and we moved into the modern era of production."

I waited for questions, there were none, so I escorted them to the next stage of the tour.

My shadow waved at the model of the bottle farm and spoke his script to his crowd as I did to mine.

"Depleted product—the words burn my tongue with acid hate—is the name for the bodies of the lifeforms that had been bred in bottles below, drained of energy and thrown into a furnace to enable more lifeforms to suffer the same fate ... reduced to product, denied any independence in the great web! Look at yourselves with your vacant stares eyeing this slaughterhouse without seeing it; you're the depleted products and I'd gladly recycle all of you right now." My shadow burned with all he impotent rage and hatred that I carried, stoked to a furious heat by the sight of the atrocities enshrined in the model. History could only be acknowledged not undone.

Showing the group through a door into a large room dominated by an enormous display of all the systems, not to scale, but a strategic political map that gave greater space to the more important locations, regardless of their actual physical scope. This had become the standard way to show the systems, so it proved a shock to view an actual scale display. The version in the room was simply another piece of the winner's history, nudging out reality and reinforcing necessary messages.

We stopped before a highly polished oval conference table in the middle of the room; every place has a nameplate and on the centre of the table was a solid state-of-the-art comms block. In its day, it was the most advanced piece of technology in the systems, often cited as the hinge of the conflict, the vital edge that cut to victory. The group spread so that every person stood before a nameplate and I took the position at the head of the table.

I straightened my shoulders and took an authoritative pose. "This is not a replica, but the actual strategic command centre for the Quill Alliance. It was in this room that the strategy that lead to the final victory in the War of Empires. The configuration of the table and the whole exhibit is the same as it was when the decision was taken to close the Archen Corridor. It was this action that proved to be the turning point in the War of Empires —and this action was only possible because that block there allowed for the simultaneous co-ordination of over 16-million separate spaceships, spread across 5,000 separate Quill Alliance fleet forces, all of whom had to act in exact sequence. The scale of the operation was what had made it so unlikely; it was never considered a viable possibility and thus never planned against. The entire process took 10 seconds to complete, done with no resistance. No action of this scale has ever been repeated and may never be. Now that the possibility has been established, it's part of defensive planning everywhere across the systems The Mengchi Centre for the Promotion of Historical Knowledge was chosen as the display location after considerable negotiation. We're very proud to have this extraordinary exhibit."

The group gazed at the antiques on display with a casual lack of interest, exactly the response that the Mengchi Centre for the Promotion of Historical Knowledge hoped to achieve. The less interest inspired by the events, in particular the part played by the Thiegler hierarchy, the better. If amnesia wasn't an option, then bored lack of interest was a perfectly acceptable alternative.

My shadow, still following after me, had a desire to shake up the crowd, to force a realization on them that history gripped them as tightly as it did him.

"This exhibit is the reason for the existence of the Mengchi

Centre for the Promotion of Historical Knowledge, just as the blade that loped off Ingea's head would be the centrepiece display in a museum housed in her palace. There have been a huge number of re-developments of the site over the centuries since; this has never changed and is always the physical centre for the place. Closing the Archean Corridor was a death sentence for twenty-two billion inhabitants in the trapped systems. They died trying to escape as the noose closed around them. This noose was the only thing that kept the inhabitants of the Sickle Quadrant contained, and if it ever fails, the future will be one long drawn-out scream of blood-soaked terror for everyone

Ingea was a one-off, willing to dream, plan and act on a scale that others simply couldn't comprehend, believe or accept. She rode that weakness for all it was worth and nearly came to victory. She lost because other wolves in the systems were willing to take big steps. The sheer numbers working together proved that a pack will beat a lone wolf no matter how powerful. One of the great absences in history is a common understanding of what Ingea was planning when she launched the conflict. That she had a clear aim isn't in doubt; the question is what it was. At least part of it's obvious, to me at least, and is never spoken of. Superimpose a map of her attack points on the display here and join them up, and what do you see?" My shadow gestured dramatically. "You've seen it recently before, no? She was shaping the systems into a frame just like the one that the lifeforms were forced into to allow their energy to be used by humans.

"Ingea was going to create the biggest power source in time and space. I've no idea what she was going to use it for. My imagination fails when I consider what possible use that power was required for. I'm positive that it was a means, not an end ... that there is unfinished business here ... and that we all hope will remain that way."

The tour group had moved to the final exhibit of my short tour, the real reason they were here: the glittering treasure of the

Centre. I could sense the group's attention awakening as we walked. The entrance couldn't have been plainer—a solid stone wall, whitewashed with a narrow-arched doorway in the middle, no signs or notices. The wooden door stood open and we entered single file. The walls of the circular room were made of the same whitewashed stone; the floor was plain hardwood. There was nothing in the room except a small table, slightly bigger than the domed glass case sitting on it. The plain setting was all that was needed to display the most extraordinary item in the combined systems: the Shoshone Circlet.

The group gathered around and stared at the blank model of a human head. On it sat a very plain band of twisted gold with a large blood-red stone that rested on the middle of the model forehead, above and between the eyes. It deliberately suggested a third eye, one that held gleaming, shifting light within. Before speaking, I left space for everyone to be drawn into the spell cast by the artefact.

"This is one of the most profound mysteries in the combined systems. There's no information regarding who, when, or how the Shoshone Circlet was made. It's not clear if it was found or discovered, or by whom. The first mention of it is found in the laboratory notes of the Shoshone farm and it's clear that they didn't create it themselves but were trying to understand how it had been created. Unfortunately, the entire farm was obliterated in an explosion linked to their efforts to replicate the Circlet. The Circlet itself had been sent to a lab at a super-farm situated here in Mengchi just prior to the destruction at the farm.

"The Circlet was the first charm, the first artefact that contained energy taken from an energy-rich lifeform. Before that the energy was always in the lifeform, it was channelled through the frame. In the Circlet the energy had been removed from the lifeform and stored to be used at will. It was at the central lab that the Circlet was first replicated ... where energy transfers from lifeforms into separate containers were performed. The energy could be stored and directed with precision. Charms meant that the power could be exported to other systems and thus the fundamental reorganization of the economies and societies of the systems started. Without a continuing supply of charms life in the combined systems would effectively stop.

"It's been stated that the existence of the Circlet was the necessary requirement for the breakthrough of harvesting and storing the energy of the lifeforms. Until it was demonstrated that it *could* be done, no one was willing to try it. Once done, however, the forces required to achieve it were again harnessed. No one knows if the second process developed by the central laboratory is the same one used to create the Shoshone Circlet. To discover this, the Circlet would have to be subjected to destructive testing and that's never been allowed. To this day the mystery and importance of the Circlet remain.

"This is the conclusion of the tour." I bowed my head to the group. "Thank you for taking the time to visit the Mengchi Centre for the Promotion of Historical Knowledge. When you exit this room, to your right is the gift shop and restaurant. Please stay as long as you wish and feel free to explore more of the exhibits not included on the tour. There's a particularly fine collection of Darkham crystals on the 15th floor and full-scale replica of the Far Deep Space Explorer craft launched 100 years ago to scout beyond the combined systems, still relaying scientific information today. The exhibit contains a live feed of the transmissions and commentary. Thank you."

The tour group exited the room after lingering for a little to gaze at the Circlet. It exerted a powerful attraction on everyone who saw it, I followed the group out while my shadow remained. My shadow stood in front of the glass case, with arms crossed, as the members of the tour pressed around to view the Circlet.

"Lanken, forgive me, I'm dazzled by beauty every time I see this death warrant for my ancestors and the ancestors of others. This glowing clot of blood is the full stop to our history; from that point on, we're lost amid human dust and can never be found. This little trinket did more than change the energy industry, indeed more than simply changing life in all the inhabited systems; it changed the possibilities of what could be done with lifeforms, and it took little time for this to be understood and acted upon. The lifeforms may have been drained of essential energy, but there were still breeding possibilities if a minute spark was left and then utilised to animate them. The lifeforms could be shaped them to any purpose. Not just a charm but also a set of living charms designed to fit any task. Work in the most hostile of environments, work in the most intimate of environments. The only boundary was imagination and the willingness to apply it. Humanity was never short of either. And look here, in all their splendid forms are some of those purposes—workers, slaves of every shape, size and capacity able to work under any conditions, ready to create waterfalls of money to flow into the mouths of their masters."

My shadow always gave an extended tour and always came to this exhibit, and this was where the danger was greatest. It was a comfortable room that held a first edition, possibly the only surviving one. It lay open to the dedication page on the grand desk where its author had completed the work. The dedication never changed, no matter how often I looked and hoped the sheer weight of the lies it held would have made the words bleed off the page.

"The spark of life burns equally in all. Let it shine forth in freedom and dignity." Such a shining lying truth or a blazing truthful lie.

"I stand before you a bottle born free citizen of the inhabited systems. I am exactly the same as you except for one matter, a minor one to be sure, I have no parents, yet I am not an orphan, humans made me but did not breed me. I do have a human ancestor and we are not his descendants. He had a name, but I won't use it. Let it rust in silence. He wrote *Radical Reason: The Spark of Life*, a rallying cry that awoke the conscience of the human race and turned a great chapter of history. Here you see a very rare first edition, ... which frightened those in power enough that they realized it was far better to have an enormous population of bottle born lifeforms on the inside pissing out, rather than risk a flood flowing in. So, any lifeform that wasn't brewed to a single specific purpose, a general-use lifeform in whatever shape they might be, was granted full, equal and inalienable citizen status of the combined systems.

"I am expected, by some, to be grateful for my status as a free citizen of the combined systems, grateful for the opportunity to have a life utterly dependent on the process of stripping other lifeforms of their essential natures, grateful that this process pushed me out to one destination rather than another. Free citizen should be more important than bottle born. Naturals who would never accept me as an equal are deeply anxious that I should not parade my differences in case it makes them uncomfortable. I cannot undo history, we are long beyond recovery as we were, we need to live in this time as we are. I want to live a quiet life without having others seeking to des... Is that the time? thank you all for listening so patiently to me, I have to finish now. "

That was much further than I could afford to travel, the pressure can be so great that I need to release it and control it, one pushing fiercely against the other. What could happen if I lose that control is on the list of things I scrupulously do not think about.

———

I headed for the small staff room to get ready to head back to my space. I had some time off and was ready to rest. It was hard to believe that I was stopped at the exit when my pass didn't open the gate. Returning inside, I walked as slowly as I could without actually stopping at the management offices. I turned the corner in the corridor and saw a long queue leading up to the Resources Office. I'd been Waved in and was now being Waved out.

The Standing Committee of Thiegler was composed of

people with a finely tuned apparatus for detecting problems that might become a danger to their continued presence on the Committee. One of the most significant problems: a large standing, if not stagnant, pool of unemployed citizens. Agitating this pool was one of the major preoccupations of the SC members and the Wave Policy one of the ways they did it. Moving large numbers of citizens of every type and stripe though jobs at various organizations decreased the total number of actively unemployed. When a very small percentage of this group actually got full-time employment at an organization, it was a triumph of public policy.

For the rest of us pool algae, we got Waved into employment and Waved out again to make way for the next set of bodies. For the most part, we were never going to get substantial employment for all the reasons we were in the pool in the first place, unless fantastically lucky or much less fantastically, *unlucky*. By the time I'd made my way up to the counter at the Resources Office, I was still hoping to be marginally lucky and get a ticket for private sector job, or even a spell on a bench filling out forms at employment agencies. When I saw the smile on Philbean's face after he noticed me, I knew I wasn't going to be lucky; still, I had enough time to harbour completely fruitless hope that it wouldn't be the worst. I was wrong.

"Mr. Mansard, how nice to meet you again. It seems that there's going to be small change in your circumstances. Let me be the first to congratulate you."

The malicious sarcasm that Philbean breathed with every word clung to me like damp fog. The only reason Philbean hadn't been clubbed to death a long time ago was that he was a three-meter high lizard with a proven taste for blood and the willingness to take it in a fight. He never started one, but always finished one, and I'd been very careful during my time at the Centre to stay out of his way. Not that that did much good; he always seemed to want to take a well-placed stab at me. Maybe it was my lack of response that aggravated him. Certainly, I was an object of unusual attention. Nowadays, I just waited for the next jab.

"We received a Quota Requirement Notice and I naturally thought of you. After your sterling service here, I was happy to have the opportunity to ensure that you found permanent employment matching your talents. It took a little effort, but what's that among friends when the results are so beneficial? I shouldn't delay you, the Public Service Allocation Bureau waits for no lifeform and, I've heard, can get tetchy if applicants aren't on time. Your appointment is at seven, so I'm sure you can make it if you don't delay."

It was a classic Philbean set-up. I could give in to my temper and jump him, and I'd lose, but I could do damage on the way down. I would be late for my appointment and be treated as an absconder, failing to report for legitimate employment. That would get me an automatic ten sentence in misery shackles, ten days in an induced for of depression that usually lead to suicide. Which was very convenient as death in service made you automatically eligible for the Involuntary Public Servant programme where you were revived and continued your career as an animated copse. I could turn and run with the already failed hope of getting to the Public Service Allocation Bureau on time and avoid a beating for being late. Beating was preferable to misery shackles so I ran, scrambling over the security gate to save time, hitting the street and trying to gain speed with every step as I raced across the square to the top of the moving stairs that dropped into the dark.

Dodging gargoyles, however, slowed me down. Now that I was no longer employed, protection had been withdrawn and I was fair game. Gargoyles infested the streets on Mengchi, one of the perks of employment was being shielded from gargoyle attacks. One of the miseries of unemployment was trying to fend them off. They were small, vicious and fast, swooping down on prey and when they landed biting through pretty much any material to get a mouthful of your blood. A very persistent gargoyle, perched determinedly on my back, bit me on the shoulder as I reached the entrance to the underworld of the Public Service Portal. I slipped on the steps and fell, hitting a hard surface with jarring impact. A voice muttered something as I exploded with body-filling pain and heard the gargoyle scream before passing out.

I woke up fresh and alert in a comfortable padded chair and looked across an impossibly beautiful desk at the most alluring woman I'd ever encountered. Soft amber lights emphasized multiple shades of red—crimson, scarlet, ruby, and berry—in her perfectly cut hair. Smiling, pale gray eyes caressed me with promises of sweet, shared pleasures. I had an erection that could have lifted her off the ground unaided, and the energy to do so as often as we wanted. All of which would start as soon as I'd signed the form she was presenting. I took it and my fingers brushed hers; more intimate contact would be a delicious, life-altering experience.

"My name is Shakbout Mansard, I am a free citizen of Thiegler. My residence number is 2269334789521."

This didn't please my beauty, nor me, but I had no control over my voice or my arms, hands and fingers, which refused to sign the form. A tiny but heart-rendering frown line appeared on her forehead and her lips pouted with disappointment that our blissful union was being delayed. I struggled to move my hand, to get on with the task. Instead, my monotonous voice droned on. "I fully and deliberately invoke the protection enshrined in Clause 7C, Subsection 36, Paragraph 78, and Item 2231 of the Establishment of Citizenship Decree, as amended by Decree AGMLZ500788453 and confirmed by ruling ODDETSGH7931 of the Standing Committee."

I had no idea what I was saying and was desperately trying to stop; I could see that each sound was hurting my heart's desire, and I'd never be able to make it up to her. The form was snatched from my hands and I found myself sitting in an old and worn office chair in a rather shabby cubicle, facing a Harvester across a strip of scuffed plastic desktop. The form was a charm that activated when I touched it. If I had signed the form, I would have given away precious rights and the Harvester would have earned a bonus. The Thiegler Public Service was not a generous employer and it systematically tried to recover value from those it employed by using very questionable means that just barely met the legal requirement for informed consent.

The Harvester didn't look like my beauty, but like a sentient flower with a large blood-red cluster of small flowers serving a vague approximation of a face, hanging on a green reed of a body. The reed would be resting in a basin of swamp water fed from a tap in a wall. One of my previous jobs had been in a swamp-water fermentation plant and had gifted me with a weight of knowledge I'd have given a less vital organ to forget.

The flower cluster rippled, and I felt as much as heard the Harvester say, "Your Notice of Service will be delivered to your habitation before the start of the third shift tomorrow. Do *not* be late." Before I could get up or move out of the way, the Harvester sprayed me with sweet smelling pollen. Harvesters were about the most mean-spirited lifeforms in the systems, which was exactly why there were so many in the PSAB; they were perfect for the work. Going forward, I'd have a hyper-reaction to any sexual attraction encountered, a massive and uncontrollable reaction that would ensure that wearing anything except very loose underwear would be a very serious and painful mistake for the rest of my pre-death life.

I was on time for the start of my new working life in the sewers of Mengchi. The good was that it was paid employment, the bad thing was everything else. The sewers were old, complicated and in constant need of repair and cleaning. Everyone new started in cleaning and you quickly discovered that shit was the very least of your worries, it was what was hiding in the shit that you had to be very careful about. Not all charms are made equal, from the precision cuts at the top end to the illegal, unlicensed bashers at the bottom, you get what you pay for. A charm that does exactly what it should, a piece of junk that will do something without any idea or indication of what it will be. When they break, are stolen, lost, hidden, discarded accidently or deliberately they fall until they are trapped in the sewers.

Broken charms are not the same as deactivated charms, broken charms still have energy. Energy that can combine with the energy in other charms which can produce unexpected results. The most serious are holes that you can fall into that lead to anywhere and nowhere. There is no way back. Each sewer worker has an alarm that warns of the any rise in energy above background levels. Getting an alarm might mean standing still with your foot in the air or it might mean run or it could mean that you are approaching a safety fence.

What an alarm means the most often is that a shit golem is approaching, a collection of charms has provided the power to move a mound of shit. Sometimes these collide and form super golems. A crew of Involuntary Public Servant s with axes hack them into small pieces, sift through the lumps and smash the charms to bits. You as the team leader get to be splattered at a distance until everything has been neutralised. I encountered my first super shit golem on day three, I got too close and nearly lost a foot to an axe blow. The Involuntary Public Servants do not discriminate, everything in range is a target.

With time it moved from being oppressively awful to being awful. There were always turds waiting to be stepped on. Then, in a depressingly familiar way I moved from stepping in shit to being in shit.

[2]

"HEY SCREW-TOP, The Knob wants to see you in his office re your achievement assessment, I believe." Lincoln delivered the news in a cheery tone, which was entirely fair since it wasn't her who'd waste precious time in the company of Thobald Ivton the Third, Deputy Assistant Sub Manager for Branch 12 of Area 96884/AQ/X, known to all as The Knob, and my direct line manager.

Lincoln was glowing with pleasure at the near miss. The day previous, she'd been stuck for three hours in a presentation on the strategic direction of staff development and was happy to use all that she'd learned, even when merely delivering a message. Lincoln was an Ornamental whose ancestors had been bred to fill giant pools and fountains on a long-lost estate; they swam and darted between water sources, their wet blue skin a perfect backdrop for the sparkling light that burst through the droplets engineered to stay on them. Nowadays, she worked cleaning sewers.

"You know that's a birth slur and an objectionable term under the objectionable terms rules, don't you?" I stood up from the bench where I'd been putting on slurry boots.

"Really?" Lincoln replied with peerless innocence." I read just yesterday that it was term of endearment among citizens who weren't subject to a natural birthing process and could be employed to indicate friendship and respect for a shared heritage."

"Stay off those Human Rights lines. They'll lead you astray. Then what will you do when you find you're the only blue-skinned citizen in a room of hungry Naturals looking for someone to blame for their body hair and lack of success in mating?" With that, I strolled from the locker room and headed up the lower depths to the Knob's office. Unfortunately, he was in. I'd hoped he might have wandered off to another meeting and forgotten all about this one.

When I entered the dim office, he looked up. I say "he", but the truth was that no one had the slightest idea what the Knob actually looked like, or if "he" might be a "she". The Knob used a glamour charm keyed to the leading cast member of the top-rated show on the lines for that day. The worst "top-rated" show had spotlighted a semi-dismembered, decomposing corpse running for a seat on the Standing Committee; a huge hit, it ran for weeks through the election cycle. The charm called up the stench, as well as the look, and that stink hung like a bloodsucker, taking at least four showers to remove.

This time he was two metres tall with broad shoulders and a nipped waist, flowing golden beard, and long thick pigtail. Piercing sky-blue eyes were set above etched cheekbones. An air of casual, yet complete, mastery was wasted once he started to talk. Seated behind the desk, he waved me to a chair, strategically lower than the desk so I had to look up.

"Ah, good. Please sit down for this important meeting. A performance appraisal is a serious career event, a time for reflection and consideration ... assessing what's been achieved and contemplating what *will* be achieved. This is a moment to look back and to look forward from the firm footing of the present. We need to use it to read the lessons of the past and sow the seeds of the future, so we might harvest success in time."

He beamed with benevolence and encouragement, and I did my loyal follower part by nodding agreement and sticking the pin I'd brought for this moment into my thigh to stop from laughing out loud.

"Excellent, excellent. Shanksworth, I believe your performance on the road-development project in Sector 15 was an example that all should follow. I'm delighted to tell you that you've been promoted to Assistant Lead Supervisor on the project. Do you have anything you'd like to say?"

I shook my head to convey modest acceptance of his gratifying, if not wholly deserved praise, and how overcome I was at his generous recognition of my efforts. I took the cue to leave and left to speak to Rosby, the Knob's guardian angel.

"Hi Rosby. Would you let someone call Shanksworth know that they've been promoted? I'm guessing that they're a Stone-Beater, involved in a road project in Sector 15."

Rosby smiled and I wished she hadn't as it triggered a major reaction barely held in check by charms. She was another Ornamental, with lovely wings on her back made of the whitest feathers; when fully unfurled, they lifted her off the ground and transported her with considerable force. Rosby was tall and muscular, with olive skin, wavy jet-black hair and matching eyes. Usually dressed in flowing close-fitting robes, she was stunning ... and enchanting when she smiled. While I struggled to move blood from my dick to my legs so I could step away, Rosby placed a hand on my arm and asked, "You okay, my friend? You look like you're going to faint."

Her gentle touch burned my arm like a heat restraint and prompted my blood to circulate; the charms moved into overdrive and I was able to regain enough control to respond. "I'm fine, just experiencing a shock of relief. I heard last week he gave an execution order instead of a transfer. Getting an *accidental* promotion was too easy."

Rosby smiled again and waved me off as I walked with stiff legs, grateful for the alterations I'd made to my suit to accommodate such events. I took the long route back to the locker to let the reaction dissipate.

Lincoln was sitting on one of the many benches, clearly waiting for me. Her work comm blinked with unanswered calls. She eyed me with concern. "You took so long, I thought you'd received an execution order and I'd have to find a new drinking partner for tonight."

I was surprised. While we'd been using the same locker room for the last 18 months, I'd been working for the Public Service Board. Lincoln worked in an office shovelling paper, and I worked in the sewers shovelling shit. As a rule, the two groups didn't mix at work or outside it. But Lincoln was a cheerful locker-room acquaintance, and we often chattered or batted insults. This was a very abrupt change. Even at the best of times (long-gone times), I'd never had the best social skills, so I was a bit stumped how to respond.

Happily, Lincoln knew how to take charge and move things forward, normally in the direction *she* wanted. "Scrub up and be at the Red Eye 20 after the shift." With a nod, she left.

I finished dressing and headed to the gates where I found my Involuntary Public Servant crew standing around like a bunch of re-animated corpses waiting to be told what to do ... which, incidentally, was exactly what they were (re-animated corpses, in case there was any question).

I formed them into a hollow square and stood in the middle. To my left, right, and behind, the Involuntary Public Servant staff were wearing chainmail trousers tucked into slurry boots. All had a nerve-stick with one setting that would kill any creature with a nervous system that it touched. The nerve-stick used on me when I entered the Public Service Portal was designed to subdue not kill, and the memory of that encounter still reverberated through my muscles.

In front were three Involuntary Public Servant members, wearing lighting rigs that illuminated the sewers for a 20-metre distance. Overlapping lighting meant no shadows for something to hide in and ambush us as we drew near. We were going to check on an blood lake inspection point. Our route would be outside any predators' hunting range, but stupidity was always fatal.

Off we marched, with the Involuntary Public Servant crew falling into step with my pace. We managed to travel as a unit rather than stumbling scrum. It had taken me three months to figure out how to get them to work together and now we fell into it perfectly. The journey to the inspection point was uneventful—no attacks, cave-ins, or gas bubbles. The inspection point seemed ordinary enough too, at first. There was an anomaly, a recess in a sewer wall that wasn't on the map or on any inspection reports I called up on the link. There was nothing remarkable about the recess in itself; it looked like an inspection port found near any blood lake.

That was the problem. We were too far from the nearest blood lake for there to be an inspection port, which made it very likely that it was in fact a smugglers niche—the point where an inbound courier dropped off a delivery and an outbound courier picked it up without the two ever meeting. Naturally, such niches had pretty serious security, way beyond anything I could deal with, and the best plan was simply to pass by.

Curiosity, perhaps the single most dangerous force in all the systems, causing more trouble, chaos and disaster than anything else, nudged me to request the nearest Involuntary Public Servant shine a light into the niche. It looked like a smugglers niche, four meters deep and empty, except for a glistening geometric-like pattern on a rear wall, above floor level.

Three things happened simultaneously. I saw the pattern, Jovial made a move, and I died.

There was a saying attributed to the Red Halls: *it isn't dying that kills you but waking up and realizing that there's no rest for the indebted.*

I woke up to the realization that my problems weren't going to be escaped by something as simple as dying. I'd have to work much harder than that. The initial moment of wakeful clarity about the cesspit of my life vanished and the shock subsided enough to let pain register. I fell to the floor and screamed. This was the best thing to do as it triggered a response from an Involuntary Public Servant who stepped over and shot me with a cool dart. This was standard protocol for someone attacked by a blood-lake predator, which usually resulted in them falling down and screaming.

The dart numbed the pain sufficiently for the person to think and be mobile enough to move from the problem area. Finding no predator to kill, the crew re-formed, two supporting me, and we marched to a pre-planned recovery spot. Once there, I took the charm from my pack; it would speed up the recovery process so that I'd be reasonably functional within hours rather than weeks. With that, I lay down on the sewer floor and slept for the remainder of the shift.

The alarm awakened me, and I headed back to the office with myself and the crew intact, which made the day wildly successful, and one I was in no mood to celebrate. Which was very unfortunate as it appeared that Lincoln was, and she wasn't about to let me escape. I saw her waiting at the Red Eye 20, and it was clear she'd seen me.

She ambled over and smiled gaily. "Ready for the night of your life? You'll never have tasted beer like this before in your life."

With that, she headed off and I followed. It took less energy than resisting and the prospect of cool beer was inviting. Lincoln walked past the office quarter and turned into the Old City, the remains of the original Thiegler, dating back to pre-war times in several places and no later than post-war reconstruction in others.

Lincoln was walking leisurely, so this time I could soak up the place. There was a jumble of building styles and sizes, no sense of underlying order, and it was impossible to keep track of where we were going. We turned at a large glass bowl of an

edifice with rainbow colours and hazy shadows cast by movements and lifeforms inside. It was suggestive of stories of other
lives and activities, and when I looked back, there was a
diamond-shaped, metal-clad building in its place.

I turned back to Lincoln, but she was no longer in sight. I
stood shocked for a second, but then she appeared from a
shadow between two identical, low-rise brick office blocks and
called to me. "Come on. Beer won't wait!"

Stepping into the shadow, I found myself in a wide room
filled with long tables where lifeforms of all types were sitting,
standing, hovering, or hanging while eating, drinking and talking. There wasn't a lot of noise however; just cheer-filled
murmurs and whispers that created a welcoming atmosphere of
unthreatening sociability. Lincoln was moving across the room
and, judging from the various greetings, was well known. I
followed her to a table beside a wall with a nice view of the
room. The only other chair was positioned so that I'd be
sitting facing Lincoln with my back to the crowd. Whatever
this was going to be, it was much more than a social event
with a colleague; this was Lincoln's event to manage as she
saw fit.

When I sat down, a natural female human came and wiped
the table with a cloth before asking for our order. The table was
already clean, but when she was leaning over to wipe it, I got a
clear view of very nice beasts supported by a charcoal-gray work
shirt and a nerve-stick in a holster at her curvy hip. It was a low-
power version, capable of disabling temporarily, but not killing.
The message was still very clear: be nice and enjoy the view or be
carried out and dumped on the pavement.

Lincoln offered a cordial greeting. "Hey Nanteer, two Top
Drawers, a mixed scald for the Screw-Top and a scale one, extra
sauce for myself please, how is the new space working out?"

"Great. It's much more convenient, and that was a good tip,
so thanks. Drinks first, food to follow." When Nanteer walked
away, the view from behind was as pleasing as the front and I

allowed myself to linger a little before turning back to a grinning Lincoln.

"All natural, not a single charm on her. She owes it to no one, but her ancestors not like you and me Screw-Top."

"If we're going to be eating and drinking together, call me Shakbout."

"That's a bit of a mouthful and very formal. Screw-Top is more relaxed, more honest."

Lincoln was needling me. Why? We shared a common heritage; we'd been built to order. We also spent our lives ignoring that fact; otherwise, it would overwhelm us and destroy us. Having it called up the way Lincoln was doing, was a dangerous game. If a Natural did this, they'd risk severe punishment in the name of maintaining civic harmony. No court would rule for murder if death were the result. They'd simply rule it suicide.

Context mattered too. At work in the locker room, it was recognized that tolerance was required to give everyone space to work with one another. Sitting in the dining hall was different. This was a public space and words had a very different weight. I was so battered by the day, and numbed by the charm, I wasn't going to take offence quickly. "Let's be honest. Why am I here? What do you want from me?"

Before Lincoln could respond, Nanteer appeared and placed two large glasses of dark froth-topped beer before us. She departed without a word.

Whatever direction the conversation might have taken was lost in the glorious, enticing sight of the delicately fragrant brew. Without waiting, I took a mouthful and realized that I was in the presence of a masterpiece. The hoppy taste filled my mouth and then my brain with pleasure.

Lincoln put down her glass. "Sorry for that, Shakbout, sometimes I speak without thinking."

"No problem. This beer is astonishing. Why is this place not packed to the rafters?"

Lincoln's expression held an are-you-joking? cast. "The Losers Lounge is in the Old City." Which really wasn't an explanation. Mengchi was a patchwork and the older sections had much more time to accumulate fallout from charms working as they should or not. Lincoln smiled patiently "The Old City was designed as a retreat for the Imperial Court if Thiegler was invaded. It's designed to be unnavigable to anyone without a trinket. Rather than try and unwind the process, the city was simply expanded around it, and the Old City became a place where you could become deliberately lost. Even the lost need to eat, so the Losers Lounge came into existence and it developed from there."

"How does anyone find their way around the Old City if the spell is still in force? I don't think Imperial trinkets would have survived that long."

"True, they didn't," Lincoln agreed. "However, you're forgetting something: The Imperial Court required a lot of support staff to help with relocation, as well ensure the Court could continue. Someone had to make trinkets for them, so after the Vanishing, they decided that getting lost was the safest course of action. So, they moved here, including the trinket makers. Still, getting a trinket is no easy task. The inhabitants of the Old City like to keep its secrets."

"How did you get one?"

Lincoln grinned, waved a hand, and took another quick sip. "I won it in a bet. When I saw you at the Red Eye, you looked as though you'd seen a ghost during the shift. Had you?"

The events of the day, the beer, the relaxation of tension that had been building between us all lent themselves to me being colossally stupid. "I did." The words leapt from my lips. Damn, I'd just blown up my life ... again.

Seeing a ghost was rare, with a significant population of re-animated corpses working everywhere, it seemed that ghosts should be more common. Placid, free labour for a myriad of mundane tasks needed to be done to keep Thiegler operational.

A consciousness without a body was much rarer; they needed a physical anchor, usually a charm, though there were stories of using mirrors, books and entire living spaces to make it work.

Seeing a ghost happened when said ghost was trying to leave its current anchor and take over a body, killing the person in the process so it could have full control. This was considered to be a Priority Security Threat and if you survived the process, you'd have had to turn yourself in for a full examination—one you might not survive. If you did, you'd spend the rest of your first life under surveillance, a guaranteed slot as an Involuntary Public Servant subject to experimentation in the Red Halls.

All of which was bad, but not terrible. I was confident Lincoln wouldn't tell anyone. I was much more concerned that she'd not know when to stop asking me for details, or that I'd be able to head her off without it becoming a problem. Revealing enough to satisfy her curiosity could put her in danger; then I'd have to drag her further in so she'd understand the scope of that danger, which would cause her to be displeased with me for doing so.

I was going to have to try for a fumble, enough to indicate the truth without actually revealing it, and hope that she had enough experience to recognize that leaving well enough alone was the best strategy. I didn't fancy my chances, but was pretty much stuck, and so I told Lincoln a story about a terrible afternoon I'd had many years previously.

"I was walking and not paying enough attention to where I was going, turned a corner and stepped into an arrest by a posse of Retrievers. There was an elderly lifeform on the ground with an arm raised to ward off blows. That arm had the most charms I'd ever seen on a single person ... a huge variety of sizes, shapes and colours. I couldn't imagine such a jumble would be effective. Surely, they'd knock each other out with crosscurrents, never mind the strain they'd place on whoever was wearing them. By the time I'd unscrambled my thinking and was about to retreat around the corner, one of the Retrievers spoke. It had a strange whispery voice, a little rusty as if they didn't vocalize often, but still clear.

"It said, 'Citizen, you're the designated witness to the delivery of the sentence of the sub-committee for Regulation and Enhancement of Living Citizens on escaped prisoner, Dialland Jovial.' And with that, the Retriever spun its bald oval head, which sat on a stalky neck. It had a grille for a mouth and three very large multi-coloured compound eyes. Staring at the man on the ground, it continued. 'Dialland Jovial, you were found guilty of transgressions against the community of free citizens in Thiegler. You fled lawful custody and in doing so have renounced grounds for appeal or clemency. In the presence of this designated witness, a sentence shall be applied.'

I explained how the Retrievers hummed simultaneously and Jovial shimmered until he slowly faded away. All the time, his small chapped mouth was moving, but I could hear nothing. Finally, nothing was left of him. The Retriever turned to me and told me how I, a "faithful Citizen", had performed my duty and would receive the appropriate bounty for my work. The Retriever placed a hand to my chest, and I received a download.

As I told Lincoln about that day, the events in the sewer started to stir within me. I was drowning and knew it without being able to stop it.

"Ahhh," said Lincoln knowingly. "That's why you're not in the scheme, down in the ship-pots. Anyway, tell me about the ghost. It was Jovial, right? What happened today?"

Eyeing Lincoln, I realized the old saying was correct: *the truth will shit on your head and smear it all over your face.* This was particularly true if someone had slipped a speakeasy into your beer. So, I told her.

[3]

"THYSON ARCHER WAS A BREW-MASTER." I took a long, calming breath as I scanned the ceiling, retrieving memories.

Lincoln looked at me questioningly and I realized she was Near-Natural, not directly Bottle-Born like myself. She had birth parents, her Ornamental aspects the result of cross-gene manipulation brewed into earlier generations and stabilized over time so that perfect product was maintained, and exclusivity assured by a restricted breeding program. I knew, but hadn't remembered, that the orchestrated breeding of Ornamentals had stopped long ago. It was too obvious for the post Radical-Reason public consciousness to handle, and the hidden processes of the bottle farms were much more acceptable. New Ornamentals arose from interbreeding among existing varieties, something that happened rarely due to purposeful structural difficulties built into each group to discourage such an outcome. Mongrel Ornamentals had no value to developers, whose vanity re "creation" was limitless.

Anyone who came directly from a farm like I had, knew exactly what a Brew-Master was and assumed that everyone else did. Lincoln had started from a natural-human base and been transformed into an Exotic. I'd started as an Exotic and been transformed into human form different roads to the same common ground.

I stopped, then started again. "A Brew-Master is the person who manages the technical operations at a bottle farm. The measure of a Brew-Master is in parts per million—how many in every million hatched lifeforms were successfully drained and trained, to use industry terms. An adequate Brew-Master can deliver about 150,000 on average across a full cycle, an average Brew-Master can deliver up to 250,000, and a top-rated Brew-Master can deliver up to 330,000. No one breaks 400,000. The competition for Brew-Masters is fierce. The differences a good one can add to the profits of farm owners are astronomical, as are the fees they command. They have to be, because a Brew-Master is the most dangerous occupation a natural-born human can have.

"All Brew-Masters have to be Naturals by strictly enforced law. A legal career limit spans 10 years and there's a mortality rate—from natural and non-accidental causes—of 99.98% within six months of retirement. The Standing Committee had a serious dilemma regarding Brew-Masters; they needed them to safely harvest the energy from the lifeforms and deliver the array of workers required to sustain the desired life. They fear, rightly, that Brew-Masters could use skills to deliver workers who'd do the Brew-Master's bidding and become a problem for the Standing Committee in nasty, violent ways."

I stopped to gauge her reaction. She seemed riveted and I continued. "In the north-east corner of Thiegler is a PEELO company super-farm, the first super-farm in fact, that's been burning for 450 years with no sign of stopping. There's a structure, where the top portion leads to a narrow walkway and then to a small platform, that overlooks the vat house. This is the point of origin of the fire and the hottest part of the farm —it's where the fire is monitored and also where Brew-Masters, considered threats, are taken and thrown into the flames. It's rumoured that the proposal was made as a joke during a Standing Committee meeting . . . and now it's official policy.

"Any natural human can apply to be trained as a Brew-Master and huge numbers do. They play the public lottery as well, so they're used to thinking they can beat the odds and live to spend their money. The training process is aggressively selective; one in a thousand makes it past the first training round, less makes it to the end. They don't fail. They simply make a mistake in the process and it kills them. Apparently, it's the biggest source of clerical-grade Involuntary Public Servant staff in the systems and generates significant revenue for the Standing Committee.

"Thyson Archer was successful all the way through the process and was picked up by the Orisimi Configuration to work on one of their farm complexes. One of the reasons that Thiegler wasn't ground to dust after the end of Ingea's war was the fact that energy-rich lifeforms grow more successfully here than any other location in the systems. Thiegler is responsible for 90% of total production in the systems and it's never been possible to replicate the effects anywhere else. The Orisimi Configuration, by the by, is one of the other systems that can support homebased production. They hire Brew-Masters from Thiegler to run the farms and follow a similar policy to the Standing Committee regarding them."

"And Archer?" she prodded gently when I stopped to reflect on vivid memories.

I refocused and smiled dryly. "Archer was an exceptional Brew-Master with an instinctive understanding for the process. This gave him unprecedented control over the details of draining and training. He could fine-tune the process to deliver results that would have had him burning in the PEELO vats if anyone had the slightest inkling. They didn't, because Archer chose the best possible disguise for a clever lifeform. He appeared to be slightly below average, making just enough mistakes to prove comforting to his employers while remaining worth employing.

"Archer was anxious to remain employed as he had a plan

that required unfettered access to a farm. He'd realized that the biggest problem wasn't being a Brew-Master but surviving after he stopped being one. After five unremarkable years at Orisimi, he was relieved of his job, given a bonus, and sent under escort back to Thiegler where he'd be kept under discreet surveillance for the rest of his very short life. He never made it back to Thiegler, though; he suffered a heart attack and died on the journey.

"The Standing Committee, being paranoid sceptics, brought back the body, revived it, discovered it was Archer, and dropped him into the flames. Now that he was *satisfactorily* dead, Archer could put the second part of his plan into action. He hadn't cloned himself, too easy to establish after the examination the Standing Committee would give... The body was Archer, the *original*. Archer had brewed *himself*, not a twin, but a replacement who shared all his knowledge, skills, genius and memories right up the moment Archer 'died'. At that point, the replacement was an independent lifeform with no connection to the dead lifeform, and no visible connection to the lifeform when he was alive. If Archer had given the faintest glimmer of being better than he appeared to be, the Standing Committee would have pursued the possibility of a replacement until it was found. Archer's lifelong commitment to his personal plan paid off."

As I sipped beer, I regarded Lincoln, wondering if she'd seen where this was going. She merely seemed excited and fascinated by the intrigue of it all; putting one over the Standing Committee was a dream shared by many and achieved by few. Clearly, she was admiring Archer for his skills, but soon she'd feel very differently.

"So, what happened to the replacement? Did it go off and live happily after?" she grinned. She had the brains to ask the right questions.

"The replacement took the name Dialland Jovial, settled in Mengchi, and sank as fast as possible into obscurity. He bought space in a K4739-West complex, took up a position with a scientific records office, and worked for the next 15 years as a data analyst ... until he was arrested and charged with Section 7, Political Crimes."

Section 7, Political Crimes were very specific, referring to any organized that attempted to overthrow the authority of the Standing Committee. The number of times Section 7 had been used was one of the most closely held secrets in Mengchi. Knowing that someone had actually been charged under said section put you in one of two very elite groups: as a lifeform being charged in the secret court that handled it or as a member of the group ruling on charges.

Lincoln and I now formed an unexpected and deeply unwelcome third group. I was sure, at that point, she'd have changed her instructions about adding a speakeasy charm to my beer if she could have. She'd set me up to talk and the words couldn't be undone.

"Dialland Jovial's job at the scientific records office was carefully chosen. The office had a contract from the Standing Committee to review brewing data from all farms to ensure that everything followed the rules. The office merely had a sliver of data, but Jovial only needed a sliver. He was searching for someone working at the limits of the rules, consistently enough to be doing so deliberately, and always inside the boundaries to avoid attention. Jovial slowly eliminated every possibility until he found what he was looking for ... someone trying to do what he'd already done.

"Jovial knew exactly what to look for and how to be found, and when they met, they recognized a strong fellowship—in greed, desire for power, and willingness to travel a long winding road to that ultimate destination. They built a secret farm, very small and highly specialised ... one that developed lifeforms that would infiltrate and act at the right moment. It was very successful. Jovial was an astonishing Brew-Master, an anomaly really. He'd grasped the subtle possibilities of brewing that had never been realized."

My attentive colleague's expression grew solemn.

"It was entirely possible that they arose, in part, from the brewing process that developed him. Archer was certainly capable of setting that up, recognizing his own limits and building ways around them in his replacement. The conspiracy was cracked ahead of the implementation because the Standing Committee, increasingly aware of a serious threat, had developed a solid grasp of the plan. They waited until the last second to round up—"

"But how did they know?" Lincoln interrupted, appearing perturbed. She was thinking clearly and assessing how close the danger was to her.

"The Standing Committee's as committed to retaining their position as Jovial and his companions were to taking it. They did have a considerable advantage: more money and lifeforms. Add infinite experience and they were able identify a threat, Jovial, and 5,000 other data analysts as potential entry points. They sifted through prospects until they were left with Jovial and three others. A big mistake, however, was they believed Jovial was merely a low-level player, not inner circle.

"When the inner-circle was scooped up, the members were heavily guarded—ushered straight to the Red Halls—while hired helpers were placed in a local holding block. Jovial exited the block before he could be identified, but was chased by a Retrieval Squad, which is where our paths had crossed. Jovial, like Archer, was a lifeform who took dying seriously and had a plan to deal with it. Being a Brew-Master meant managing lifeform energy a lot of the time—the energy in charms and generators, and the transfer from one entity to another. All those jangling charms he wore were simply camouflage. The real secret wasn't with them, but with me. I'm a Bottle-Born. I look human, but that's not all I am. I hold a trace of my true lifeform—like a shadow inside every cell. It was that trace that Jovial hooked when he began decomposing ... jumping into a shadow.

"So, when you asked if I saw a ghost today, you were almost

correct. It was the ghost of Dialland Jovial reaching out of the shadow, trying to place *me* in the shadow. Jovial had never expected that his host would have Retriever download installed, so the takeover was only partially successful. I got access to his memories and his active personality switched off."

"So, you were only *partially* completely fucked then," Lincoln summarized with a dry smile. "Well, this has been fun and very informative and exciting, but now I have to get completely smashed. You'll have a bit of a headache too. Sorry about that." She waved at someone behind me. The charge from the nerve-stick was intense, but much less than what I'd received before. Still, it was enough to knock me out.

————

I came too with the promised headache, one that actually encompassed my entire body as I sat on a metal bench at the transit point where I normally caught the tube back to my space from work. At least, they'd dropped me here instead of leaving me on the street. I owed Lincoln thanks.

I recovered enough to made it onto the third tube that blew by and slumped onto an uncomfortable seat. How lucky I'd been. I'd not actually wanted to do this; an involuntary reflex simply took over and demanded to be seen and heard. I had keys to a plot that could overthrow the current administration of Thiegler and possessed knowledge of secrets that the Standing Committee would repeatedly kill and revive me to access. The parts were all in place; they just had to be activated. I'd told someone about the plot, which realistically meant that the safest course of action would be to sell me to the highest bidder, take the money, and run!

This was still the best possible outcome; Lincoln had never asked me what I was doing when I encountered the Retrieval Squad. If she had, with the speakeasy charm still in force, I'd have told her and that would have been the end of everything.

The disaster that *hadn't* happened had be acknowledged before dealing with the one that *had*.

When I made it to the door of my space, I was ready to follow Lincoln's lead and get inside any alcoholic drink but hope of that vanished upon entry. They were sitting about, drinking my wine, and looking very comfortable. The senior one, (she had that "senior" look), waved to the seat alongside her, which I humbly took.

"You're late," she said sternly, not offering any wine. "That's quite inconvenient, so don't be late again. I don't like people who work for me to be late. Is that clear?"

I managed a nod. Agents of the Public Relations Office were the less visible and more powerful security section of Thiegler law enforcement, concerned with events and activities that had a broader, deeper scope that regular criminal activities. Political activities in particular were a focus of attention, because there was an election coming up for the Standing Committee.

Elections always brought a spike in Public Relations Office activity, a standard plot frame for countless shows on the lines and had become general knowledge about the Public Relations Office. Those shows were how I knew they were Public Relations Office agents. Both sported the standard uniform: scarlet-red tailored robes with a slight sheen. If you touched the robe with an energy wand, it would absorb the charge, which could be used against you.

"Good, the time hasn't been entirely wasted. We've accessed your account and have set up relevant arrangements. It's always much better if done from a verifiable location. Right, pay attention citizen, Mansard." She peered more closely at me. "You look bad. Have you been drinking to excess? Sober up fast and take a shower, because you smell rancid."

I rose without a word and went to the washroom where a hot shower did a world of good. A change into comfortable robes followed; if I was going to be fed to predators, at least I'd not be trying to pull underwear out of my arse crack at the same time. I returned to the chair and looked, hopefully, agreeable.

Both were Naturals. The Public Relations Office only hired Naturals as agents, blatant illegal discrimination no one complained about. The senior agent was female, sable-black skin and hair, and dark bark-brown eyes. Her male partner had flame-orange skin and hair, and sun-yellow eyes. She was satisfied enough with my clean up to move to the main event and my place in it.

"Citizen Mansard, as you're aware, there's an election for the majority of the seats on the Standing Committee, to be held in a month. A majority election only occurs every eight election cycles, so it's very significant and is normally contested by numerous candidates and groups. One of those groups is the United Platform for Citizen Respect. They represent non-born citizens like yourself. The United Platform for Citizen Respect is trending positively and is steadily gaining electoral support among non-aligned groups and could gain four seats in the election. That would make them an important force on the Committee and very influential over public policy. To ensure the community's stability, it's important to establish, definitively, that the United Platform for Citizen Respect is committed to upholding the foundation of the community and isn't a threat to the future of Thiegler ."

Which translated as, "We have a problem—a wild-card group that looks like it could become a threat, which we won't allow that. We're going to find out if they need to be eliminated before the election or not. You'll have a part to play in this process."

I nodded again when she paused. Her partner continued to stare.

"You've volunteered to assist our investigation by becoming a campaign worker at the United Platform for Citizen Respect election centre. You'll examine all the candidates and party officials at close range and assess the distance between their public and private policy limits. You'll report everything you find directly to us in face-to-face meetings. If you speak of this investigation to anyone, you'll be demoted to Involuntary Public Servant status for a period to be determined by a competent authority. Meanwhile, you'll continue in your current role in the underground maintenance division and not make any major alterations to your living patterns. Any changes will be considered a security breach and accordingly responded to. Do you have questions? No? Good. You have an appointment at the United Platform for Citizen Respect election centre in 90 minutes for a position as a campaign worker. *Be persuasive.*"

I had to ask. "Why *me*? I have no track records with campaigns."

The fuzzy-haired agent spoke, his tone slightly impatient, as if having to explain was a burden. "You've been identified as the correct resource for the task. You're expected to do your civic duty and you've been furnished with the information required to do it. Additional information and instructions will be provided, as necessary."

I returned to nodding and looking as pleased, welcoming, and civic minded as possible. They regarded me for a full 60 seconds with aggressive silence before leaving. The evening promised to keep getting better and better.

One of the generally lesser known side effects of being Bottle-Born is a higher sensitivity to the presence of magic; we detected the presence of a charm even when shielded. Well, some of us could. The 18 months spent at the Fogler & Twist Warehouse had sharpened my focus. Fogler & Twist were high-end charm developers. While their custom work required considerable time and design, they used mass-produced items as the base item for that work and had a warehouse full of them.

Sorting and checking charms all day for defects was the sort of detail and boredom I'd been seeking, and constant exposure to them increased my sensitivity—that, and actually getting burned by one (another "lucky accident" of the type I seemed to attract). The charm that had burned me had been stuck on a high shelf without the owner's awareness. I'd discovered it while on clean-up detail; when attempting to pull it free from whatever it was snagged on, it had burned me.

The burn charm was potent and had a specific user profile. All security-force issued charms would burn non-staff personnel on contact. Essentially a security device to prevent the charm from being used by an unofficial party. Most provided a sting as warning; this one gave a full-blown shock, designed to disable. The only reason I still had a hand was that I was wearing full-protection gloves, as required by warehouse policy (they'd not want grunt staff contaminating wares, would they now).

The charm self-destructed as part of the energy release of the burn. I'd had a chance to see it clearly—for a stunned blink —as I was propelled across an aisle. Working at Fogler & Twist did have advantages—in particular, access to a treasure trove of private information about charm patterns. As such, I was rather interested to check on mine. They didn't have any information on the one I'd seen but did suggest a likely source. It was likely the charm had been made by and for members of a highly committed Human Rights group who wanted to abolish rights for Bottle-Born. I didn't investigate beyond that suspicion and was now strongly wishing I had. The male Public Relations Office agent sported a similar charm on his wrist, made to mimic a standard Public Relations Office charm, and I noticed the hidden pattern.

I was being sent to investigate a Bottle-Born political group on the verge of political significance by someone who wanted to return the Bottle-Born to slavery. Well, if I survived long enough to worry, I'd worry about it *then*.

4

THE UNITED PLATFORM for Citizen Respect campaign headquarters were in the middle of Thiegler's business section, a
good decision to reassure everyone that the United Platform for
Citizen Respect was in tune with the money and didn't want to
rock any profitable boats. The office was relatively low-key with
a small rectangular front plate displaying the party name and
logo. They weren't doing anything to draw the wrong kind of
attention ... the kind I was about to give.

I ambled into the bright reception area buzzing with
people and chatter and filled with positive energy. Someone
wearing a gray United Platform for Citizen Respect armband
greeted me as soon as I'd taken a step inside. She had a sincere
smile and a flexpad in her hands and was clearly a natural born
human.

"My name is Reyan. How may I help you?" She extended a
slender hand as she spoke, and I shook it. She looked pleased
and excited.

When I told her, I had an appointment to be a volunteer, she
checked her flexpad. "Mr. Mansard, how nice to meet you. You
have a meeting with the Director of Campaign Staff, Dr Sand."
She paused to check the time. "Right now, in fact. Thank you for

being so punctual." She headed through the crowd and I followed.

The crowd held many more Naturals than I'd expected. Clearly, the United Platform for Citizen Respect had done its work well to capture the guilty vote ... and make them feel they weren't doing it from any sort of guilt at all. If and when the United Platform for Citizen Respect got onto the Standing Committee, they'd stop feeling guilty and start feeling entitled. Handled properly, it would become a reasonably reliable voter base. The United Platform for Citizen Respect was serious and could score well in the election; the PR agents were right to be concerned.

We sauntered down a short hall lined with unmemorable campaign posters with the usual blur of phrases and pictures. Reyan stood at a narrow door she'd just opened and waved me in, announcing to the being inside, "Dr Sand, Mr. Mansard is here to see you." With a pretty smile, she closed the door behind.

If I could have turned and run, I would have, but when a rifle was pointed at your face and a cannon at your back, not moving seemed the best course.

I glanced at a slightly battered desk, a cheap put-together item that would do the required work and give a message of no-nonsense pragmatism by the very big lifeform seated behind it. He was a StoneBeater, with the usual flat features, grey skin, and hard muscles that gave force to the name. Wearing expensive robes, custom-made by the way they fell, they emphasized the strength of his bulky frame. Sloping, almond-brown eyes stared. He radiated sheer physical power. It was too perfect and had to be a cover for a gentle giant; the Naturals out front would be thrilled for seeing through the disguise. Except I knew it wasn't a front. He was everything he appeared to be and didn't scare me a fraction as much as did the slim, elegant Avian seated to his right, smiling with far too many teeth.

Dressed in a form-fitting sea-blue robe slashed with red and yellow, Zusak Sedge was a clear and present danger to every

Bottle-Born creature in the known systems. Finding her here was an unmistakable sign that I was several kilometres in shit over my head.

"I see that you know me. Fine. Introductions are tedious. Sit and listen very closely. While I may say this more than once, this will be the only time that it will be painless. You've been sent by the Standing Committee to spy on us so they might prevent us achieving our deserved win in the election. That's good, because we need a pipeline to them. You'll report what you're told to and that will keep them happy.

"The trickier problem you have is keeping *us* happy. In your unalterable history, you've chosen to embrace those who've enslaved and deformed you. I'd have you flayed, and your skin tanned for shoes but, in this exceptional case, you're marginally more useful alive."

She fell silent while she assessed me again. Zusak Sedge never shouted or raged; she had a beautiful voice, clear and pleasant, making everything she said sound calm, rational and trustworthy. A calm manner suited those serene features and sparkling brown eyes. Topaz-yellow hair with amber-orange streaks was carefully arranged on her head so that it looked like an explosion of colour. If you looked at her and knew nothing more, you'd feel the warmth of her presence and be willingly bound by the shackles of that subtle charisma.

This could easily happen even if you knew she was the most dangerous, politically motivated, mass killer in the systems, pursued by multiple organizations that had "mysteriously" never managed to capture her. Someone dead from severely unnatural causes had likened her to Empress Ingea—of the Bottle-Born.

She claimed to work for the liberation of the Bottle-Born, but the countless wracked corpses in her wake spoke to a very different agenda of power and domination. She was the single biggest cause of fatalities for independent Bottle-Born lifeforms like me; we were the rungs on her ladder to success. Zusak was also considered—by those who couldn't actively prevent the thought from crossing their conscious minds—to be in league with the furthest reaches of the Human Rights fringe.

"You're going to complete a task for me. If you fail to do so, I'll add you to my calculator. Achieve the task and I'll grant you a swift death and use you to mulch my flowers. It will make the worms happy. We'll contact you with task details. You may go now."

I understood perfectly. Being part of her calculator meant being physically wired into her personal neural network. I'd become part of her, literally. Diversity was critical to long-term success and Zusak Sedge followed the logic with ruthless efficiency—captured diverse lifeforms were grafted onto an organic matrix that ensured their physical wellbeing. Linked charms ensured they were a mental collective comprised of individual voices. They thought about the best methods for Zusak Sedge to achieve her aims. She'd use me to think of better ways to create fear, hurt, death and chaos. I'd resist as much as I could but, undoubtedly, I'd contribute to the horror.

The StoneBeater rose and circled the desk. Up close, he was even more imposing than I'd initially thought. He handed me an infogem without a word.

I stood up and, looking directly at his heavily veined throat, took it and walked from the room without my bowels betraying me (the muscles of my buttocks were clenched so tightly, they'd have held a planet in check).

I walked back through the throng of happy faced Naturals, who had no idea what was transpiring. As I left the building, I was thinking all I needed now was a transit breakdown so that I'd have to walk back to my space and an unscheduled storm to soak me to the bone as I did so. Neither happened and I returned to my space safe and dry ... where I engaged in a screaming panic fit in the comfort of my bed.

———

The following morning, I dropped off the infogem at the nearest security drop box on my way to the transit. The poster on the drop box that loudly proclaimed the lie that any lifeform who dropped off would remain securely anonymous was clearly designed to mock me personally. I had been sold out before I had even dropped off any information.

At work I was assigned to an emergency team to work on a blood lake predator breakout in an Emergence Corp super-farm disposal system. There was no time to think about anything except avoiding predators chewing up Involuntary Public Servant staff and spitting the bones at me. After surviving another day at the blood lake, I headed out of the staff portal to return home for a scrub and a sandwich. I'd invested in a personal protection system, not the most sophisticated, mind you, but functional enough for my purposes. It had assessed the movements as not being threatening and allowed it without a primary alert. As such, I wasn't startled when I felt pressure on my arm.

I turned and was surprised to see Nanteer, more discreetly dressed this time. She wasn't smiling and looked a little worried and off balance. Clearly, she was outside her geographical comfort zone. I was very glad to see her, more than I'd have expected, and hoped this would be a chance to re-establish contact with Lincoln. I hadn't seen or spoken to Lincoln since she'd seen me slammed at the Loser's Lounge. I'd been so busy going to United Platform for Citizen Respect rallies, setting up and running message shots, and generally being the active volunteer, I was supposed to be, that I'd no time outside of work to think of anything else.

All lifeforms, Natural or otherwise, are creatures of communication. We crave a chance to jump across the isolation of individual consciousness to share with others. A speakeasy loosened more than your tongue, and speaking the truth was a crucial act of communication; it created a deep bond between speaker and listener. Professional interrogators knew this and used the speakeasy as a lever to open the door to creating a bond, starting with something trivial and unrelated. They'd then use alternative means—exploitation—to get what they wanted. A speakeasy was also a much sought-after love potion, found in so many entertainment stories.

I had a bond with Lincoln and an aching need for friendship that I'd held at bay for years. Lincoln had breached my defences at their most vulnerable point and I was feeling the pain. Any hopes I may have had were quickly swept aside when Nanteer spoke.

"Lincoln doesn't know I'm talking to you. She'd explode if she knew, whatever you did to her wasn't right." She waved away my attempt to speak. "Her mother is seriously ill and needs medical help. The clinic will only accept a clean card. Lincoln thinks you have one and can't bear to ask you for help. I, however, can."

I removed my card from its holder and handed it over. "Use my name, no restrictions."

Nanteer looked more shocked than surprised. Obviously, she'd been expecting a price. This left her dumbfounded. I couldn't help those I had most desperately wanted to, but I could certainly help someone in need. With a curt nod, I headed to my evening of volunteering and high wire balancing at the United Platform for Citizen Respect.

———

Lincoln had noted that I was working in the Public Service and not on the scheme. In fact, 99.99% of all non-management staff in the Public Service were in the scheme—the Public Service Staff Benefits Enhancement and Elaboration Scheme, to be precise. That those 99.99% were also Bottle-Born free citizens wasn't coincidental. The Public Service had become the default employer for bottle born free citizens, a solution to a significant problem. Naturals and non-Naturals made each other uncomfortable, tolerance was achievable, and acceptance and genuine integration, were purely aspirational. Mixed workforces were more potential trouble than employers wanted so the solution emerged in silence.

One of the problems inherent in the Bottle-Born was medical. The process of brewing lifeforms had possible medical repercussions, not for every lifeform and not all the time, but enough to make it a lifelong threat to us. Medical insurers realized there were profits to be made and struck a deal with the Standing Committee to provide medical cost insurance for the Bottle-Born population. The vast majority of all Bottle-Born were specialized lifeforms with reduced lifespans—disposable labour for extreme conditions, cheaper and more productive than machines. The target group: the free-citizen Bottle-Born. Big enough to be a market, sick enough to want protection while not sick enough to be unprofitable.

The Standing Committee provided unlimited, universal medical insurance for all Bottle-Born free citizens. If you asked a Natural, he or she would tell you it was a "Guilt Tax", a charge for the sin of existence. At least one seat on the Standing Committee went to someone who traded on the injustice of such a tax and received an angry vote in return. This way, everyone got something, despite the awkward reality of it all.

Every new Public Service employee was offered an opportunity to join the scheme—education and housing benefits in addition to priority access via the medical insurance deal. A good deal on the face of it, basic education at all levels was free, enhanced education was expensive. Sometimes you had to wait months for medical treatment with regular insurance, months that could result in unceasing agony, so most went for it. It was made more attractive by the process I'd endured, where the camouflage increased sign-up rates. The problem was *how* the premium was paid—not in cash, but in working time. The working time for cash exchange was set by the Public Service and was the least transparent process in the whole of the systems.

The only thing that was absolutely certain: once you were in, you *never* got out. You were in debt to the scheme until you retired, which you only did when the debt was paid. Death wasn't the same as retirement by the way, as many had discovered.

The reward from the Receivers was automatic immunity to the enhanced sign-up process, which would override charisma and allow me to assert my right to refuse joining. Of course, I also cost that damn plant commission, so I paid a price in different way. The net result: I worked in the Public Service and still had regular medical insurance, which was an anomaly (and anomalies existed to be exploited). The specific anomaly: the assumption that everyone in my grade was in the scheme. Therefore, to extend the reach of the scheme, any Public Service employee could share insurance with another individual but carried the cost burden. This way, the scheme pulled in the entire family, not just the worker, and tied up everyone (tightly).

A very lucrative, niche industry had developed whereby insured lifeforms—with insurance and not trapped in the scheme—rented out their cards. It was entirely illegal to benefit from another lifeform using an insurance card, if the lifeform made a charitable contribution to registered entity completely unrelated to the use of the card that was entirely legal. The owner of the card could be the patron of the registered entity entirely legally. Nanteer had been expecting me to nominate my favourite charity and the suggested donation.

Thinking about Lincoln and her mother as I was strolling down an incline to the transit, my security system gave a quick jab. Standing at a food broker in the transit hall was the male PR agent I'd last seen in my space. As my belief in coincidences had suffered a fatal blow long ago, I assumed he was there to talk to me and wandered over to join the queue. By the time I had soup and sandwich in hand, the agent was sitting at a counter facing the window, there was a free seat beside him. I sat and started on my soup, which was surprisingly good. Most food brokers thought tasty food meant lower profits.

The agent didn't actually speak, but I heard him clearly enough—undoubtedly achieved via secret PR stuff. "Step up your work at the United Platform for Citizen Respect. We need a definitive read on the situation within the week. The information so far has been good, but we need more access to the upper rings to be sure. Get into them and get more information. A major rally is being set up tomorrow."

I'd already known this; thanks to contact lists I'd been slaving over the last days. My task had been to ensure anyone with the remotest interest would be there, a big push for the United Platform for Citizen Respect.

"There's going to be trouble. A highly motivated opposition group intends to make a statement. This will give you the opportunity to demonstrate your commitment and get on the *real* inside."

Demonstrate my commitment clearly meant getting into the middle of the riot that was going to take place and being seen. Truth be told, I was terrified by violence. Running away had always been part of my agenda and no matter what I was presently being instructed to do, it was *still* on the agenda.

Naturally, the PR agent already knew this. "We'll have additional eyes inside the rally and they'll specifically observe you … assisting you to get into the action … and ensuring that you're prominent in the ensuing animated discussion. You'll be reported on the lines as a prominent United Platform for Citizen Respect organizer who was willing to take action when required. We'll gauge the overall level of support the United Platform for Citizen Respect have and push you into the right position. Your participation is appreciated and I'm confident you'll rise to the moment, even if you need some help to do so."

The PR agent rose and left without waiting for a reply, not that I had one. I was too knotted up. High visibility of any sort was exactly what I'd spent years avoiding. Finding myself the centrepiece of a report on the news lines, one that would carry a lot of momentum to gain maximum exposure, was a death sentence. Killing myself would merely make me more vulnerable; dead I was easy prey. A solution to the problem was what I had to come up with, and fast.

Necessity never made you cleverer, which seemed unfair; being squeezed should include inspiration. All I had was dull desperation, which had me realize how unsolvable everything was ... without the slightest notion how to resolve it.

I was in a complete slump by the time I strode into the campaign office and fell into my seat. Logging onto the campaign system, I stared at the cascade of news and messages about tomorrow's rally. Nothing required effort from me, which was nice—much nicer than the message I received telling me to go to Dr Sand's office. It appeared I'd soon learn my mission.

This time the StoneBeater was alone, but he didn't look any less threatening. He peered closely, clearly assessing me. He must have been satisfied, because he didn't kill me. Instead, he gestured the chair before his desk. The small narrow chair was surprising comfortable ... maybe a little too comfortable I thought, aware I was stuck (another word for "trapped").

Dr Sand continued to regard me, then finally leaned forward and folded his hands on the desk. He had a deep, reassuring voice that surely had to be modulated by a charm. No lifeform had that precise mix of assured warmth and confident authority that garnered trust in a listener. Clearly, it was a trap—and knowing something was a trap was useless, as I was finding through repetition.

"We're expecting trouble at the rally tomorrow based on a reliable source. A radical and militant Human Rights group will attempt to start trouble. They're hoping we'll respond, so they can gain attention as martyrs and stir up their base." He waited for acknowledgement.

I nodded vigorously, then offered a lame shrug. I might as

well have jammed a finger in a power outlet and experienced a spasm. I had no idea what to say, but looking blank didn't seem safe, either.

"We see this as an opportunity to reach undecided voters, so we're going to manage the process to demonstrate how peaceful and law-abiding we are and how well we can manage the inevitable friction that our presence on the Standing Committee will create."

It sounded almost credible. It was exactly what a sophisticated, self-aware non-Natural lifeform political coalition would have chosen to do during a strategically important election.

"Mansard, *you'll* take a lead in this process by directing the response to the group." His gaze was intense and a twitch of a smile—or smirk—pulled at his dry lips. "You'll spontaneously lead rally attendees in vigorous and vocal opposition to the group. You'll interact with them physically and engage the leaders in discussion on the merits of our platform. You'll be a natural United Platform for Citizen Respect spokesperson ... arising in the heat of the moment ... providing grassroots energy for the platform.

"Of course, Human RIghts thugs won't take lightly to your impassioned defence of a diverse and inclusive social community, and they'll fall back on violence. They'll beat you, at which point our security group will intercede and escort them from the hall. Your transportation to the medical facility will be in high position, as will bulletins re your recovery. The press conference that will take place on your release from the facility will bring us a 5% increase in approval in the polls and a 7% increase in voter turnout in key targeted locations."

Dr Sand stopped speaking and resumed staring. I'd have wriggled if the chair didn't have a most effective grip. I opened my mouth, then closed it and concentrated on the happy part— when I'd be in the medical facility, recovering from the vicious beating. Temporarily, thankfully, I'd be beyond reach. Not only would I rest, I'd be on another plateau, thanks to painkillers.

"We need to capitalize quickly. The medical facility will use accelerated regrowth techniques to recover you within 24 hours, so we can hold the press conference before the Human Rights team has fully regrouped. You'll have the required responses dialled into you as part of the process, and you'll appear a little hazy—but very passionate—about returning to the struggle.

You've been sent scripts to prepare you for tomorrow's event."

With that, the chair relaxed its grip and I was free to leave, which I did—swiftly. I went to my campaign desk and did my voter-reach activities like a good campaign worker before heading back to my space to consume those scripts.

The game kept getting more complicated and the possibilities of my surviving it more remote. They had reasons for pushing me into the public frame—the reasons they'd told me and the *real* reasons. Sooner, rather than later, those real ones would conflict, and I'd be burned by the friction. The last time, running away had appeared successful; I was sorely tempted to do so again. The problem was, to remain successful, I couldn't risk the attention that running would bring.

5

WHEN I GOT off the transit, I joined a street syndicate and bought a lottery ticket. The Natural lifeform organizing the syndicate assured me that, given this was the last draw of the night, it had a higher proportion of clearances than any other. He didn't mention that it also had a greater number of entries, which pretty much cancelled this. I decided that when my syndicate had failed, I'd take the hit and run, whatever the consequences. I just needed to shift the decision-making process from my shoulders.

Standing at the rear of the hall, watching the United Platform for Citizen Respect volunteers finish the set up, I wondered how badly everything would go. My street syndicate had had the entire basket cleared; the odds against this were so large they could not be easily stated. The syndicate shark asked if I wanted to double down, and I did. I bought another number from a different basket, one with quoted odds. I got the message that it had cleared as I walked into the hall. When probability was flat out against you, caving in to the inevitable was the way to go.

I was ready for anything and completely surprised when a soft persistent cough sounded near my ear. I whirled. Lincoln smiled amiably. She was wearing a stunning set of elegant robes with scatter of vivid sparkling colours. She also had noticeably more prominent breasts than I remembered. She started talking as if we'd only seen one another a few hours previously and had parted on the best of terms.

"Hi Screw-Top. Just heard the Knob has been moved, upward no less, for outstanding performance. You thinking of throwing a spear at the target?"

I couldn't have been more thrown off balance if Lincoln had grabbed my ankles and was hold me upside-down which may have been the plan, given her sly smile. A teeny hint of embarrassment could be viewed in the amused expression. With a playful slap to the back, she continued.

"You should get yourself out of the shit pots for a while, before they discover you're sane and put you back down. You get to the keep the money; they change grade but not salary if you're not on the scheme."

She regarded me intently and I could read the challenge. I'd found my med card slipped into my locker two days before and seen the statements before that. Someone received special and expensive treatment, and I'd approved everything. There had been a discharge notice with the last statement but didn't indicate if it was a warm or cold version (and I'd not dared check). Seeing Lincoln, I decided that it had been a warm one; her mother had recovered, and this was Lincoln wanting to see if any non-medical complications had occurred.

I shook my head and took Lincoln's cue. "No, not really interested if it's true. Being a manager is asking for more trouble and grief, and I've more than enough of that, thanks," I advised with a rueful smile.

Lincoln smiled in return. "I can understand that." She looked at me as if seeing me in the hall for the first time. "Why are you here? You staffing with the United Platform for Citizen Respect?" Her tone had changed. This was a genuine question.

I decided ducking the issue was a better plan of action.

"Yeah, leveraged action. Someone I know is involved and they asked me to come along ... show of strength really. How about you?"

"I'm providing the security for tonight, a late entry I should say. The regular team had a problem down at the docks when they decided to go headfirst with a set of Hartigans over a case of unclaimed deliveries at a storage pick-and-buy. The Hartigans put them in a liquid nitrogen tube and gave them a moonshot. Anyway, it created a vacancy and I was the only one available at such short notice. So here I am. Should be easy money—political rally in a major election with a breakout group ramping in the polls. There'll be more PR agents here than voters. My team only needs to be visible and meet public assembly requirements." She grabbed my arm and pushed me against the wall. She'd read my face with complete accuracy; my shock and concern could have been viewed from across a field. "What? Are you going to fuck my night again? Is this a fucking cover for some stupid stunt you've in mind?"

Shaking me, not roughly, but enough to stir me from my stunned state, I thought about what was about to happen. "No stunt by me, but yes, there's going to be trouble and you should take your team and leave now. I can't share details, but there's a major riot scheduled, and I assume the security team has been fully briefed. If you haven't, then you could have a serious problem. Leave before it boils over."

Lincoln remained calm as she studied me for a second before speaking.

"Okay, that explains the lack of bidders. I knew there was something wriggly going on, and so we've been booked to be the punching bags. Security failure will be on us. We're not connected, so no one need worry, and there's probably someone lining up to strip our base after the show. I think there's going to be an unscheduled change to tonight's program." Lincoln lifted a hand to her mouth and spoke code into it, waiting for a reply before speaking again. "Now, Screw-Top, tell me what you know."

I nearly laughed. That was exactly what I wasn't going to do, but I needed her to know enough to not get killed, so I gave an edited version. "I was told yesterday that a Human Rights group was planning to make a scene here tonight and that the United Platform for Citizen Respect would use it to give themselves a lift. I've been marshalled into fronting the response and am going to be a star on the lines, so I've been told. Should do wonders for my career."

"Marshalled how? No, don't tell me. You're the most impressive trouble magnet I've ever encountered, and I really don't want to know more. These skinbags have tried to net me and I'm very unhappy and intend to deal with it. Go home. It'll get more than a bit raucous here shortly and I don't want to have to worry about you getting under my fins."

"I can't leave. I'm being tagged and if I go, there'll be more trouble. Anyway, what about you? This isn't a bar brawl; this will be a serious breakout and there could be weapons"

Lincoln's laugh was genuine and amused. She finally took her hand off my arm, stepped back, and looked at me. I realized that she looked different, and not just because of the robes. There was a different attitude. I suddenly realized that I'd not bet on anyone who crossed her. She held an edge, like a long shiny knife that caught light in a murky alley.

"Thanks for the thought, Screw-Top. Like the robes? They will turn a Broccian filleting knife and absorb the full charge from a nerve-stick. Not my own, unfortunately; hence, the stuffing up top. You need more chest thrust to get them to hang properly. This is going to be a bad night for some people and a really good night for others. Find a bolthole and stay there till the froth is gone. "

She walked across the hall, talking into her wrist while I decided whether this was good or bad. Reyan, the Natural I'd met on my first visit to the United Platform for Citizen Respect office, an assistant to Dr Sand, came over. "Shakbout, we need someone to test the audio levels. Would you mind doing the readings on the stage, please?"

I nodded and followed her across the hall to the stage where equipment for the speakers had been set up. Dutifully, I read prepared scripts in various locations as levels were tested for various degrees of crowd density. This took over 90 minutes, as there was an intense and inscrutable struggle between Reyan and the audio manager over dead spots that required repeated readings. Finally, Reyan emerged triumphant and some equipment was re-configured to her satisfaction. I was free to wander off but didn't get very far before I encountered Dr Sand, who pointed to a spot on the floor. It had a faint X on it—the spot I was to stand until I leapt into action.

The hall started to fill with lifeforms I recognized from the campaign office. More Naturals started to arrive that I didn't recognize. Evidently, this would prove an important rally for the United Platform for Citizen Respect, an all-out pitch to swing Natural votes, specifically those active enough and curious enough to be willing to take a closer look at candidates and supporters. The willingness of a Human Rights group to make a move also made more sense. This was exactly the sort of mixed event that their core support required action against. Everybody was going to get a slice of the pie ... except me.

The rally went off without a hitch, which was the problem. Various speakers spoke convincingly and passionately about whatever they'd been scheduled to speak convincingly and passionately about. The crowd seemed engaged and there was a buzz of excitement, and delicious risk-taking about being there and making a deliberate political decision. There was no impact on the rally from the "spontaneous" race riot that took place outside on the streets.

The general agreement was that it was in fact "spontaneous" and a race riot, with the majority favouring a confrontation between an (unknown) Natural and an (unknown) Ornamental.

Apparently, the Natural referred to the Ornamental as a "stinking blue fish-head", an entirely plausible reason for a fight between the two. How exactly this confrontation became an all-out riot was unclear, however.

What was beyond dispute was that, over the course of 30 minutes, there were 18 different fights between individuals and groups. No fatalities occurred and property damage, while extensive, was limited to public furniture and paving. Benches and litterbins were torn from bolts and used to beat people. Under the circumstances, the lack of fatalities was very mysterious unless everyone involved had, coincidently, been wearing high-grade protective wear ... which would undermine the "spontaneous" aspect the Standing Committee had been so anxious to assert.

Not that I was in any hurry to dispute the conclusion. I'd dodged a nerve-stick and wasn't going to pick up one. Dr Sand appeared unruffled by the turn of events. He simply stared at me when speakers had finished and nodded curtly to signal, I was free to go, which I rapidly did. When I left the hall, I saw Lincoln still in those dazzling robes, talking to a tall and fat bald lifeform, who must have noticed my attention because he looked over. He spoke to Lincoln, who turned and also looked, without malice or emotion, though she did offer a slight smile of recognition before they returned to their conversation.

———

Any hopes I'd had about extending my streak of luck were removed the next morning when I got a promotion that I really, *really* didn't want, and couldn't escape. The Knob had indeed been moved somewhere where he could do more substantial damage to a greater number of people. Rosby caught me as I clocked on and advised I was wanted in the office.

I walked into the Knob's old office and saw a natural male sitting behind the desk. He was about two metres tall with a slender build; his pot belly looked out of place. A set of plain, mid-priced robes indicated that he was from the lower reaches of upper management. Who had he offended, to be dumped down to this spot? He waved me to the chair before the desk, equal level with his. He seemed to have his own hair and skin, and those charcoal-gray eyes looked unadjusted. A beacon of quiet self-confidence and assurance, I hated him from the start.

"Mr. Mansard, may I call you Shakbout? Let me be the first to congratulate you on your new position. I'm sure you'll be every bit as good as you've been described." He then smiled and appeared to be waiting for me to say something.

I smiled and said thank you, hoping what I strongly suspected was happening was actually not happening. No such luck.

"I'll tell you that I was seriously considering taking you for my new group, managing resource allocations for targeted sub-sectors that need performance support. However, with the vacancy right now, it was deemed better to slot you in right away. Particularly given the strong support for the move from your predecessor."

The look that accompanied this gave a strong impression that the gentleman greatly admired my oral sex prowess and had been looking forward to experiencing it first-hand, only to have the chance snatched away. Fair enough. No one advanced up the greasy pole without laying it on for the rung above. What I didn't understand was why I was there; as far as I knew, I got borderline acceptable reports, enough to stay in place, not close enough to put me on the promotion line. This was either a set-up or a fuck-up, and I'd have to wait to see which. The lifeform stood and extended a business card, which I took.

It showed that Allson Gala was Assistant Deputy Director of Resource Allocation. This made it much more likely to be a fuck-up, which was a relief. Sooner, rather than later, wheels would grind, and I'd be returned to my rightful place, and my time in the chair would never be spoken of again.

With a smile to remind me that he had his eye on me as a future acquisition, Allson left the office, and Rosby entered and closed the door behind.

Leaning against the door she said, "It's not a fuck-up. You're here because I worked to have you here, and you need to understand what's going on. With the election coming up, *everything* is under scrutiny. Nothing makes the top layer feel safer than offering up the sacrifice of some low-performing section to their new masters, as proof that they're awake and earning bonuses. With the Knob in charge, we were heading the list for clerical staff in the Red Halls. There's a limit as to how far I can distort numbers without actual assistance from someone in this office. I created an obligation to have him pulled up and create a vacancy. I submitted your reviews and recommendations to ensure that you'd be put in place when that vacancy arose."

"I'm not grateful," I told her, holding back the real words I wanted to shout.

Rosby stepped across the room and stood directly in front of me. Looking up, I could see she was burning angry. Her tone was as heated as her expression. "Fuck gratitude. This is about survival and I'll do what I must, to ensure that I and the 350 live staff and 600 Involuntary Public Servant sacks here survive. At the moment, you're the best chance we have of doing so, and you need to know that if we go down, we'll be leaning on *you* as we fall. We have little time to drive up productivity over the average for the sector. In fact, we need to be in the top five to be sure we're in the clear.

"You're here because you're the sole reason we have any productivity at all. Since you aren't on the scheme, you're not having the will-to-live sucked out of you every day. Now, I need you to figure out how we're going to achieve 75% of the annual targets before the next audit in four weeks."

Rosby turned on her heels and left, closing the door with enough force to make a point without actually slamming it. When you were in a blood lake and a predator was coming for you, it was much better to swim than to stay and argue, so I set about swimming as fast as I could. I decided to avoid being clever and to concentrate on the obvious and left the office. No sign of Rosby at her usual spot, thankfully.

I headed for the Involuntary Public Servant hot box. The process altered the Involuntary Public Servant's body, so it was considerably more durable and injury-resistant than a living body. They were destined for rough work and needed to be capable of tremendous wear and tear. The work did take a toll and the Involuntary Public Servants gradually started to buckle under the strain. To extend their useful productivity period, they were refurbished in hot boxes. It was like going to a vehicle wash. An Involuntary Public Servant was picked up on a hook and moved through a steam-filled tunnel, and then dropped the other end, looking slightly less work-stained.

We had a hot box that had puzzled me from the first time I'd herded a crew through it. It was wide enough to accommodate 10 bodies in a row—a batch—and took three hours to process. This created a constant backlog of bodies waiting to be steamed. The work we did was rough on them. What was puzzling was a sign on the box that gave instructions for a continuous feed rather than the batch process used. I felt compelled to check why.

News of my new position had spread. When I asked at Procurement about the box, they provided relevant information. Delivered by error, it was too big for the requirements of the section. Signed for, it was stuck here and set up to run with minimum power, without anyone giving any more thought to it.

I took a bolts-and-sparks tech with me and went to look more closely at the box. She checked the power feed and connected it to the major junction, and I dialled in a set-up code. The box extended to five times its previous length and a plat-form extended beneath it that raised up two metres off the ground; ramps slid out at each end. The length of the hot box steadily changed colour from off-gray to navy-blue, with crimson-red horizontal bands running the length.

The tech looked on with surprise and then turned to me. "Lanken's Tears, that's a Metro Double G-Weight. What's it doing here?"

I just nodded. It was indeed the top-of-the-range hot box, made by the best manufacturer contracted solely to the military, and this unit was designed to return near-death fighters to good health in the shortest possible period. A living human could tolerate three trips through the box, but a fourth had unpredictable side effects, a subject that sparked considerable rumours and official silence. For an Involuntary Public Servant, this was the nearest they'd come to having a living body again.

I was very relieved that I was right. I'd read the sign bolted to the box and been curious about is several months ago, and now hoped it wasn't a joke. The box was the key to my plan for the section. The tech correctly interpreted my silence as a command for the same from her. She grinned and ran up a report that covered her time as maintenance on a misfiring spritz pump. I signed it and she walked away while I admired the box. The lights stopped abruptly, and the stripes lit up together. This meant the system was operational and it was time to get customers for my new wash-and-go service.

I returned to my office. Rosby was back at her desk and didn't look up when I sauntered past. I closed the door (two people could play the ignoring game) and spent the next 20 minutes enmeshed in the bureaucracy of the largest catering company in Thiegler. I was impressed by the sheer persistence of indifference and poor service, I had to force my way past. I'd been positive that Public Service had a near monopoly on such hostility aimed at external callers. Based on this, Profit Service provided serious competition. Finally, I managed to connect to the person I wanted to talk to, by accident. It was clear that I wasn't whom they'd been expecting. Still, to his credit, he did provide an opening that I readily stepped through.

"Hello, my name is Shakbout Mansard, I work in the Sanitation Department of Mengchi and I've a fully operational Metro Double G-Weight with a great deal of excess capacity. I was wondering if you'd be interested in using it?"

"When can I see it?" was the quick response.

"Right away, if you have the time. I'll meet you at the main entrance of the Sector 67 drainage section."

"Be there in 15 minutes." The call was over.

I sat back in my chair and breathed a huge sigh of relief. I hadn't thought it would be this straightforward; clearly, there was a bigger gap in the market than I'd thought or the report on the lines had suggested.

I left the office. Rosby still wasn't looking at me; maybe she was considering that she'd put the wrong romper into the race. No matter. I had a plan and that made me happy. For now, I was the one driving events rather than being whipped on by others.

Standing by the main entrance, I gazed absently across the empty car park. A very nice glider crossed towards me. When it stopped, five people got out, none of whom looked like the figure I'd spoken to earlier ... which was not a surprise, since it was a construct, designed to shield the real faces listening to the call. Unsurprisingly, they were all Naturals. What was surprising was how the family resemblance spread between them. I'd stood on a nerve all right. I had the majority owners from the founding family of the company come see if I was bluffing or if I was about to save their skins and money.

We skipped introductions as I opened the doors and ushered them inside, three females and two males sharing the same gray eye colour and energetic confidence. I led them to the lift, and we descended in silence, which was maintained until they sighted the hot box. I deliberately stood several feet away from them, so all I heard was subdued murmuring that stopped as one of the females approached and held out a hand. She was my height, with a round cheerful face and slim figure that didn't look like it had been corrected. As we shook hands, she introduced herself. "I'm Saba Magellen and am very interested in the excess capacity you spoke of."

"I'm very glad to hear that," I responded with a quick smile. "I have a simple proposition. I need full-depth catering for 370 families in an assembled eating space, run continuously for three shifts a day, every day of the year. You'll have similar access to the box for all your staff, live and re-animated, and transport will be provided to collect them from the basement of the central warehouse, as well as return them on a schedule provided by you. No paperwork, no cash, and you get three days advance service as a down payment. A like-for-like trade. We're ready to start as soon as you have staff to be washed."

She didn't blink or hesitate, "Do you have transport ready now?"

I told her I did and with that, the trade was sealed. I'd have the eating space assembled and running in three days and she'd have the first crew in the box within the hour. The rest of the clones nodded and smiled, and we left in silence that continued until they got back into the glider and departed.

I went back down and gave the Involuntary Public Servant waiting in the drain-bus the address for the collection, and it drove off. Now, it was a matter of waiting for the space and the food to arrive before I could take the next step.

———

I lost the next three days to paperwork. The Knob had believed that if he ignored it, it would cease to matter. Rosby assured me that auditors wouldn't share that view.

She worked at an extraordinary rate, constantly finding missing information and ensuring that finished product was circulated properly. This was no mean feat as she was in a struggle with every other marginal section, all of whom saw salvation in the defeat of others. It was a zero-sum game; there'd be winners and losers, and everyone knew the stakes.

Signing, stamping, formatting, backdating, and polishing turds by the dozen for 16 hours a day helped time to pass. There was no pressure to attend the United Platform for Citizen Respect meeting from either side, to my relief. Allson Gala's visit had a none-too subtle agenda. We were part of his empire and he was sizing up potential losses and how to manage results. He wouldn't assist in any way. If we made it past the winning line, he'd accept congratulations on our behalf, with becoming modesty. If we looked like we were irretrievable, they'd cut us out before the axe fell from elsewhere. Cleaning your own house was greatly favoured over being written up in an audit report.

I did get to walk every day and saw that construction was taking place in a previously idle space near the staff entrance. The eating space was being assembled. On the third day, it was ready to open. The company had done a very nice job. It was full of little niches and booths that didn't make it look like a public dining room. Time to spread the word.

Mass-produced (affordable) food was created with processes driven by magic and allowed for a controlled scale that couldn't be achieved otherwise. Plants and animals were grown to maturity under controlled conditions that ensured consistent maximum disease-free yield. All to the good and utter necessity of feeding the population on a non-fertile planet like Thiegler , the planet was devastated during the war, compounded later by a disastrous misjudgement. We were all crowded into the remaining, viable 20%, which meant that living space tended to crowd out growing space. The solution: ultra-productive, sky-high food farms.

The problem for Bottle-Born lifeforms was the residual sensitivity to magic, which meant we could taste the taint in farm food. We spent our lives eating food that never quite tasted right. There was a saying that a Bottle-Born would be your slave for life for a slice of natural bread. I was going to find out if that was true or, at least, if I could receive vastly increased productivity for untainted food.

At the office, I requested Rosby collect the living staff at the shift change down at the disaster assembly point. I went there and stood on a table and put a broadcast charm around my neck. The staff filed in and when everyone was waiting for the latest round on management nonsense, I got started.

"A new eating room has just opened by the staff entrance and will operate around the clock. All staff members and their first and second-degree relatives are free to use it. It's being run by the Tallester Group, which some of you may know are the largest catering company in Mengchi. There's no charge for the food or limit on what anyone may eat at a sitting nor on the number of sittings anyone can have. The price for this facility is that every shift meets *every* shift target in full. Targets were posted as I've been speaking. These targets are high; if we fail to meet them, we'll be dissolved and reallocated to activities that are guaranteed to be considerably more unpleasant than the current work. For this shift change, and this shift change only, there will be a 60-minute delay so that everyone can try out the eating hall and test the accuracy of my statements. Please go and eat."

The assembly area emptied faster than it had filled; within a moment, there was only myself still on the table and Rosby looking at me with a strange smile.

"You're not hungry?" I asked as I jumped from the table and took off the charm.

"Starving, as it happens, for answers and food. How did you do this? The cost is more than can be hidden and when word gets out and the food stops, there'll be twice the trouble than if it had never been."

"Let's sample the wares in the food hall and I'll feed your curiosity at the same time. It'll be good to have someone to show off to."

6

Rosby and I sat in a quiet corner with laden trays in front of us, the smell mouth-watering. Until you put food into your mouth, there was no knowing, but in this case the knowing was truly wonderful. Every morsel tasted of food, no taint of magic. We ate in silence until we'd cleared the plates and our trays had been removed. Facing each other over glasses of spring water, Rosby indicated with a wave of a hand that it was time I satisfied her other hunger.

"About six months ago, I was browsing the lines, looking for nothing in particular, when I came across a report on the Curse of the Natural Farm. Frankly, I thought it was a story about farming Naturals, so I was a bit intrigued. Unfortunately, it wasn't, but it was interesting nevertheless. There are 20,000 hectares of uncontaminated land about 500 kilometres north-west of the city, which had been a country estate at one time. Now it's the sole source of naturally grown food. It's far enough away from the city to escape the pressure to maximize output and fills a need for natural products that citizens are willing to pay for."

Rosby appeared sincerely interested, so I happily continued. "The Standing Committee awarded the contract to run this estate to catering companies that also have ongoing management stakes in a forced farm operation. They want managed food growth industry experience and commercial trading expertise when handling the estate.

"It's a big deal. The potential profits from the estate easily overshadow the returns from the forced farms and the contract is seen as a mark that the company's the best in the industry. According to the report, the contracts always followed the same pattern. The first two years would be fabulously profitable and the following three would incur increasing costs that would finally reduce operations to a loss by the close of the contract. The existing contract holder always had first refusal on the next award, and to date, no one had ever held the contract for two consecutive terms. Plenty of companies had held it more than once, though, and a few have held it multiple times, always with gaps of no less than 15 years between awards. None of the companies involved were willing to talk about the contract, and neither was the Standing Committee, all for reasons of 'commercial sensitivity'. The writers explained that the Committee needed to have the land farmed. Food and revenue were always important, and the companies wanted initial profits and prestige, so they mutually agreed to bury the problems. So, the Curse of the Natural Farm has become a subdued legend in the industry.

"Still, the writers were intrigued enough to research and estimate the problem. They learned the roots of said problem. The estate's located out in the Ribbed Band, so forget mass automation. There has to be a very high proportion of non-machine labour. Growing the workforce in a farm for a five-year contract isn't cost effective, so a different plan has been informally put in place. The Standing Committee provides the company with an allocation of Involuntary Public Servant labour to work the estate and support the automated infrastructure. The only problem is that the natural environment wears out the Involuntary Public Servant s at a higher-than-average rate."

"Fascinating," Rosby murmured, leaning forward, her eyes never leaving mine (Flattery works).

I nodded absently. "The replacement formula is set at the average wear-down rate, so for the first two years, the Involuntary Public Servant labour force turns over nicely, and productivity and profits are high. Then, the wear-down rate starts to exceed the replacement rate and the supply starts to slow down. The productivity starts to fall and more has to be done by less Involuntary Public Servant bodies, thus leading to a higher wear-down rate. The spiral continues for the balance of the contract. Productivity remains level enough to pay the Standing Committee fees, while actual realizable profit falls to minimal levels. If you renew the contract, you don't receive a re-set on your labour terms; it's a continuation.

"A nice piece of work, I enjoyed how they'd drawn the story together without thinking further. I also knew we had a serious hot box. I'd been detailed to clean it my first week here all information without purpose. Then you put me in a body clamp which was when I realized that someone had food and a problem, and I had a hot box and a problem. It seemed possible that we could provide solutions for each other."

I paused to take a breath and put my concluding thoughts into place, which prompted Rosby to gesture impatiently for me to continue.

"The hot box we have boosts the Involuntary Public Servant recovery by ten, which makes a standard average replacement rate a very comfortable supply. I needed to get the staff here to work and food was—is—the quickest way to motivate them. The Tallester Group is two-and-a-half years into the contract and has a strong desire to avoid the curse. Their other enterprises won't easily absorb the strain from the contract, another handy item from the report. So, in this case, one plus one equals four."

I sat back. As I'd told the story I'd been leaning closer. If I hadn't sat back and relieved the pressure on my work suit at waist level, I'd probably have cut my hard-on in two via an inconvenient fold that had trapped it.

Rosby was suitably impressed and a little worried. "How long can you hold this up? Sooner or later, word of this will leak and it will be taken over by another, and we'll be squeezed out. Taking away something is always much more trouble than never giving it."

"That's a very accurate summary of the position and I look forward to seeing how you resolve it."

"*Me* solve it? What are you talking about? This is your idea!" Rosby looked very unhappy.

"How could I solve it? I know nothing and nobody. You, on the other hand, are as wired in as possible, without being actual infrastructure. You're the only person who could solve the problem of ensuring that this process continues uninterrupted, so that we retain production at non-threatening levels. To level up, you threw me into this blood lake and now you get to keep me and everyone else afloat. I can't do it by myself and neither can you, but we might be able to do it together."

Rosby smiled fleetingly and touched my hand, which had the same impact as being brushed with a nerve-stick (the blockers I ate as part of my breakfast kept it down to a tolerable minimum). "Nice play. I wasn't sure if you had it in you, but you were the only one available and you've done it. There's no way I'm giving up this food for anyone."

She stood and left the eating area, and I stayed for another hour while the reaction slowly wound down. As I was about to leave my contact charm jangled. I didn't recognize the caller ID and answered in neutral mode. We'd be able to talk, but no system or location data would be exchanged.

"A very good afternoon to you Mr. Mansard." The voice was confidential and inviting, and breathed an unforced intimacy between people who didn't know each other. "I hope I'm not calling at an awkward time."

"No not at all"

"I'm glad. I won't take much of your time. We have an acquaintance in common, Lincoln Bluefin, she has done security work for us. She mentioned that you'd be a suitable person to include in the planning of a new health related project. Would you be free to attend a planning meeting tonight? Lincoln will be there, and it really would be most convenient for everyone if you could attend. I can assure you that it will be a mutually beneficial meeting. I'll slide you the location details."

"I'd be glad to attend," I replied, and with that the call was severed and a note delivered. Someone was using Lincoln to get to me; if they could put a grip on Lincoln, then I had every reason to be horribly scared, which I was. I thought it likely that the lifeform I'd seen the night of the rally was involved. He looked like the managerial type, not staff, and I'd definitely recieved a call from staff. Suddenly, I was furious. All the rage I tightly held about placing those I cared deeply about in danger filled my entire body. No running this time, I'd have to deal with this directly and headed up to my office to consider exactly how I'd do so.

When I entered, Rosby was standing next to what looked like a very large upright snow-white worm. The worm had wide, nearly circular feet and its body seemed to be a stack of fat and rather wrinkly white circular tubes. Its round bald head rested on a beanstalk of a neck, emerging from the middle of the topmost tube. Big ocean-blue eyes blinked slowly behind large magnifying glasses that appeared to be a feature of the face rather than an addition. It had a small narrow nose, a wide blubbery mouth, and thin arms that connected to the tube below the head. The worm wore a book bag—jammed full of books—with a long strap diagonally slung over the body at the neck. The creature was surprisingly strong to carry it so effortlessly.

Rosby gestured the worm. "This is Aikon, our information specialist."

Information specialists were usually referred to as Book-Worms, a name I'd thought to be a reference to their work. Now

I saw the real reason and words flew out before I could stop them. "What heartless fuckwit thought this was funny? They'll pay in full measure when they have to explain the day the hammer falls. Lanken will shed no tears for them." There were times when the knowledge that we were merely clay in the hands of stupid Naturals was too much to bear.

Aikon bowed his head a little and, after looking at Rosby, left the room. The backwash from the rage caught me full on. I'd insulted a lifeform to its face and demonstrated that cruelty really was universal. I turned to Rosby to explain and stopped at the expression on her face. Sporting a huge smile, she was obviously entertained.

"You have no idea, do you?" She shook her head and laughed. "I should worry about you, I really should. You're going to be quite the box of surprises. I hope you've nothing you want to keep hidden, because your life is an open book now. Of course, that's the usual trade-off isn't it: privacy or security? If you want security, you have to give up some privacy. For the kind of security, you now have, I guess it comes with no privacy at all."

"Rosby, what are you talking about?"

She looked at me in surprise. Thankfully, the depth of the shock I had after she'd spoken was enough to make me appear calm. I'd been waiting for this for ten years and was as unprepared as if I'd never given it thought when it actually happened.

Rosby peered more closely. "You should sit down. This may take a bit." She waited till I was sitting behind the desk before she, too, sat down. "The information specialists are Intercessionists."

With that, I saw the breadth and depth of the new hole I'd thrown myself into. No one had any idea of the religious belief patterns of Bottle-Born lifeforms in their native states and contexts. All lifeforms now believed in Lanken the Blind, weaver of the great web that connected all living creatures together. In the name of justice Lanken cries tears for the terror and horror of our lives, each tear collected and placed in a balance against those who caused them to be shed. The judgment of Lanken will take place when the web is finally unravelled and it would be a full measure of the weight of her tears and then it would be the time for others to cry.

Intercessionists had added another layer to the mix. For them Lanken was both blind and deaf, and it was only when their situation was recognized by another and that other demanded justice on their behalf, that Lanken would see them and cry the tears that would grant them their due on that last day. Whoever interceded on their behalf got the eternal loyalty and devotion of the group. The flaw in this plan was apparent to everyone, so a qualification was included in the fine print. The intercession had to be entirely genuine and made without thought or hope of future reward. It had to be honest and self-less, which ruled out it ever happening. Until it did, it took something extra to beat the odds and the absurdity to success-fully fuck yourself.

The last thing I wanted was to have anyone pay attention to my life and actions. Rosby was correct. I'd surrendered all slivers of privacy to the devotion of the information specialists, who'd investigate me with appalling completeness to understand how best to serve and protect me. What they'd do when they found out went beyond imagination, mostly because I didn't dare imagine it.

"They have put you in their pocket now. You should make yourself comfortable. There'll be no leaving it." Rosby looked at me thoughtfully. "I'm going to have to be nicer to you as well. I don't know if they have a sense of humour and I'm in no hurry to find out." Ignorance was such bliss, I could have shrieked, stabbed her, stabbed myself, cried, laughed, or done something calm or crazy if I'd possessed a spark of energy; instead I was anesthetised.

The door opened and Aikon entered, followed by four iden-tical information specialists. They stood in an arc around Rosby and me. Akion stepped forward. "I am Akion, information specialist and saved being. Through your intercession, Lanken has seen our situation and cries for us. For this gift of salvation, we thank you with our devotion."

Akion stepped back into the arc and another information specialist stepped forward and spoke. "I am Belkirk, information specialist and saved being. As you saw the great wrong that has been done to us and spoke for us so we, too, see you and speak for you to Lanken. Your life will be added to the terrible balance on the final day."

Belkirk stepped back into the arc and the fear that had flooded me receded a little. It looked like this might be prayerful rather than inquisitive. I could certainly do with extra prayers. A third information specialist stepped forward and spoke. "I am Chador, information specialist and saved being. It has become my happy task and duty to record your life for the edification of all saved beings, so that we may see you truly and serve you deeply."

With that pronouncement of doom, Chador returned to the arc and the final two information specialists stepped forward and spoke in unison. "We are Dalok and Efrin, information specialists and saved beings. We speak for those who cannot be here to speak for themselves. We see you as you have seen us; you have saved us so shall we save you. You have changed our sorrow to peace, and we place our lives in your hands." The pair stepped back into the arc and no one spoke.

My throat was clamped shut with fear, but I did manage a seated bow. That appeared sufficient. Four of the information specialists left, but Akion remained behind and blinked slowly.

Rosby moved to the door and said. "That was unexpected. Still, there are unsaved beings to get organized." With a quick nod, she departed.

Akion continued to stand and blink while panic steadily lessened. A thought finally managed to make itself heard and I was ready to inflict damage on someone. The address I'd been sent was in a very nice, quiet section of the city, residential properties mixed with unadvertised business premises, set among tree-lined streets. It wasn't the most expensive part of the city; it was the most *assured* part of the city. You were very happy with your money if you lived there and you earned it very discreetly if you had an office there.

———

I walked up several narrow steps to the door—the steps unusual for street buildings and I assumed there was a security device to delay hostile forces seeking to enter. When I saw the front door, I realized the steps were there for show.

The front door was beautiful, with Vesper woodwork, the shapes and colours of the wood grain drawing eyes from one point to another. To have this amazing piece of art casually on display explained the wealth and power of the inhabitants more effectively than words. The cover also hid the fact that the door was a blast-grade block; the building would crumble before the door would. I was familiar with them from the drains. They were used extensively across the system to prevent floods or other events. The door cover didn't include the seals, which were warnings to those who could read them.

The door opened as I neared a nice smooth movement. The walls of the house were braced to support the door and withstand a direct hit from a mid-range missile. It would take a combination of blows to crack this shell. I stepped inside and was greeted by a small lifeform. He reached my waist, with a slim muscular body emphasized by a snug, dark-yellow one-piece uniform. He was bald, shaved rather than genetic, and smiled widely. He was a Natural; I'd never met one so short before. Genetic variations must occur randomly, as well as being designed.

"Mr. Mansard, welcome. Mr. Constain does greatly appreciate punctuality. Would you come with me, please? Leave your coat there on the rack." He pointed to a beautiful piece of crafted sea-stone that came straight from the soul of a Stone-Beater, and I did as requested.

I was carrying no weapons or charms. As I followed the life-form down a long corridor, I could feel the prickle of full-body scans. The building used a similar charm to confuse a sense of direction used in Old City. It was very effective. As I walked, the distance in front shifted constantly. Not enough to make you lose your footing, just enough to confuse or baffle. After what seemed like a long walk, we came to a set of wooden doors with no decoration, save for the beautiful grain. The short lifeform knocked and waited, and upon an unheard signal, pushed open one of the doors and ushered me inside.

The room was smaller than my entire living space by several centimetres, with a stunning late period Mreves hanging on the wall to the left, an abstract of lovely colours and space that demanded attention. The flooring was plank-cut Ragan wood with a delicate grass-green glow from heated volcanic slopes where they grew four systems over. While I didn't see them right away, they became clear in my memory later, because my attention was focused on a large metal desk at the far end of the room, with two people sitting on either side. Behind it, in a very comfortable looking chair, was the lifeform Lincoln had been speaking to the night of the rally. I had not realized when I had seen him at the rally just how big he was, not just tall but also wide enough to suggest a very compact mass. Bald head, pale skin with no wrinkles, wide topaz eyes set over a straight nose and a smiling mouth. Common Man robes that cost more than my annual salary, worn with assured confidence that rested on the strong exercise of power. I knew his name, he was Mr. Constain. He was the a deeply serious criminal, with a very extensive organisation under his control.

Lincoln was sitting on equally comfortable looking chair on my side of the desk positioned to the right of Mr. Constain. She didn't, however, look comfortable, but furious and frustrated. The two lifeforms who stood behind her with nerve-sticks were probably what was keeping her quiet. There was another chair opposite Lincoln, positioned so that Mr. Constain could look at both and have an unobstructed view of the door. I was waved forward to the empty chair before the desk. I sat and smiled at Lincoln, who gave me a look that would have toasted a boulder.

"Mr. Mansard." Mr. Constain had a strong, confident voice. Whoever he spoke to would listen fully and carefully. "I don't wish to delay yourself or Lincoln any longer than necessary, so this is what will happen. You'll deposit your health card with me and sign all account statements delivered. When I have the card, you and Lincoln may leave unharmed and unencumbered."

He leaned back and waited for a reply. A tunneller came through the floor and the nose lifted the desk before it split in two and fell on either side of Mr. Constain. Three Involuntary Public Servants, armed with doubled-headed ballet axes, jumped out of the tunneller. One held a long blade against Mr. Constain's neck. The other two lurched at the guards with the nerve-sticks, who went straight for the invaders. Nerve-sticks were only good against creatures with nerves. An Involuntary Public Servant was a revived corpse and nerves weren't part of the equation. Battle axes, on the other hand, were good against any type of flesh and in a short time, the guards had been chopped into bloody lumps. The Involuntary Public Servant trio stood still, waiting for the next instructions.

I spoke to Mr. Constain. "I don't wish to delay anyone, so this is what will happen." I handed him an info cube. "This contains details of all your accounts, including deposits with the Royal Bank of Hinjer and the transfer stream that the Insol crew are using. I'll give this information to the Financial Intelligence Department if I think you're casting a shadow in our direction. Lincoln and I have a dinner reservation and need to leave. We can find our own way out."

Mr. Constain didn't speak, but the hand with the cube remained relaxed. I stood, turned to Lincoln and smiled, and motioned the door. Lincoln's face was blank, impossible to read.

I led the way out of the building, with the map of the interior primed in my mind before I'd entered.

When we stepped outside and descended the steps, Lincoln stopped.

"Mud Slayer." She spat the words at me. Her rage needed no words, her body was shouting it as loudly as possible. Apparently, there were too many words in her brain and mouth right then to spit forth anymore.

The words cut through my haze. I was timed to be sober after leaving the building, if all went to plan. Lincoln's rage sped the process and left me reeling. A Mud Slayer was the most dangerous predator on the planet; it rested in unexpected shallows out on the waters that covered most of the surface. In keeping with the name, it resembled a piece of mud. Step on or move near it, and it would attack with fatal results. Sometimes, you could tread on one without any reaction; the unpredictability of the Mud Slayer was what made it so dangerous. The other was that it would attack anything of any size or nature as long as it was alive and eat *anything*. Next to nothing was known about Mud Slayers, because no one had ever caught one to study it. After 15 failed expeditions and no survivors from any, curiosity had been replaced by self-preservation. There was a theory that they were an invasive species, not manufactured, but transported from another system.

Lincoln was talking again, angry, defiant and defeated. "My mother always told me to watch out for hidden shallows. Mud Slayers resting and waiting, striking when you don't expect. But I would see the Slayer in its home and *know*. Instead, you were waiting all the time, hiding beneath my feet and I never knew it. Then, suddenly, you move, and everyone sees who they should really fear. How you must enjoy your little game, let the prey think they're someone, don't disturb their dreams until it suits you." Punching a fist into her palm with force, she regarded me balefully. "You casually show everyone what force really is, a lesson on how to do it for the blind and foolish."

One of drugs in the mixture I'd taken was to heighten perception of other people, to read them more effectively. I saw the humiliation than Lincoln was feeling. I'd stepped on her ground and resolved a situation she couldn't, and with finality that could be considered insulting. It was time to reveal the truth. I'd thought I could do it over a companionable drink, with a shared laugh, but I was presently in a situation more dangerous and inflammable than when I'd been sitting in front of Mr. Constain.

I grasped Lincoln's elbows so that we had a direct connection as I spoke. "I have so many drugs in me right now, I've had to book three sick days off. I've been assured it'd be the same as if I'd taken a full pack of Sour Jumblys, only worse and longer. You hardly believe that I could have managed that situation in cold blood, do you? I'm not you; I'm a seriously frightened lifeform who responded the only way I knew."

Lincoln looked at me and said, "Dinner reservation? somewhere nice I hope."

In silence, we strolled to the bar I'd had in mind and took seats in an un-crowded corner.

After several quiet moments, Lincoln took a long sip from a rainbow-colored alcoholic mixer and regarded me thoughtfully.

"So, drugs? Still not everything, fill in the blanks, please." She took another sip and sat back. I could see her relax and this gave me the space to finish what needed saying. But before I could speak, she regarded me sternly and said, "Edit for length, without leaving out anything significant. It's been a long night."

I briefly told her about the BookWorms and my new position, to which she nodded thoughtfully, and I could hear possibilities and calculations flash and crash in her mind. When I started on the details of the events, I got her full attention. "When I got the call about you, I knew I had a choice. I could hand my life over to another person who'd nibble me to death, or I could jump straight to the conclusion, where I was either fully dead or the problem had been fully removed. Managing the problem to a better conclusion wasn't within my grasp, so I choose to jump. I'd have one small chance to do it, so it had to be credible. Given that I was dealing with a very rich and ruthless lifeform, no one who could capture you was anything less than fabulously dangerous and utterly competent. I had to go all out." I scanned her rigid face and she nodded once.

"Akion got me information about Mr. Constain. His weakness was always going to be money. He likes to spend it, a lot of it, so he'd need easy but hidden access to it. The required information was packaged nicely for me. I'd be directly threatening him without offering him any reason not to kill me right away. I needed to set up the circumstances so that the threat was a way *out* of the circumstances, rather than simply a full stop. For a lifeform who prizes his security, a comprehensive breaching of it was a route to take. Working in the shit pots gave me tools to use a nice bit of theatrics to *over*-make the point.

"All I needed was the ability to do it without becoming unglued or fumbling. As far as I know, I've been given ten different doses of mindbenders to allow me look like I was in control the entire time. There was also the scent trace that the tunneller was locked on. No charms, because they'd be screened for. The mix was calculated to react to give a clean first-wipe profile if I was tested. Truthfully, I never expected to convince you. I thought you'd see the plot and react. Your response was probably what convinced Mr. Constain that it was all clear running and to take the deal."

Lincoln tried to recover some ground. "I was off my game a bit and being caught by the fucker upset me and made me doubt myself. I walked into his hook like a Struckle Fish and I was furious with myself. Seeing you walk in so easily and loose should have warned me. I wasn't ready." She eyed me curiously. "How did the bodies get away?"

"They were set up to depart in the tunneller 10 seconds after I left the room; the time calculated that it would take for us to exit the building via the most direct route. The tunneller would have backfilled on the descent, so there wouldn't be a hole in the floor." I paused and scanned her face, feeling uncertain. "Are we okay with each other?" It was the only question I really cared about, because I'd realized that I had an unexpected and precious degree of affection and concern for Lincoln. She'd slipped under my skin with me only realizing it when she was in danger.

Lincoln's smile was warm and suggested friendship and laughter. "My mother warned me about people like you, Screw-Top ... told me I'd meet someone sincere who'd lead me into more trouble than I could possibly imagine because they were trying to make things better. No money, just trouble. *Interesting* trouble. You're going somewhere, Screw-Top, and I'm with you for the journey."

With that, she slapped me on the shoulder, stood, and left the bar. I stayed a little longer to enjoy the unusual moment: someone who wasn't trying to actively ruin my life while becoming involved in it.

7

I MADE it home without any trouble and passed out on the bed. I awakened to find myself holding a small baby close to my chest while Asher told me it was a historical necessity and the walls melted away to reveal huge hands reaching for both of us. There was an explosion of fire and I felt the baby wrenched from my arms. I kicked wildly and threw myself out of bed, onto the floor and into wakefulness.

The dropdown from recent events, as well as the drugs, had finally arrived and it was going much worse than I'd have imagined. The turmoil was shaking loose something that could never be released, something that should never breach my conscious mind. I'd embedded charms and schemes to protect myself, but they couldn't withstand the onslaught they were receiving. I was going to have to do something to lower the tide, move the stress from my brain to my body.

I slapped on a numb patch, which slowed me down enough to get to a local pharm where I explained I was having a severe reaction to badly cooked Fry Beans. The assistant nodded knowingly and gave me a leech and six litres of replacement plasma. He also instructed me to put a mattress on the floor of the bathroom, because I wouldn't be leaving it for at least two days.

I made it back just as the numbness started declining. Pulling in the mattress, I threw my clothes out of the bathroom, pieced the plasma, and needled myself. At that point, I could feel the cracks in my mind. I slapped on the leech and fell straight onto the mattress. The theory was that one pain would balance the other. Not true. The pain from the leech obliterated room for anything else; it was worse than a nerve-stick. Then it came— happy, delightful, desired blackout.

When I came to, I was covered in blood and exploded bits of leech, as was the mattress and bathroom. The leech had drained all my blood and decaying drugs and suffered the consequences. I was filled with replacement plasma and would suffer a bit longer. Technically, I was alive, where I'd dropped, and had the prospect of being able to move in the next hour or so. This was the happiest moment of my life.

I managed to reach the room-clean button and press it hard enough to activate it. The room filled with steam and warm water showered everything. The steam quickly turned red and then slowly turned white as it was spiralled from the room. Everything was clear and the water stopped. The bathroom, mattress and the remains of the leech were blown dry. I lay still for hours after the cycle had finished, not thinking anything, simply conscious of the mattress under my back and the ceiling above. It was peaceful and easy, and if I could have, I'd have stayed there forever.

The alarm rang stridently, announcing the start of my next working day; it was loud enough to be heard in the bathroom and persistent enough to force me to turn it off. I found I was back in my shabby reality. I went into work and breakfast at the food space did make it a lot better right up to sitting at my desk and looking at the mountain of bollocks I'd have to clear before I could do anything else. Fortunately, I remembered I owed Rosby a turn or two, and moved it all over to her. Her glare should have reduced it to ashes in an instant, except she became even more furious when I advised that she'd been promoted to

Executive Assistant and the interoffice requests were now her responsibility.

I left to do actual work, the kind that would ensure we could meet targets and stay out of the chopping line. It made me feel strong and productive, a bit "leadery" really, and I enjoyed it for the few seconds it lasted.

I was pinged to attend a meeting. Allson Gala wanted to discuss matters of pressing urgency with his extended staff. I made my way up the sixteen levels to where Gala's conference room was located; his office was another sixteen levels up again, among the lower branches of the great management foliage we supported. Since I liked to firm up prejudices quickly, I was annoyed to have to revise my opinion of Allson Gala. He was competent, knew how to manage his staff to get work done. A summons to a meeting wasn't just an opportunity to have his grandeur polished by his minions, it would be about something that impacted us all.

I stepped into the large conference room and nodded to those I knew and took a seat at the far end of the vast table, which proved to be a really good idea when Gala walked in flanked by a woman I'd never seen before. I felt Dialland Jovial stir as he admired his work and unwanted information flowed into my mind while I struggled to control my face and body language.

By appearance, she was a Natural from the Belteeq Affiliated Systems. They had a longstanding staff-exchange program with the Standing Committee, off system administrative experience was a valuable commodity. It also meant that Belteeqrs were a well-known, integrated sub-group on Mengchi with no apparent interest in disturbing any part of the structure. Hiding where no one was looking was a *very* good plan.

Jovial was admiring how her blonde hair fell which, evidently, had been a detail that had proven to be surprisingly troublesome to "get just right". Her bright cornflower-blue eyes, sallow skin, broad shoulders, and long legs were easy. Jovial was pretty pleased with the results. I was having difficulty remembering to breathe.

I'd thought the plot had been interrupted before it had started. Far too late, it occurred to me that action by Jovial's group must have rung the alarm; now I could see that the house was burning down.

Jovial didn't know operational details, work was strictly segregated for security. He was given requirements and a free hand to implement them. I had no idea if the woman would explode in the room or do something relevant or suspicious. Gala nodded, a signal to be quiet because he was taking the floor. With an amiable smile, he began. "Before I turn over the meeting to Ms Hiba to explain why I've called you here at such short notice, I'd like to make an announcement."

He paused and peered directly at me. "I'm very pleased to announce that the Secure Disposal Resources Section, led by Shakbout are now number five in productivity for the service-wide sector ranking. I'd like to congratulate Shakeout on this significant achievement, and I look forward to a peaceful post-election transition."

The congratulations weren't fake we'd just sidestepped a visit from the audit death squads. They never stopped with the obvious victim; they liked to root around. Normally, my extremely rapid rise would have been enough to prompt a visit. With the pre-election rush, they simply took everyone who qualified and didn't bother with anyone who'd scrambled to safety. No one was going to question how I'd done it. The risk of breaking something that had been fixed wasn't a good plan. The food service had survived the biggest threat and from here on, it would be part of the furniture.

Gala gazed around and gestured dramatically. "I'd like to introduce Ms Hiba from the Central Security Compliance Directorate and hand it over to her."

He sat back and Ms Hiba sat forward, looked around the room (I didn't flinch under her intent gaze, though I did experience an odd internal quiver), and began to talk. She had a very nice voice, somewhat deep, very confident, and very clear.

"Thank you. As Assistant Director Gala has noted, I work in the Central Security Compliance Directorate and am here to talk about security compliance. We're now in the closing stages of the pre-election timescale and the levels of attempted interference with the Public Service information infrastructure increases hugely during this period. Based on previous events, we anticipate attempts to penetrate the infrastructure to increase by 800-fold per time fraction while actual breaches also increase. Significant breaches will actually decline as the sheer volume of activity crowd out long-term tunnellers. The risk of an amateur cutting across their set-ups is very great, so they usually rest up and let election waves subside before returning to active service.

"To prepare for the storm of activity that will hit the infrastructure during the active voting period, Central Security Compliance Directorate has developed a protocol that gives us temporary oversight over the whole infrastructure. We don't have any greater access, nor can we make changes to any part of the individual security modules that each of you manage. The protocol is to give an infrastructure wide view so we can see where the pressures are changing to identify patterns of interference. We don't take action ourselves—we're simply an information clearing house and accelerated provider to the relevant enforcement divisions."

She paused and waited for questions, but none came. "What this means in action terms for everyone here is that, as security module-key holders, I need permission from each of you for temporary access to your modules to copy activity logs for the previous sixteen months. This is to create a valid picture of ongoing activity as a baseline for the analysis." She passed encrypted sheets to everyone. "Please complete these today and don't change any security settings right now. After the election has been confirmed, there'll be a requirement to change them. Please wait until you've received that notification."

There were still no questions. Gala closed the meeting and we filed out. Gala and Ms Hiba remained behind, engaged in an animated discussion. I walked back to my office, filled with appalled admiration at the superb brilliant simplicity of the plan so much under everyone's nose, they'd not see it. The Public Service information infrastructure wasn't designed to be fantastically difficult to penetrate. It was, however, time-consuming to obtain critical penetration and control without detection. Any section that had been penetrated could be easily shut down, without disabling the rest of the infrastructure.

This was done by sacrificing efficiency for security. Each section of the Public Service infrastructure was self-contained and linked by feeble reporting lines that allowed the minimum required information to flow sluggishly from one point to another. Penetrate any module and you'd have to repeat the process from scratch for the next one. The links wouldn't support a leap from one to another with sufficient power to actually breach the module. This meant the Public Service was epidemically inefficient, with costly duplication and confusion across the whole service. No one cared. The BookWorms were the hidden information infrastructure that provided enough operation effectiveness to be acceptable; when needed, a centralized process could be temporarily implemented, which created an opportunity for attack, something everyone on all sides of the situation knew.

The solution to this problem was encrypted copy-write, which again harnessed the limitless power of distributed inefficiency. When I wrote on the paper Ms Hiba had given me, it would be encrypted and part-copied to three other sheets distributed at random through the service. To decrypt, each sheet had to be touched in sequence by designated persons; a fourth person then received the entire encrypted scheme and had 120 seconds to unravel it with the key charm they'd been handed. The theory behind this was that the coordination required to successfully enter was so great, it couldn't be secretly maintained long enough to break codes. Doing so was a staple of a sub-genre of dramatic fiction that I really liked; some proposals floating around were monuments to ingenuity.

Someone, somewhere, had realized the power of the process —a shiny, sparkling lure that would trap and absorb your time and attention. People desiring to penetrate the Public Service information infrastructure wanted to show how clever they were. Give them a difficult problem to solve and you tapped into their vanity, and they were hooked. The group didn't want to penetrate the Public Service System but take it over as part of a greater project. Possessing a very different sort of vanity, they sidestepped process distractions and simply asked for access to the entire system. We'd offer it with a smile and relish the satis-faction that came from another box ticked.

The encryption didn't matter, since all the information would flow steadily to those people waiting hungrily for it. Access to every module, to read activity logs, was an open door and I was sure they had enough skill to stroll unnoticed into the infrastructure and do whatever they wanted. This strongly implied that someone, or multiple someone's, very close to the top were involved. Getting Jovial's carefully brewed lifeforms into the positions they were in, required influence and political muscle.

When I returned to my office, Rosby was sitting at a her almost clear desk and smiling angelically. My heart sank. This could only mean trouble. I made a light swerve towards the workshops and Rosby smiled even more brightly and shook her head. Whatever it was, there was going to be no avoiding it. I stepped into my office and found the female PR agent in my chair.

This time she was alone, which I didn't like at all. She motioned the door and I closed it. I was about to point out that that she was sitting in *my* chair in *my* office, when she spoke, her tone matter-of fact. "Nice office and nice chair, too, not exactly standard issue, but very nice, lucky you."

She was correct that it wasn't standard issue and it was very nice. Akion had decided that I should have a better chair and had one delivered; it mixed comfort and support in very pleasing proportions.

"This is your office, please, there's no need to stand. Take a seat. We have matters to discuss and you standing there looking uncomfortable won't do." She waited for me to do as requested. "Let's get started with the nonsense that you've been reporting from the United Platform for Citizen Respect. Apparently, you think that I'm an idiot and would accept any box of rotting predator shit that you choose to serve up ... and that this could transpire without consequences. And, speaking of consequences, we might as well get that out of the way right now."

She zapped me with a small nerve-stick she pulled from a pocket, and fire spiralled through my body. It was over instantly, but the after-effect would linger for hours and I'd have pink piss for a couple of days.

"Now that we've established a fuller understanding of what you've been chosen to do, you can tell me directly what's actually going on."

But I couldn't tell her, because my tongue wasn't willing to cooperate, and I was busy remembering how to breathe without thinking too seriously about it. Finally, I was able to talk and breathe at the same time. I'd expected something like this, having believed the PR Agency wouldn't be satisfied with the reports I was to deliver. I wasn't ready to mention that Zusak Sedge was involved, either. I'd developed what I feverishly hoped was a suitable cover story that contained sufficient truth, so that omissions wouldn't attract attention.

"They were expecting me. They know I'm a plant sent to gather information and they told me that my continued good health was utterly contingent on my conveying the information they'd provided and not adding or amending it in any way. I don't know how they knew, because I never said anything."

"They know because they were expecting you and you fit the

profile. They knew we'd investigate them, so we sent you in the front door to divert attention from real work being done at the rear. That had been going well until this morning ... when we found our assets distributed across several floors and walls of what was supposed to be a safe house. It was a Zusak Sedge signature piece. "

The only good thing about being zapped: any involuntary spasm that might otherwise be a screaming indicator, was accepted as an aftershock. Given the spasm I'd had at the mention of Zusak, I was grateful for this smallest of mercies.

The PR agent hadn't stopped talking for a blink. "If it turns out that she's involved ... I'm sure she'll be working with a local network. She always likes to plug into one that's active locally and use its resources." Her lips drew into a trim line as she studied my face. "Now that they've eaten, they're going to be more relaxed. You're considered window dressing, so you're not a threat. There's a small opportunity to check out what's going on. If there's any sign of Sedge, back away. She's too big a problem. What I want are the names of her local associates."

"I'm watched all the time. Dr Sand is suspicious enough already, so how am I supposed to avoid him?"

"That'll be easy. He was my asset and keeping on top of you was part of his cover. You're on the inside now and considered to be contained. Over the next four days, I want you to see who's talking to whom and when. Whatever's being planned is going to come to the boil soon or they'd have not taken the risk of cutting up Sand. Their mistake is my gain." Standing, she walked to the door, turned back, and nodded. "Nice work with the food space. Use that kind of thinking and find out where the leak is."

Since she'd come alone, I had a feeling she was using me as window dressing again. As I watched her leave, I realized having a broken leg didn't stop a headache.

―――――

Fortunately, the rest of the day continued without any other life-threatening circumstances. As I left the office, I tapped Lincoln to meet me at the Whirlpool Fountain, and she replied she would.

I took transit to the Fountain, located in one if the oldest and most exclusive parts of Mengchi. If you had a residence here, you not only had the money, you had the history as well. Beyond subtle walls and rising plants were generations of string-pullers working very hard to retain their positions. It bothered me a bit that I was going to help them tonight. It was reasonable to consider them the enemy; they were feasting on the flesh and blood of countless generations of lifeforms like myself.

I turned the corner and entered an open space where the Fountain was located and saw Lincoln sitting by a wall, near the pool. She was studying a charm on her wrist and I was struck by how well she looked. Aquatic Ornamentals were not designed to live full time on land. Placed in water and the difference became clear. They possessed a healthy energy glow in water that was dimmed on land. As I approached, she shone a little, appearing as if she'd just stepped out of water. It looked good on her.

The charm was a simple bracelet made of multiple, loosely braided strands. Its simplicity belied tremendous craft and power and was a masterpiece of custom manufacturing. How had Lincoln afforded it? Even with her alternative activities, which were undoubtedly well paying, such a charm was astronomically expensive.

Lincoln glanced up and smiled. "A mysterious summons to a lonely location. I have a feeling there's heavy lifting required."

"True." I sat beside her and nodded to the charm. "Beautiful work."

She moved it from view. "Just a bangle I treated myself to."

I laughed. "A custom-built charm that captures moisture from the atmosphere and ensures you're constantly surrounded by the required depth of water for maximum health is a bit more than a bangle. Controlling your own personal climate is nice work."

"Controlling the actual climate *would* be nice work, but that storm last week created havoc at the docks. No one in or out for hours. You'd think that clever heads would be solving a problem like that."

Lincoln stared when I guffawed.

"Sorry. It's just that what we're sitting on is a monument to the utterly misguided attempt to do what you've been talking about. Climate and weather control was one of the first major projects undertaken on Thiegler after the super-farms started to make mass power a possibility. A researcher called Larch Unfos developed a theory about how to control wind and temperature to deliver desired weather results. A huge chain of weather stations were constructed around the planet in a configuration that would amplify the power supplied from specially built super-farms.

"It was a long-term project and it took 50 years to build everything and organize the power distribution before being switched on. Nothing happened at first and for the next 30 days there was a scramble to alter the configuration to achieve results ... and then they did. There used to be 10 different major land-mass formations on the planet, all inhabited, eight of them submerged under water. One had every living creature trans-formed into a tree before it sank slowly over the next 150 years. Thiegler became the spiral shape that it is today and Larchfall became a wandering landmass that submerges and rises at random. At least as far as anyone knows it is random, no one has actually landed on it and sent any information.

"The two most popular explanations are that climate is so complex, trying to map it to a charm would in turn create a charm of such complexity that it wouldn't function, and the other is that one of the changes created a malignant configura-tion with visible results. The storms that you were speaking of are one of the results of the attempt. No one's going to stop them, because no one knows what might transpire if they do."

"Right, storms, but why the laughter?"

I winked. "That's the lesser known part of the story. Larch Unfos was here, on this spot, when disaster struck. This was the site for his laboratory, part of a much bigger academic and government research facility. When disaster arrived, the laboratory exploded and there was no trace of Larch Unfos. Two hundred years later, a fishing ship hooked something near the main fishing grounds and reeled it in. For a long time, there'd been stories of iceberg sightings, which made no sense as it was warm water. The fishing boat crew had seen something, and the captain was curious and persistent enough to track and capture it. It was an iceberg all right, with something trapped inside. The iceberg had resisted all the efforts the crew had made to crack it open. Finally, they brought it in for a reward.

"The iceberg was hauled here to be studied at the rebuilt laboratory. They cleaned it up enough to be able to see a human shape inside ... and that it appeared to be alive. Nothing they tried made a dent or scratch on the surface of the iceberg until a woman, Kim Lanseer, attempted to communicate with the human with a simple far-cry charm.

"It worked. There was a reply. No one knows what it was, since the research site imploded and all the structures, and everyone and everything in there, vanished into a large hole, which had quickly filled with that whirlpool we have behind us."

Lincoln was silent as she collected thoughts. "Have you ever given a *short* answer to a question? I'm really glad you know stuff, but it's more than enough for the both of us."

"That's a little harsh. You didn't request a short answer," I replied quietly, upset at the jab. True, I did talk more than I should when interested in a topic; I sometimes failed to read stop signals from the audience.

Lincoln could be gracious when she wanted to be and smiled

amiably. "You're right and I'm very sorry. From now on, please give short answers, unless I specifically ask for more details."

I smiled in return and nodded.

"So where are we going?"

"I chose not to mention it earlier, given the situation with Jovial is live and we need to take action tonight. The farm is here, so we can get into it and do what we can." I provided Lincoln with details of the day.

She mused for a moment. "This could be a corpse action. It has been years by your own admission since you encountered Jovial for the first time. The plot was speared then, this is just a stray loose end. Just because you saw the woman doesn't mean the plan is active. The parts could have been in place for a while and they're simply sunk in their cover. No one has actually activated them."

"True and I have thought the very same things. There are a couple of other factors at play as well. Brewing fully grown lifeforms is rarely successful, for unknown reasons successfully Bottle-Born lifeforms need a period of growing time, never as far as I am aware, less than eighteen months. It can be much, much longer. Ten years is not unusual for very complex lifeforms. Given that Jovial was extraordinary the timescale could be shortened for sure. There is the lead time to get into place a well. Jovial was not surprised to see Ms Hiba, he was engaged in admiring how effectively his work had turned out to be. Finally, do you want to take the risk?" I asked, hoping that she would yes as the scale and scope of what we were trying to do had started to come home. I had started to cool down and question if I was rushing off to just waste my time and walk into trouble for no good reason. Lincoln cocked her head and looked thoughtful for a second before grinning hugely at me and replying.

"We need to do something to make sure it's properly cancelled, so what's your plan?"

"Get into the farm and do something to stop it."

"I don't mean to be picky," said Lincoln, who clearly *did* mean to be picky, "but that's hardly the tattered ghost of a plan. Do something to stop it? I had hoped you have something more substantial in mind."

"I do. I'm sure that these people have a failsafe in place. There are so many things that could go wrong; they must have had a built-in emergency shutdown protocol. We need to set that protocol in motion and to do that we need to be in the farm control centre."

"Do you have a backup plan if we can't get into the control centre?"

"Not really."

"Then we have to do something to stop it, don't we?" she smirked. "Where's the farm?"

"We're sitting above it. This was a brilliant choice. Farms need huge quantities of water. It's one of the major tracking signs the Standing Committee uses. Here they have all the water they need without anyone noticing."

8

I TAPPED the code on the fountain wall we were seated along-side. The receptors in the surface read the presence of Jovial Dialland through my skin and responded positively. Below the surface of the water, a large rectangular shape could be seen. It looked as inviting as the entrance to Jalwar Funnel and was equally dangerous.

I swung around and put my feet into the water. Contrary to Lincoln's often told version, I didn't scream like a 10-Bay Sucker bed being pulled from its feeding patch, nor did she have to dart me into tranquillity and carry me to the farm while I offered my life savings to return to "the light of freedom above". I did have a moment, however, when the combined weight of everything happening became palpable and I wanted to run far, far away.

Lincoln read the situation accurately and pushed me into the fountain. I fell headfirst (perhaps I did scream at this point, but purely from surprise and nothing else) through the opening and landed on drop-nets at the bottom. Lincoln landed after me, at which point the entrance closed and we were stuck going forward.

"Where's the blood lake?" I asked after we'd walked a few paces. Lincoln had brought star-lights, so we had enough illumination to move by, without being bright enough to be seen farther away.

"The blood lake?" asked Lincoln, perplexed. "Why?"

Lincoln didn't have the knowledge of bottle farm operations that every Bottle-Born lifeform did. Remembering her request for short answers, I tried to pare it down to the essential details. "A blood lake is the disposal system for a bottle farm. Any farm generates a huge quantity of biological waste. More than half the results of Brewing aren't usable and have to be disposed of. They're dumped into a blood lake."

"I thought any surplus was recycled via incinerators into energy to power the farm? That was one of the steps that allowed mass commercial development of the farms."

Lincoln had clearly absorbed the "almost information" the Standing Committee displayed everywhere to obscure the real purpose of bottle farm operations.

"That was true a long time ago, when energy recovery was important. Since then, far more effective methods have been developed. Farms are powered by biological charms ... lifeforms brewed to be part of a charm that provides power in a much more predictable and controllable way. It's also considerably more cost-effective. The use of incinerators recovers less than 40% of the potential energy while biological charms deliver 87% of the potential energy for less investment. To deal with biological waste, an interim measure was to store it in huge external reservoirs. Very quickly, those reservoirs attracted a range of hungry scavengers, who in turn attracted predators. The predators have a hormone that allows them to fight infection and is also very useful for humans. The blood lakes became a planned revenue stream for bottle farms and are secondary farms for blood-lake predators."

"Thanks for the update, but why are you asking where it is?"

"From what I understand about this farm, we've entered the waste-processing section, and there should be a blood lake nearby that it discharges into. But I can't smell one."

"And?"

"And a blood lake that's not continually topped with fresh waste will start to decline. It won't support the population of scavengers, which will impact the population of predators. When the predators' supply of scavengers runs out, they don't die, because they're tremendously tough, but simply start to hunt further afield. Eventually, the lack of a sustainable food source will eliminate them, and that can take up to two and a half years as they prey on each other … before they finally become extinct. I can't smell a blood lake, which means that the lake has finished decomposing and dried out. The supply of scavengers is gone, and the predators are scouting for new sources of food." I drew a deep, calming breath. "I have a concern that could be attracting very unwelcome attent—"

Lincoln clutched my arm. She was keenly alert, sensing something I couldn't. Suddenly, she started to run, pulling me along as she raced down a service tunnel. She let go of my arm so we could run better. I had no idea what was making her move and didn't care. If she was moving fast, so was I. Then I got the first whiff and I started to run even faster as fear ignited my muscles. I knew that smell from the sewers—a sweet, not-so-subtle smell of a predator.

Predators weren't fast on land, and not fast in blood lakes either, but they didn't have to be because food came to them. They simply waited near the farm outlets where waste was pumped out. Scavengers came to get it and the predators got them. A scavenger with a full belly was half asleep, so a predator could easily get within range and clamp onto them before the scavenger was aware of the danger.

We had the marginal advantage of being awake and aware; they had the advantage of expecting us. Lincoln switched tunnels. I began to think they were herding us. When Lincoln and I arrived at an open area with four tunnels leading from it, I could see we'd indeed been herded. The ground was covered with predators. Even if we'd been wearing chainmail waders, it would have been a problem.

Lincoln halted before she stepped into the death pit. "Which tunnel?" she asked in a remarkably calm voice.

I didn't have the breath to answer and pointed at the one diagonally across. A scraping sound came from behind. There was no going back, only forward.

Every lifeform had a stress indicator, some physical sign of the toll stress was taking. According to a thoroughly unreliable source, mine was a high-pitched snort, emitted at regular intervals like a manic teakettle.

Lincoln glanced at me and nodded tersely. "Follow me." She started to blast predators to create spaces so she could walk.

I had no idea if I snorted, squealed or squeaked. My entire field of vision had narrowed to the steps in front, rapidly diminishing space Lincoln had cleared. I began to wobble and raised my arms sideward to stay upright. I regained balance and stepped forward less forcefully. I could hear predators filling the space. My heart had decided to cease beating and my lungs were filled with sloshing fluid (I could hear the splashes as I tried to breathe). Suddenly, my heartbeat returned, racing so fast that I thought it might explode, but this, too, suddenly stopped.

I realized I was dead, that I was simply going to topple over into the hungry mouths below ... and it would be a relief. I could no longer manage the processes needed to put one foot in front of the other. In fact, I could no longer see in front. I was in complete darkness the only sounds were breaths whistling from my body and the hypnotic shuffling of the predators.

Something heavy landed on my left shoulder, with enough force to make me stagger, a movement that didn't quite reach my feet, which were stuck in time and space. I'd been welcoming the jaws of death until they bit into me.

Life and sensation returned at gale force as pain poured through my body and I shrieked. My eyes, functional again, saw Lincoln put her hand across her waist and shoot a second weapon without turning around or interrupting her movements. The predator on my shoulder blew up with a loud bang. An appalling stink filled my nostrils and would remain until I was ground to dust.

I stepped on a predator as I moved forward, the movement beneath my foot wriggling to get a grip on my boot; it was enough to release pent-up fear and aggression. I lifted my foot and the predator, persistently hanging on, sailed across the death pit where I kicked it. A feeding frenzy started where it landed. I kicked another and then another, following Lincoln who'd increased her pace. She never stopped blasting, however, and I didn't stop kicking until we'd cleared the pit. How long the experience lasted, I couldn't say.

Access stairs were in the tunnel ahead and we raced up them. At the top, I coded a retraction into the control panel and the stairs sank into the wall. Predators couldn't climb steps, but I was in no mood to be proven wrong. Lincoln eyed me and then knocked me to the floor, stepping over me and removing grabbers from a pocket. She yanked out the jaws still embedded in my shoulder. The pain was intense, and I was ready to die when Lincoln opened my jacket and shirt and slapped hot sauce on the wounds. I was fine.

To be honest, being fine disgruntled me. I was glad to be pain-free, but it seemed strange to be beyond being shit-scared after an attack by a predator and then so abruptly feel *fine*. It was hard to shake off the feeling that I'd somehow been cheated. If the recovery were so quick, did it mean that I'd never been in trouble to begin with? Luckily, Lincoln wasn't looking for gratitude, because she was too busy surveying the area.

Then she asked the question everyone did. "Where are the bottles?"

"There are none," I advised. "When the farms first started, there were brewing vats that were called bottles and the name stuck. There are 100 kilometres of high-density glass fallopian tubing underneath our feet, where the brewing is done."

Lincoln looked over to check if I was being funny. "Fallopian tubing?"

"That's the actual trade term. The farmers are famous for their rich and generous sense of humour." Sharing details of the process used in the tubes would have been too blatant a reminder about where I came from.

Lincoln shifted back to business. "Where to from here?"

I took a few seconds to orientate myself. Accessing Jovial's knowledge was tricky. I could simply have thought his memories, but this also gave Jovial access to me, and I wasn't confident he was fully powerless. I used osmosis instead and let bits of information seep into my memory. Details became clear and I knew the path to take.

We were standing in the reception area of the farm. There was no direct physical access from this part to another; it was all done through charms. In most locations, they simply returned you to where you started, but here they led somewhere fatal. I knew the walk-through would read Jovial, but I had no idea how to get Lincoln past the charm. I glanced over and realized, again, that this was her area of expertise and I should concentrate on the real problem: me.

She was wearing a skeleton key, a charm that confused identity security charms to allow unrecorded access. The PR service used them all the time and rigorously controlled who had them. It was a guaranteed trip to the Red Halls to be found with, or near, one. A thorough lack of discrimination proved to be effective in limiting production, distribution and possession of these charms. That Lincoln had one didn't completely surprise me; it was the key itself that caught me off guard, clearly of Empire vintage, and a priceless antique that would be significantly more powerful than a contemporary version. It was likely that Lincoln could pass through the Red Halls with a charm like that.

She regarded me with a furrowed brow.

With a shrug, I waved at the niche and quite needlessly said,

"We go through here". Obviously, there was nowhere else to go, but I was more than a little scattered.

I headed for the niche, which transformed as I drew nearer. It became a transparent glass panel through which I could see the farm operations control room. I felt Jovial stir and stepped inside the room. A push from behind made me move aside and create space for Lincoln.

She looked around with interest. It was a typical set-up for a farm with large conference table and functional chairs in the middle, a large wipe-clean to write on and, most significantly, an L-shaped metallic desk with a single chair before it. On the desk was a complex cube array; each cube had enough information-processing and revival power to run a small farm by itself. Even the biggest super-farm had a three-cube array, which included 100% redundancy and additional capacity. This one had seven cubes and a White Glass Control Display sheet with a separate feed from each cube.

Whoever sat at that desk had an unimaginable level of control over every aspect of the operations within the Fallopian tubes. Jovial stirred again at his workspace; this was where he imposed his will on creation to brew singular, custom lifeforms. I'd known he was extraordinary, but the set-up on the desk suggested I'd grossly underestimated him ... and how unprepared I was for what happened next.

"I'm a bit disappointed. I was hoping for something more intense. This is merely a conference room for bankers or lawyers. Where's the deadly intrigue? Lanken's Tears, these people have no sense of how to do things. Where are the uniformed minions streaming from hidden locations to defend their master's secrets?"

"This is how they work, no matter if the problem is a traffic offence, an expired credit line, or secretly overthrowing the government. It's nicely discreet and corporate all the way."

Lincoln nodded and asked the question I'd been trying to avoid. "Now what?"

I took a big breath. "There's always an exit strategy. But too many things could go wrong before the final act. Never mind removing traces that could lead back, which is imperative. They were caught before they could push the button on the plan, so *we're* going to. Somewhere in here is a key to starting the exit process and fleeing the scene. We need to find it, start it, and get out."

"Can't fault your logic, so instead I'll point to the inherent problem ... any clues as to *where?*"

I nodded and took another breath. There'd be no returning once committed. "Jovial was a member of the inner circle and probably the designer of the exit process. He knows exactly what to do, so I'm going to ask him for the information. The problem is that this is Jovial's home ground, where he's most powerful. I'm going to wrestle his most guarded and vital secret from him. I have no idea how it will play out, so if I make any move, sudden or otherwise, kill me and leave the way we came in. Jovial's death will trigger security protocols, which will destroy this site and maybe close down the plan."

She winced and drew a long breath. "We're here now, so we better get to it. How do you want to do this?"

I walked over to the desk and moved the chair to the wipe clean. If it didn't work, Jovial would have to get to the desk and I hoped that Lincoln would have enough time to kill him before he managed it. The taste of fear flooded my mouth with metallic flavours; breathing was proving difficult. I sat in Jovial's chair and felt him stir; he was powerfully present.

I glanced at Lincoln, who stood back and well out of lunging distance, the weapon in her hand pointed at me. Time to play. I closed my eyes, rested my head against the headrest, and walked into the room to meet Jovial.

Jovial didn't have clear features and his voice was a hodge-podge of other voices I'd stored in my memory. I hadn't really seen him when we encountered each other and didn't have a sharp image of him. He was trapped in my mind. The failed takeover attempt had weakened him, but not completely reduced him.

Jovial was sitting at a small table in a standard-issue kitchen. I spent considerable energy every day not thinking about that kitchen or hearing the voice that was clearly speaking comfort to a baby from the room beside it. In this location, at this moment, aided by the knowledge he'd just looted, Jovial was clearly hoping to make another attempt for complete mastery. Just as I had access to Jovial's memories, Jovial had access to mine, and here was the proof that he was willing to use them against me in the ensuing fight.

Jovial smiled cheerfully and waved at the chair opposite him. I did as requested and he spoke first. "Nice kitchen. I used to have one of these back in my flesh days. It is amazing the awesome and wonderful things that can happen in such ordinary surroundings."

I lunged at the indistinct shape and forced it to give up the secret I wanted. It was like arm-wrestling an octopod. He wrapped multiple arms around me, pulling me into an embrace. I heard a door handle rattle and threw myself toward it to stop it from opening.

Jovial swallowed me as I yelled ... just when the force of the blast from Lincoln's weapon propelled me back into the chair. I hit the wipe-away hard enough to impel me onto the floor and lay there, a storm of sensations demanding attention over the disorientation in my mind.

I appeared to be alive and in the operations room. Clearly, I'd been shot and was still alive. I had the knowledge we needed, as well as a huge bruise on my chest ... and Jovial was finally silenced. None of it made any sense. Jovial had defeated me, yet I was present in the operations room. I cracked open an eye, the least painful thing to do, and saw Lincoln standing where I had last seen her, still pointing her weapon at me.

"Screw-Top? That you?"

I was too sore to respond or signal, so I simply closed my eye again. Apparently, that was enough as I heard her come over. She stabbed me in the neck with something freezing cold. Here was a handy household hint: if you were going to undertake an insanely dangerous and probably fatal trip, make sure that you included a companion who packed a military-grade make-up kit and knew how to use its contents to restore the nearly dead back to full-strength living.

"Why didn't you kill me?" I stood up and stretched, enjoying the feeling of being awake and well.

"You're not the first ghost attack I've seen. A shock is enough to disable them; they're not as rooted in your body as you are. If it hadn't worked, I had time for a final shot."

Just what sort of people did Lincoln work with if she had such casual experience with ghost takeovers? ... Right, Lincoln worked with people like *me*.

She dropped a bomb. "Who is Petra? You shouted that name just as I recovered you."

Sometimes plain, context-less truth was the most effective lie. "A girl I once knew once." Lanken's Tears, I'd spoken the name. We were in one of the most secure places in Mengchi, yet very keen ears may have heard that. The secret I had to hide to protect those I loved; the reason I was running had nearly slipped free. I was being battered too much I would have to make a final decision soon.

Lincoln smiled and nodded, and thankfully didn't pursue it. "Did you get what you wanted?"

"Yes, there's an exit code that has to be entered in the cube array here, and then we have five minutes to get to a blast-space before the whole location melts. The code also triggers a suicide command in all active lifeforms. The Standing Committee will have a rash of sudden deaths among the staff. I don't suppose it will take long for them to launch relevant cover stories. Security is going to be top-notch once bodies start to drop. Once they read the heat signature from here, they'll be all over it, so we can't leave traces."

"How long before the bodies drop?" Lincoln asked.

"Same as the melt: five minutes."

"So, we have minutes to get from the blast-space to a safe distance for the initial inspection and then to get outside the security orbit. Not bad. Let's get to it!"

I sat down at the array, placed a palm on the cube in front of me, and thought the start-up code. The cube warmed as it sent out feelers to read the code or kill me if it didn't. A demand for the secondary start-up code prompted me to tap it onto the plate my other hand rested upon. The plate also warmed and held me firmly in place while the array considered my request, I felt feelers on my body, assessing the possible threat I posed. Jovial was no longer active, but I had his signature and that was enough.

The array connected with me and I was in. The rush of information was exhilarating. I knew every molecule of the farm. I could organize the data as I wished ... create a lifeform to my exact specifications ... build an army and fix all my problems. All I had to do was will it and it would be so. The astonishing possibilities drifted to me like an intoxicating cloud, and I wanted to do it. Then it passed, because I wasn't Jovial, and his dreams and desires didn't pull the same levers in me.

When I found the exit strategy line, I entered the code and waited. There was a delay while the cube array considered the request. As a semi-autonomous item, it had a vested interest in not processing the code. When it tried to kill me, I had my response. Feelers attacked my hands and attempted to invade my body but failed because they were coded to Jovial's physical structure and not mine. During the brief interval, before they adapted to the change, I repeated the exit code. The override opened and the feelers retracted. The exit strategy line was engaged, and the first step uncovered.

I had to solve a standard brewing equation; hidden in it was a subset that only Jovial would be able to resolve. As I unlocked the sequence, I felt as if I were wearing Jovial's heavy boneless body like a flesh suit. I popped the trap and resolved the inherent contradiction to create a new version of Jovial/myself.

The simulation then asked a question. "Five to the left then?"

"A thousand steps up the ladder to the sun," was my reply and the simulation opened a door through which it entered.

I followed and ended up in a huge, empty room. The ceiling was high and painted to look like a clear night sky. The simulation vanished and something shimmered not far ahead. A tall, lithe and stunningly handsome human male smiled. He had glossy raven-black hair and deep bark-brown eyes and wearing custom-made robes with twisted gold threads and tiny glistening jewels. He radiated friendly, warm charisma; he was your best friend the moment he met you. You were happy and relaxed in his company.

The lifeform spoke with a rich, deep voice that caressed your ears and inspired confidence and trust with its confident tone. "Hello there. We need to go this way." He turned and started to walk.

The stress of the past hours ebbed, and I was content . . . and my knife plunged into his ribs before slicing into his back. A spray of blood, hot and sticky, splashed over me. The lifeform fell without a sound and blood pooled around him, turning black as it continued to flow. It reached my feet, flowed up my legs, and quickly covered me.

I was back in the chair, looking at the cube array. My hands had been released and the wipe-away had swung away from the wall, revealing stairs that led downwards into darkness.

Lincoln looked at me with a what-now expression.

"You first, I have to close it behind us."

She strode to the entrance and began down the stairs, stopped, and returned to hand me a small crystal disk. I hooked the communications link behind an ear. When she stepped back down, I placed a palm to a wall plate. The wipe-away closed silently behind and subdued lighting emerged, just enough to navigate by. I had to hurry to catch up with Lincoln and found her climbing into an open pipe in the wall. Following, I began to crawl.

Thanks to the shot she'd given earlier, I was full of energy, so when the reaction set in, it was at gale force. The sight of Lincoln's bottom wriggling in front gave me an erection the size of a lamppost. I became dizzy from the lack of blood reaching my brain.

The tunnels were narrow enough to brush my back and shoulders as I moved, and an expanding sense of enclosure started developing.

"Hey Screw-Top, don't you think this is a bit weird? Here we are, crawling along the fallopian tubes of a bottle factory. Sort of a multi-layered moment, don't you think?"

I remained silent—and uncomfortable—thanks to the claustrophobia and mixed emotions. Lincoln took my silence as an invitation to pursue the topic. "This is as close a return to the womb as you can get, isn't it? A rebirth experience. A chance to re-consider all the possible choices you can make after you emerge. I have to say it's not something I'd go for myself. I'm pretty happy with my choices. Still, for someone as tightly wound as you, this may be a breakthrough. "

That stab brought forth my voice. "What do you mean, *tightly wound?*"

"Every word you just said came out at different volumes and tones. You're waiting to explode. Stop projecting into the future, grasp the moment, and deal with it. The past is closed, and the future is unwritten, so capture 'now' and make it work."

It was too much and I laughed helplessly. Lincoln had imitated one of the stars of the lines, a peddler of platitudes and clichés, and delivered with soulful seriousness and synthetic sincerity. I hated her empty verbiage right at that moment, but I quickly recovered and crawled forward faster, conscious that I'd lost time. Finally, I caught sight of Lincoln.

"Dead-end, Screw-Top. Any suggestions?" she asked when I reached her ankles.

I started to speak when the wall behind whispered, drawing our attention. Several blades formed a seal behind us. We were trapped in a confined space, with no going forward, no going back—so down we went instead. The section of the pipe we were in moved forward at increasing speed. I was flung into Lincoln, which intensified my reaction. I wriggled to avoid touching her with my erection.

The pipe section halted abruptly. We were able to stand upright, with space between us. Without a sound, a section opened to reveal an array of sinks and wash stations. Lincoln didn't hesitate and stepped forward with me immediately behind.

She grunted softly and turned. "That won't do." She removed a small silver box from her pocket, slid open the lid, and took out two small gems. One she placed on my forehead, the other on hers; they were low-power image charms. Lincoln now had ivy-green skin and looked a decade older. Her cloths were business-neutral robes. She was an office drone, and no one would pay enough attention to her to spot clashing details. I assumed that I was something similar, but it had to be trickier to manage, given I had blast marks and blood to conceal.

Satisfied, Lincoln nodded and headed for the exit just as several commuters walked in. I hurried after Lincoln who seemed to know exactly where she was going. She took a turn off a corridor and we emerged onto a suburban transit-stop platform. A transit was pulling up and Lincoln and I hastily boarded.

"That was good work, Screw-Top. They mixed with dangerous people. It's just as well to have rolled up the carpet after them." Lincoln was still using the link we'd put on back at the farm, so we could talk quietly without being overheard.

"I think they were dangerous enough by themselves," I smirked.

"This exit route wasn't set up by lawyers or bankers, or by Brew-Masters, no matter how talented. I recognize the architecture and that worries me. This was designed to return them safe and sound to their cover lives and be free to try again. They were playing with Mr. Constain and he never plays for anything except the highest stakes. This exist route is his design and if he's involved, trouble is deep and wide, and very present."

I was amused by what it took to make Lincoln believe that the plot was serious: for me it was the presence of a Brew-Master of Jovial's ability, for Lincoln, Mr. Constain's involvement. We exited the transit and boarded another and did these four more times. At every change, there was a visible increase in security, and always concentrated in areas we were leaving. The final stop was my normal one, thought I have no idea how we got there. At the exit, Lincoln grinned and headed into the crowds. I made it back to my space without further trouble, placed my clothes in the recycler, showered, and had the best night's sleep in year.

9

I WOKE up at the usual time, ready to start the day. Checking the message line, I saw the usual flotsam and jetsam that evaded my filters and one real alert from the United Platform for Citizen Respect campaign office. It was short and to the point. "Meeting tonight, 8:30." I felt a sliver of unease and nausea settle in my stomach. A second update noted that Dr Sand had been replace as campaign manager by Mr. Hennessey, Dr Sand was moving on to different work for the organization.

At work, there was considerable buzz—chatter and messaging about the deaths of a number of senior staff. A bit too many to be random was the consensus, followed by the determination that a purge had been implemented. This was good news for everyone still alive, because danger was now past. I avoided discussions and concentrated on work as much as the nausea would allow. The day finally passed, and I had to head to the United Platform for Citizen Respect office and discover what was waiting for me there.

It was Reyan who was waiting as I entered the campaign HQ, which had moved to a new location. The United Platform for Citizen Respect was getting deep traction in the electorate and becoming a serious contender. The new offices were impressively low-tech, which made Naturals much more comfortable because mechanics were out of sight. She'd been promoted to a permanent staffer for the campaign. As Deputy Director of Outreach Services, she'd have a slot on the Standing Committee staff for one of the United Platform for Citizen Respect representatives. This made being nice to her imperative.

"Shakbout, you have a meeting with Mr. Hennessey, don't you?" she asked flatly, with a slight frown.

"I do. I was told about it this morning. Are you coming, too?" So, I hoped.

"I'm not," Reyan replied stiffly.

The lights came on. Reyan was concerned that I was being called to a private meeting and she wasn't, and she was wondering if this was bad news for her.

"I'm sure Mr. Hennessey is just taking a look at staff. We're in the final days and he's taken over, so he wants to ensure we're all to his liking. He'll want to make sure that there are no legacy issues." I smiled and beamed all my bureaucratic experience at her.

Reyan appeared relieved. "That makes sense." She motioned me to follow her to Mr. Hennessey's office, knocked loudly, and opened the door without waiting for a response.

Mr. Hennessey was a Disguised Ornamental, a fairly rare subgroup. Their features didn't show except under specific circumstances. They were often the showpieces at parties where the lighting or air composition would suddenly change, and they'd be revealed. He was a tall human male with brown-toned skin, tar-black eyes and hair. He looked strong and fit, and his robes were tailored to display his form.

The large kidney-shaped desk of polished stone he stood behind supported stacks of multi-coloured papers on two corners: security briefs from the Standing Committee. Mr. Hennessey motioned a small table with three chairs, and I sat down. The man strolled over with papers in hand, sat, and then tapped the papers against the table.

Zusak Sedge quietly entered and took the third chair. She smiled, overflowing with good fellowship and humour; in fact, she glowed with relaxed charm ... which was utterly terrifying.

"So, Shakbout, how are you?" she asked with a tone of friendly interest.

I managed a smile and nodded, not trusting my voice.

"Snapper got your tongue?" she asked with an amused chuckle. "No need to be shy, because you're among friends. Tell us how you are. We'd like to know."

My mouth was suddenly so full of saliva, I was on the verge of drooling. After swallowing a bucketful, I responded with a quiet, "Fine, thank you."

"Enjoying your promotion? Slick work with that food space it was a smart solution to a tricky problem. The sort of thinking and action we look for in our associates, don't we Mr. Hennessey?"

Mr. Hennessey leaned towards me and I could see a small circular scar on the side of his right eyebrow. I realized that I was wrong about Mr. Hennessey. He wasn't a Disguised Ornamental, but much rarer than that, so rare as to be considered a myth. He was a Scar Carrier. For every lifeform he extinguished, he grew a scar, the more appalling and inventive the process, the smaller the scar. They were enforcers for their creators, easy to create and fabulously difficult to control. Very few lasted long before being extinguished themselves. The scars were usually internal, hidden in the skin, visible only in the right light or if the Scar Carrier revealed them. Mr. Hennessey's scar was visible only because he wanted me to see it.

He spoke with a calm voice that would have made him a fortune on the advertising lines. "That is correct, Honoured One. We look for such mental energy and ingenuity as Mr. Shakbout has consistently demonstrated. A supple energy that allows him to fit into all sorts of situations and find solutions that others might not."

"Why don't you tell Mr. Mansard about our little problem

that's sure to engage that supple energy?" Zusak Sedge suggested happily.

"We want you to bring us the Shoshone Circlet on Election Night," he with a straight face.

I stifled a chortle and waited for the real problem to be revealed. An uncountable number of nanoseconds crawled by and I realized that this wasn't a joke. I opened my mouth to provide rational objections about trying to steal the most closely guarded item in the systems and the likely impact such an attempt would have on social relations, only to have them turn to dust in my mouth.

As I regarded these two insane creatures, I grasped that they had a full understanding of what I was about to say, and that *they* were the precise reasons to make the attempt. The Shoshone Circlet was wrapped up in so much history and extended meaning that a serious attempt to steal it by a Bottle-Born life-form would be the contemporary equivalent of the Empress Ingea splitting the leader of the Wrexen Federation into two with an axe. The difference: it would be an entirely subterranean war.

Surface appearances would remain the same. The perpetrator would be subject to unbiased justice. Below ground, hatred, fear, shame and lust would burn fiercely; the hidden cost would be paid daily by everyone. The winners would be those who used the conflict to draw the populations into their orbit as the only reliable protection from the other. It was brilliant.

"How?" I finally asked.

"Mr. Hennessey, I believe you owe me for our wager." With a smug smile, she turned from him to me. "Mr. Hennessey thought you'd mouth objections and require persuasion about how serious we are. I always knew you were much smarter than that. No worm sent here would have been that guileless. Now you've deprived Mr. Hennessey of something he'd been looking forward to ... and he tends to become upset things about that."

The smug smile evolved into a cheery one. "We're leaving the 'how' to you. I'm sure you know the rule. You can own the result or the process, but we own the result."

Silence followed. Because no one was speaking or because my hearing had shut down in response to the overload in my mind wasn't clear.

After several seconds of eyeing one another, Zusak Sedge spoke. "Off you go. You don't have long, so I suggest you get started right away. It would probably be a good idea to involve that blue-fish friend of yours; she has skills you could use."

As I rose from my chair, Mr. Hennessey smiled for the first time. I was being told that no matter the outcome, he and I would have another meeting, a private one that would be held on his terms. I made it out of the room and building without falling. Standing outside the campaign HQ, I tapped a contact request to Lincoln, asking her to meet me at the Losers Lounge and to send a guide. I received one that would allow me to navigate through the Old City for that single journey only. A step off the path and the guide would cease, and I'd be lost.

———

When I entered the Losers Lounge, I saw Lincoln wave. She was sitting at the same table we'd used before, which seemed fitting since I was bringing bad news again. At least the food and drink (not to mention the view) would be good.

Nanteer greeted me as I sat down, put a big mug of Top Drawer on the table, and went off without waiting for a food order.

"I've ordered for both of us. Food first. Then tell me about the trouble we're in."

That casual "we" was, in spite of severe competition from food and drink, the single best thing about the whole day. Once the food was gone and plates cleared, Lincoln looked at me with a raised eyebrow.

"Zusak Sedge has given me a job," I said nonchalantly.

"Zusak Sedge?"

I had an awakening, a moment when you find that you are in the same place but the meaning of everything around you has irrevocably changed because you were asleep and now you are awake to reality. I hadn't been concerned that Lincoln didn't know what a Brew-Master was or much about bottle-farm operations. She came from a different process and there was no reason for her to want to know about farms. Zusak Sedge was a different matter, however, because she was centre-square in the world that Lincoln moved in, she should be semi-public knowledge to lifeforms who travelled the dark corridors of the systems. Only now it was clear that Zusak Sedge was highly specialized knowledge, only known to those who actively sought out said highly-specialized knowledge. It was *deliberate* knowledge, found in much less crowded locations where those who visited weren't lost in the multitude.

The visitors came individually and, no matter how well-disguised, could be identified and tracked by watchers with the resources to track visitors to unfrequented areas. Watchers like the PR Agency. They'd not picked me at random for this task like I'd imagined; they knew exactly where I'd been, that I'd know who Zusak Sedge was and be delicious bait for her. There were others with even more resources than the PR Agency and they'd also simply watch and wait, but they wouldn't have to find me because I'd simply walk into view. All the time I believed I was hidden; I was visible to all who looked. All the time I thought I was hiding in darkness and protecting those I love I was walking a stage under a spotlight. It was the audience who were cloaked in darkness. The only relief was that I hadn't crossed the line. Now, though, I'd have to take action.

Zusak Sedge and her Human Rights allies via the rogue PR agent had what they wanted, to start the war to achieve aims of blood, power and dominance. The PR Agency had what they wanted, an active line to Zusak Sedge. Those I could not even think about were closing in on what they wanted, delivered into their hand by myself. The outcome would rest on my increasingly tired and weakening shoulders. Ten wasted years to reach the point I had known from the moment I had held Petra in my arms.

With a soft sigh, I asked, "Do you know about the Seedling trade?"

Lincoln shook her head. "This sounds like a conversation that requires serious lubrication." She waved at Nanteer. "A bottle of House TopLine please. Thanks."

House TopLine was the most expensive and sought-after wine in the combined systems. It was produced in limited batches for export by a dozen estates on Pradndor. Most of the wine was held locally and used to bargain for major diplomatic concessions. Lincoln's smile was dark, dangerous. "Fear not. I won't ask you to split the bill. It's from my private stock housed here."

When Nanteer returned with a blue-green crystal bottle and two matching crystal glasses, I merely sipped in silence. The reputation of the wine wasn't exaggerated, and I refused to consider what Lincoln had done to acquire it.

"You know the Breeding Stations?" I asked, taking another enjoyable sip.

"They're space-based bottle farms, up there to reduce problems if something goes wrong on the ground."

I was impressed at the spread and depth of the "almost information" that had been so carefully developed by Standing Committee functionaries. I'd expected Lincoln would know about the Breeding Stations, because they were the critical connecting points between the smuggling operations across the systems, located in a semi-unclaimed pocket of space that allowed them to serve the widest range of markets for their headlines business and develop an equally lucrative alternative revenue stream from the smugglers. The money was distributed widely. Large number of vested interests provided a high degree of security, stability and plausible deniability—a winning combination.

"They aren't bottle farms. I'm not just showing off. This is important." I waited for her response, which came in the way of a terse nod. "Thiegler was the epicentre for the Empire War but wasn't reduced to cinders because those who could have, had a more powerful reason *not* to. Naturally occurring energy life-forms are vanishingly rare. Thiegler i is one of the few places and by far the most productive, for reasons no one's been able to establish. Altered energy lifeforms are crucial to the economy and civilization of the systems. A reliable supply is a big deal and that means that Thiegler had to be left intact. It's been estab-lished that the initial development of the embryos must be done here—the development can be continued at other locations—so, hence, the Seedling trade and the network of Breeding Stations."

I sipped to allow my pulse to lower and manage the anger that flowed through my body every time I broached this topic. Lincoln was sitting with focused attention, listening, weighing and evaluating the information, obviously assessing the implica-tions and how she could use them.

"The Seedling trade is the source of 80% of the revenue for the Standing Committee and while it's not officially a secret, it's well camouflaged. The number of farms multiplied by production levels would make no sense if they were only serving a domestic market. It's the export of embryos that are developed at the Breeding Stations that takes up the majority of output. This means that cargo shipments from the farms are fantastically valuable, blanks that can be developed in any desired fashion under the correct circum-stances. The technology to develop an embryo is less complex than farm requirements, so setting up a Breeding Station is within scope. This makes it a consistent threat to the governments of the systems that depend on the Seedling trade and the breeding farms."

Lincoln grinned as she picked up the thread. "Security there has to be significant a quiet security operation or rather multiple overlapping, feuding and corruptible security operations, sub-operations, and independent force managers all swirling around. This is a bit humiliating, Screw Top, that I didn't know something like this." Lincoln took a thoughtful sip.

I waited for her to ask the obvious question, Lanken help me.

"It must be very useful having the best information service in the combined systems at your beck and call. It's fascinating. Tell me more."

I grinned, relieved, and pushed away from the dangerous ground I was skating on. "Security is definitely the issue. Zusak Sedge was bred for security and worked on the Seedling trade until she decided that working for herself would be more lucrative. Do you know about the flare-up at the Hoxleth Breeding Station?" Flare-up was the preferred term for a bloody attempt to hijack a Breeding Station that was defeated by the single-handed actions of a resident technician. It was serious enough and included headline grabbing heroism that made it public news.

Lincoln arched an eyebrow.

"It was Zusak Sedge behind the hijack attempt and, as far as anyone knows, it was her first major act. Being beaten by Hiral Lakeview was a painful lesson that she fully learnt. Acting to get a profit was too narrow; being the burning branch of bottle born liberation was a much better disguise. Lifeforms would feely give you their lives and loyalty. No act was too absurd to consider for the cause. Zusak Sedge is every justification Human Rights militants need to drive their platforms. She's the most wanted lifeform in the systems, but strangely has never been caught, and now she's in Mengchi and wants me to do something for her." I did not say that Zusak Sedge also knew who Lincoln was.

"Hiral Lakeview has a lot to answer for," Lincoln jested weakly.

Hiral Lakeview is my personal hero. She'd made a choice to fight and proved it could be done. When faced with a colossal threat I had run, might have been the right thing to do but I could not lose the gnawing thought that Hiral Lakeview was correct and I was a coward. Lincoln must have read me correctly and offered a soft smile. "Hiral Lakeview was a serious person who acted with courage and strong tactical smarts under pressure. I admire her greatly." Another smile. "So, what do you have to do?"

"Steal the Shoshone Circlet." I took a mouthful of wine to calm myself.

Lincoln's glass froze close to her mouth and eyed me intently. When she realized I was serious, she took a large gulp, smiled, and sat back. "Okay, tell me how. I know you have a plan." She searched my face and chuckled quietly. "Lanken be thanked, you're the biggest bag of excitement in the systems. I've never considered how quiet my life had been before you arrived. Now, I'm enjoying myself".

A love of reckless adventure had been included in the mix somewhere back in time, when her ancestors were being developed. I was sure if I looked hard enough, I'd find flashes of blue in the strangest places, where the stakes were the highest, and the odds of success the longest.

"I want to meet with whoever made your bracelet," I stated.

Lincoln touched the charm that maintained her water atmosphere and regarded me curiously. "It's impossible to make. No charm-maker capable of anything serious is allowed in the room and the surveillance team at the Centre is very good."

"I know. I worked there for a while, but I still need to get into contact with a maker to test an idea, and only they'll be able to tell me for sure." I didn't want to share more of the tattered ghost of an idea I had, nor did I want to subject it to more scrutiny than I had to.

Lincoln nodded. "I'll ask if I can share. Now, I have something to ask you." She smiled cheerfully, which wasn't reassuring. "I know where the Claphain Jewel Box is, and I need your help to get it."

Now I knew why the House TopLine had been produced; this was space-pocket stuff, so insane that it made mining space pockets for gravity seem reasonable. When defeat was finally recognized as inevitable, Empress Ingea gathered the inner circle of her cabinet for a final discussion. No one had any idea what was discussed, but it was known is that Empress Ingea left the room and vanished. It was claimed, documented, proven, and demonstrated that Empress Ingea was on a vessel destroyed during an intense battle. The group it was part of tried to breach the border of the Sickle Quadrant. The group was detected at the exact time it would have taken for them to arrive at the border, if they'd departed Mengchi at the time Empress Ingea left.

The problem with the Claphain Jewel Box, which was the same problem with Empress Ingea, is that it did exist; in fact, it was Empress Ingea's personal Jewel Box and possibly most treasured possession. The box contained a matched set of ten firestones, which provided a source of energy, enough to power a private bottle farm. It had been given to an unidentified courtier, who'd placed it in safekeeping, ready for Empress Ingea's triumphant return with the hordes from the Sickle Quadrant. If you believed that, then I had a map that showed the location of the Claphain Jewel Box, yours for an entirely reasonable price.

The potential value of the contents of the Claphain Jewel Box never diminished over the centuries it had actually increased as technology to utilize the power of firestones developed. Matched firestones produced more than double the energy of a single one and increasing the number of matches had a wildly disproportionate increase in input. A set of ten matched stones today would provide enough power to make the most ambitious space-mining programs economical and profitable. The Claphain Jewel Box remained a historical footnote and hobby mystery item for centuries; if previously located, it would have triggered a new war over who was entitled to it. All that changed with the passage of time, the steady dimming of memory, and the discovery of the Lahhosen Deep Vault.

A 95% success rate in correctly developing charms and implementing energy-bearing structures sounded impressive, but what it hid were the numberless years it took to get to that rate and the dangling 5% that still existed. Unintended consequences could be significant where charms and energy-bearing structures were involved; the lifeform who fell from the sky 1,000 years after stepping through a tower door was the most famous example. Following the demolition of a wharf at the Lahhosen inner port, a second structure appeared in its place: a deep vault designed to remain hidden within the folds of other structures. It *should* have remained hidden. The demolition, however, had been incorrectly implemented, inhaled rather than exhaled—and the vault was revealed.

The vault security was all in the disguise; it was relatively easy to unlock. Inside was an archive of documents from a very rich, rather bored and quite obsessive mystery hunter from the Inquon System, who'd come to Mengchi to search for the Claphain Jewel Box. Finding the archive had two outcomes. The first was that the Standing Committee issued a ruling that whoever found the Claphain Jewel Box would be the sole and exclusive owner of it. The second, the search for the Claphain Jewel Box went mainstream and reliably provided 15% of the annual Mengchi tourist revenue. During the following 400 years, the fever didn't abate ... and was still as potent as ever from what I could see in Lincoln's expression.

"If we assume that the Great Destroyer wasn't stupid then it's reasonable to assume that she knew that she was in an endgame and that she had a plan," she mused aloud.

"Sure, it's safe to assume that there was a tactical retreat being implemented. Giving up was never an option."

"Very good, then you'd agree that a return was planned for when that next required step had been executed?"

"I would."

She cocked her head and scanned my set expression. "Would you also agree that a point of return had been established, just as a point of departure had been prepared?"

"Agreed."

"This point of return would be behind enemy lines when the return occurred, both for tactical reasons and because the enemy would have been actively searching for her ... returning to places that had already been searched and would be less secured, thereby increasing chances of successful re-entry."

"I can see the logic to that, but so would her pursuers," I pointed out.

"There'd be logistical constraints at work, because they had to guard places that hadn't been fully cleared. Reported sightings would have to be investigated. The greater balance of force would have to be at the forward positions and follow-up searches. The rest of the locations would have to be more exposed. Not stripped of forces, just having less to cover the area, so blind spots would be more frequent. Just a fractional advantage. She never showed that she needed anything more than that."

"Then she was killed at the Sickle Quadrant border," I said with feigned innocence.

Lincoln shot a don't-be-stupid look. "A bag of replacement body parts, sufficient to leave trace evidence and varied enough, could easily be stuffed into a costume and placed in a command chair ready to receive a direct hit. The perfect headline for those desperate enough to believe it. Now may I continue?"

I raised my hands in surrender and reached for my refilled glass before she might take it back.

"Then the unexpected happened and she didn't return. This is the worst possible result, an information vacuum filled with mutually contradictory stories playing to the hopes and expectations of various survivors. That's where it stands today: same vacuum, same stories. There's been no new information since the Sickle Quadrant play."

That surprised me. I thought there'd been a steady accumulation of information as archives had been released, looted, found, copied, translated, leaked, and in at least one case turned into DNA and replicated organically.

Lincoln followed the line of thoughts crossing my face. "Nothing new," she repeated. "An extraordinary multiplication of information, coloured and weighted with subtle differences, crossbred with academic opinions and directed research that reassembled parts into different pictures ... which then become parts for next-generation pictures."

"That's your biggest claim so far tonight."

"The WZPROS Group did a search-and-filter exercise for me and found that all routes returned to the same set of data points, all dating from the week of the Sickle Quadrant firefight. Everything after that descended from that information, which is in itself a pretty substantial piece of information. Someone managed the process very effectively."

"The WZPROS Group did work for you?" This was unexpected, Lincoln getting the attention of the largest research organization in the systems, an organization that routinely shrugged off requests from ruling elites and governments ... to accept a proposal from an individual, and a proposal as insane as researching the validity of information about the Claphain Jewel Box.

Lincoln offered a brisk wave. "It was a straight exchange. I had something they wanted, so we swopped."

I'd seen Lincoln wear an Empire skeleton key, so I found this easy to believe. "How did you sort through all the confusion?"

"I didn't, I ignored it. I started with one indisputable fact: *she didn't return.* That's the real problem. Why? The simplest answer: *she couldn't.* Something went wrong that prevented her return, something accidental or something deliberate. If it was accidental, then it was a random event that could never be traced. If it was deliberate, then there'd be traces, and if I found them, I'd I have a trail."

"I follow your logic, but—"

"But I could hardly be the first to think this? If other searchers had found nothing, is it likely that I would have?"

"Something like that" I murmured.

"Which is what I thought, then you came along and it all changed."

"What do I have to do with anything?" Lanken's Tears I would not cope another unforced error.

"The farm we visited wasn't built by the people who used it. It was Empire construction, in fact."

10

"The farm technology is current, only developed the last 15 years," I explained, watching Lincoln closely. "Everything in that farm was current to the timeline. A bit out of date now but nothing antique and absolutely nothing Empire."

Lincoln offered a got-you smile, arched an eyebrow, and leaned back in the chair. "Did you notice the floor as we navigated the predators?"

I recalled a faint and unmistakable mark on the floor, the ladder and sun of the Empire, Empress Ingea's personal stamp used to indicate that construction had been completed by Imperial commission. Those marks weren't wildly uncommon and could be found in the layers beneath the city, but not in that particular quarter. Another recollection: during the Empire era, that location had been beneath the sea, so it must have been utterly secret.

Lincoln did some mindreading again and picked up where my thoughts had left off. "Correct, an unknown reserve location waiting to be utilized, out of sight and mind. So, what went wrong? I went back to survey the—hey! No need to look like I jammed a fork into your arse! I came at it from below and stayed away from the hot spot. Anyway, I found the command centre, which had been stripped and dusted."

"Looters?"

"No, this was a deliberate, ordered shutdown ... completed at the same time as the Great Destroyer's vanishing. The base commander had orders to take everything back to fallback location if they were not contacted within a specific timeframe. Following the instructions, the base commander left a plain text log identifying the actions taken so the trail could be followed in the event safe part arrived at the base. The key let me in, the base is rigged to melt if unauthorised access is detected. She complied with the orders in full."

I had to spring the trap that Lincoln had so carefully set. "What base did they fall back to?"

She leaned forward and gazed intently. "The Red Halls."

I was horrified, but not surprised. This was what I'd been hoping Lincoln *wouldn't* say. The Red Halls were Empress Ingea's personal bottle farm, the place where lifeforms that haunt the Sickle Quadrant were first developed. They were planned, brewed, and removed to the Sickle Quadrant for further refinement, a safe distance from Thiegler . If any place could be considered the engine room of the Empire, it was the Red Halls. Naturally, this made it a prime target for incoming forces, not to destroy, but to absorb ... to inhale the information, procedures and techniques that had been developed ... and capture the living intelligence that laboured there. Losing the Red Halls was the loss of the Empire.

The bargain that had been struck to clear out knowledge and leave the infrastructure for the Standing Committed to develop as they wished, created a second history for the Red Halls, which obliterated the first. The Red Halls are the security fulcrum for the Standing Committee, easy to enter and impossible to leave without the Standing Committee's stamp. Getting into the Red Halls wasn't a problem. Thousands streamed in there every day, but getting in unobserved and, more critically, getting out unaltered, was a gigantically difficult problem that had never been accomplished.

"If I unwillingly grant you everything that you've said, there's still the substantial problem that no military installation was discovered in the Red Halls. So, when you say fall back from the secret location, why are you *so* sure that they fell back to the Red Halls?" Just because I was losing, didn't mean I was giving up.

Lincoln smirked. "They said so. When they left the command centre, they also left details of where they'd gone."

I snorted with disbelief; Lincoln was so deep in the mine; it'd be impossible to haul her out. She reached into a robe pocket and took out a small egg-white box and slid open the top so I could peek inside.

There was a tiny Empire military insignia, the ladder and sun motif of the Imperial Corps, except this time the sun had a teeny berry-red jewel in the centre. Only one group in the Corps had that; they guarded the Red Halls. It was obvious it was genuine from the power that lay within.

Lincoln placed it on her palm and we both stared at it. "It was left on the commander's chair for the next one in the chain to find."

It dawned on me that this was business for Lincoln; my problems were a fun wild ride, but this was serious and needed to be treated as such.

Most likely, Lincoln had considered that there was a non-zero chance of succeeding, but it was the depth of the non-zero margin that was the point of concern. Lincoln changed all the calculations by stating, "BookWorms have free access. They come and go without restrictions."

"You want to recruit the BookWorms?" Astonishment had to be etched on my face.

"No, I want to get information from them. Getting in isn't a problem; it's finding what we want in the time window and exiting. If we know exactly where to enter, we have more of a window for the exit. I know what I'm looking for, but don't know where it is. The BookWorms would know but would never tell *me*."

The odds had doubled in our favour, though doubling a really, really small number still left a really small number. Lincoln now had an info crystal on her palm; it looked multiple generations old ... and was as secure as posting on the lines. Regardless, I put it in my pocket before draining my glass and standing. Lincoln settled back in the chair, obviously not going anywhere, and neither was the bottle. Clearly, there was more business to be done tonight. "There's a return guide in the crystal. I'll be in touch regarding the maker."

I strolled from the lounge with an increasingly "normal" feeling that I was pulling one foot from a sucking-tar pit and stepping into a bucket of glue. I followed the guide to the Square of Arts and Knowledge, the location of the Mengchi Centre for the Promotion of Historical Knowledge among a cluster of insti-tutes that actually did promote knowledge. They were housed on the same campus, a sightseer attraction in its own right. A dim line of light bisected the unadorned square. If you crossed the square from north to south, you'd see nothing, and if you crossed from east to west, you saw an extraordinary glass pane that ran the length of the square. Completely unsupported, it rose so high it vanished into the sky. The glass reflected activity from across the city, a great collage of Mengchi public life and movement.

There were public benches from where you could watch the vivid city tapestry, which was never the same one second to the next. I sat on my favourite one and stared at the lives that might be robbed if I got it wrong.

There was a doorway in the pane that never changed, the only entrance and exit for the campus within. Inside, you were in a beautifully landscaped business park with enticing walkways, unexpected vistas, and fascinating buildings. The Centre for the Promotion of Historical Knowledge was the closest to the entrance and drew the biggest crowds. The campus was a visible answer to the question of how a small sliver of ground like Thiegler could contain a population of 200-million lifeforms and still not seem crowded. Location space warping was one of the most advanced aspects of energy-controlled engineering, creating living room out of the space between molecules. After sending a request to Akion regarding the location of an unknown military command centre in the Red Halls, I went home.

The next day, I never actually reached my office. I was captured by an agitated mob as soon as I walked into the administration corridor. Fortunately, I'd stopped by the food space before this and had lunch and coffee with me. This was a regular event, which was why I had lunch and coffee ready. I sank into the day, as required. By the time I had more or less solved, or put off, the issues of the day, I was ready to leave. Back at my space, I slumped into my comfortable chair and stared into nothingness, devices switched off. Nothing would disturb me.

When I did switch everything back on, I noticed a guide from Lincoln. It was stacked and torn, so it would only be readable a section at a time, and then only when I was actually in motion to the destination. I washed, put on a transparent Stop-All under my public clothes. I could see no point in making it too easy to stab, beat, or shoot me, given that I was going into what would likely be hostile territory.

The guide started me off at a nearby transit point, not my usual one, and steadily brought me through a series of loops and returns that seemed to have been created solely for the pleasure of making me walk up and down a never-ending series of steps.

I'd never realized how many sets of city steps connected walk-ways and pass-throughs.

Eventually, I arrived at a doorway. Where it was, I couldn't say. I touched it gingerly and it swung open, revealing a bright, clean hallway with beautifully laid natural work planks. I took the silent invite and stepped in, feeling prickles as the door vanished and the charm expired. A door open to a room at the end of the hallway which contained a plush chair beside a small oval table with a translucent bottle and etched wineglass on it. Ruby-red liquid filled the bottle. The room was shadowy, except where soft light fell on the chair and the table.

"Welcome Mr. Mansard. Please sit down and help yourself to wine. It's not what you had the last time, but I do hope you'll find it acceptable."

The voice was high-pitched with a whistling sound. It told me what I needed to know, and I sat gratefully, poured a glass of wine, and sampled it. "Thank you for both. This wine deserves no apology and is very nice." I took another appreciative sip. "Has our mutual acquaintance told you anything, or should I start from the beginning?"

"Anyone who comes here wants only one thing, but I don't know the specifics in your case, so if you don't mind..."

"I want a copy of the Shoshone Circlet that can pass a first-order inspection. I need it in five days."

There was a burst of whistling laughter. "And I'd like a clean liver."

"I can do that for you. Can you do what I want?"

There was strained, heavy silence. Finally, a twisted branch of an arm that had a hand resembling a bloated red spider attached to it, slid out of the darkness. The spider picked up the medical insurance card I'd put on the table and the branch withdrew into the darkness. All that could be heard with whistling breath.

I had an idea what was happening in the darkness and beyond. The card would have been passed to someone further back and they'd have gone to check if it was valid. Once established that it was, there'd be a search for a suitable match and when they were found, a rapid negotiation would have been conducted with a third party. Time would be the subject of the negotiation: how soon, how long, how fast, how lengthy. Everything rested on the quality of the match.

Most charms were manufactured in highly automated factories assembled in the Cobhouse Quarter; an entirely artificial concept made to mimic an artisan workshop cluster that never existed outside of tourist propaganda. If you wanted something out of the ordinary, there were shops that could customize charms, and if you wanted something built from the ground up, you had to trade with an Avian.

I had no idea why Avians possessed the talent for creating charms or copying any charm that they saw. This talent for forgery was perceived as promise by some and a threat by others. The Standing Committee responded to threats with speed and vigour, reducing the downside to keep the upside, their motto I was once told. All Avians had a twist in their genes, which gradually developed disabling disfigurements that could be read by security scanners. If an Avian tried to get close to a guarded item in order to copy it, security systems would capture them, no matter how heavily disguised they were. Their lumps illuminated scans, as they are intended to do.

Avians had migrated to private work and had a natural dislike of displaying themselves in public. For my plan to start, the Avian had to look at the Shoshone Circlet, which the security in the Mengchi Centre for the Promotion of Historical Knowledge was actively set up to prevent. They'd look for lumpy Avians, but if they had no lumps, they'd not attract attention.

The Standing Committee loved collective punishments; they were self-enforcing and very effective. Still, demand would eventually create supply. There were routes to acquiring a clean Avian —the key was a health card that could be used to create a chain of surgical and medical work, and headline patients that moved money and spread activity across many places, so that no single act proved significant. Matching a headline patient with a real one was where blade met flesh; it had to be exact.

Ten minutes of silence passed as I relaxed and enjoyed the wine and chose not to consider much more than the simplicity of the moment.

"All seems to be in order. Where would you like the item delivered: domestic or employment?"

This was a new voice, but it too held the faint trace of a whistle. "Domestic would be good, thank you." I rose, bowed to the extraordinary talent that rested in the darkness, and left. The door reappeared as I approached, and I exited onto the street where my space was located.

All I needed now was to survive a break-in into the Red Halls, leave with a fabled treasure trove, and follow my thread-bare plan to steal the most closely guarded artefact in the systems—and see it come to perfect fruition. Then, I'd be free to kill myself and secure the future of my family and the universe. It was good to have goals.

———

When I arrived at the office the following morning, Akion was standing by my desk, which was unusual.

"We've investigated your request. The location you seek in the Red Halls does exist. It is NoWhere."

"Fuck" flew out of my mouth before I could stop it. If you wanted to hide something, NoWhere was a really good way to do it. NoWhere was literally nowhere, a non-existent location that could never be found, except under highly specific circum-stances. If you stood in the correct spot, and had the correct key, then NoWhere could be uncovered. The key could be anything, the correct spot could be anywhere, and either or both could be, and frequently were, lost or forgotten.

"The location has been found and the key has been identified," Akion advised.

"Oka-aaay." I smiled fleetingly and wiggled my fingers in a give-me-more gesture.

"The location is in the Records Section in the Red Halls, and the key is the Shoshone Circlet."

11

AKION STOOD WAITING while I thought through the situation. Finally, I asked the most important question. "Can you get us to the location?"

"Yes."

Evidently, details were not required. I nodded and watched Akion leave.

This was a severe complication to my plans. I had not intended to actually steal the Shoshone Circlet, just make an apparent attempt for cover and have a copy to give to Zusak Sedge. This would buy me enough time to finish the rest of my plan and finally secure a safe future for my family. Now to I was going to have to actually steal it. I had no idea how I was going to do that; I have planned to simply avoid it now I would have to solve it.

I sat and doodled to encourage my mind. It did not help much. Lots of swirls and circles, all leading to the same conclusion, I was stuck. To distract myself I took my memory bracelet out of my pocket and fingered the crystals. All the carefully created fake memories of a life and family I never lived or had flowed into me. I admired the work in the same spirit that Jovial had admired his work, it was nicely done. Part of my camouflage, they were carefully created and curated to mislead and distract anyone who found them.

They also allowed me wallow in a huge bout of self-pity and footless recrimination about what could have been if only circumstances and reality had been what it should have been instead of what it actually was. Misinformation and replacing reality with manufactured memories, everyone including myself did it right up to the Shoshone Circlet. It was an artefact that managed to bury an appalling history under some powerful charisma that captured every lifeform that saw it.

Which is when an idea slipped into my mind, fully formed and vibrant, it must have been waiting for the opportunity to present itself. My shadow had looked at the Circlet every day I worked at the Historical Centre and every day had fallen under its spell. Acknowledging power was not the same (I hope) as accepting it. Power is a relationship and a perception, reframe the perception and the relationship could change.

The problem was not actually stealing the Shoshone Circlet, I knew how to do that the problem was what to do after we had stolen it. I had been ducking the issue by pretending that giving a replica to Zusak Sedge would work without a proper context to sell the deal. I had been sitting with my eyes closed holding part of the puzzle praying desperately that it was really the whole picture. Other stray pieces of information started to become relevant and steadily a more coherent plan developed. Lincoln would have ideas and information as well that could support or change the plan. Time to get to work.

———

The days prior to the election were extremely busy. The United Platform for Citizen Respect machinery had cranked into full force and hordes of additional volunteers were busy spreading the word. The momentum that the United Platform for Citizen Respect had gathered was clear and it was inevitable that they'd take some of the open slots on the Standing Committee. But how many, and how would that change the existing power groupings? This was what my PR handlers wanted to know, and I tried to find out.

I was never included in any strategy meetings, but I soaked up and reported all the gossip and leakage I could find. Two days before the election, there was a general gathering of the HQ staff. I had told Lincoln the plan about the Shoshone Circlet some days before and had arranged to meet her after the gathering. Seeing Lincoln at the gathering was unexpected. She was there in some unspecified security role that she was annoying vague about. We were addressed by a handsome Golden Ornamental. He was an actual candidate. He was "The acceptable face of bottle-farming" according to Lincoln who then added an appreciative critique of his physique.

The candidate spoke to the campaign staff, "Thank you for your work in this vital election. This is the first time we've been able to stand for ourselves and express our own requirements and desires. This will be a historic moment, regardless of the results. We'd still like results to be historic, as well. We need ideas from you about how to capture the spirit of the campaign, the inclusive and tolerant spirit I feel so strongly here today. There are citizens who want to vote for us but are hesitating to do so because they're still not sure what we represent. I'm appealing to you, you who've worked so hard, you who embody the spirit of this campaign and the United Platform for Citizen Respect, to present ideas that simply and effectively capture this moment, ideas that others can share and declare with confidence and pride."

He stopped speaking and looked around the room, and I realized he was actually asking for ideas. This was an unexpected opening; I had wondered how I would make my suggestion there was very short space of time to get it accepted let alone implemented. Everyone in the room had an idea. We offered our ideas to a team of recorders I'd not noticed before. We weren't asked for identification, just details. I gave my idea and moved away, but not quickly enough. I was touched on the arm and turned to find Zusak Sedge and her shadow. Lincoln had vanished; I neither heard nor seen her go.

"Clever, worm, very clever I'm feeling satisfied with you, something that's unfortunately rare. You're close to restoring my faith in humanity." With a wide smile to push home the joke, she glanced around the room before continuing. "I'd go so far as to say that your plan won't require support from me to be accepted."

I didn't speak in case it encouraged her to stay longer. She stood alongside Mr. Hennessey, both looking as innocuous as glasses of water, as the Golden Ornamental drew up. "I'm sorry to interrupt, but I'm looking for Mr. Mansard."

I raised my hand and he continued. "Mr. Shakbout what an astonishing and compelling idea you've proposed. It's bold and imaginative and captures the spirit of the United Platform for Citizen Respect and the election. We think it will provide exactly the edge we're looking for, a powerful symbol that will bring everyone together and reclaim a piece of our history that has remained unseen for too long. Not to be officious, but would you mind coming with me? There are a number of release forms that you'd need to sign before we can proceed with action." He smiled broadly and stepped aside so I could follow him—which I did, with immense relief.

I'd not been sure when I submitted my proposal if it would be seen as outlandish or provocative. I was a little surprised that it gained acceptance so quickly. I followed the candidate out of the hall and into a large office that was nearly full, with lifeforms seated at tables and standing around boards covered in writing. Everyone had pictures and posters that were being examined and discussed; this was the final meeting to set the media messages for the end run of the election.

I was taken to a small wooden desk in a far corner where a small SilverScale sat with an empty chair in front of him. I recognized Dr Fleet, the campaign communications manager who'd been taken on after Dr Sand' departure. I had had no dealings with him and when I was directed into the chair by the candidate, he looked at me curiously.

The Ornamental spoke before I could. "This is Shakbout and he's here to sign the release forms." He may have thought that I'd change my mind and hold them to ransom after his ill-advised bout of enthusiasm. There'd be no problems; I wanted the idea to fly even more than they did, and if signing away rights would do it; I'd spend the day with pen in hand, signing them away.

"Ah, thank you, Junger. Let me assure you, sir, we're not trying to take away any of your rights. We need release forms for the manufacturers to start working. In the event that we cover the initial costs and there's a distributable profit, you'll receive full entitlement. Yes, that form please, and this one," he said casually as he pointed. "If you'd put a thumbprint there—and yes, a retina copy ... a little further from your face. Yes, that's it. And, finally, if I could just jab your finger for a blood smear on this one ... thank you. We're done." He twisted in his chair and called to someone name Lathall.

A small StoneBeater sauntered up and looked at him expectantly.

"Lathall, take these to the distribution centre. We'll need work to start right away and have the first batches ready for the launch at ten tomorrow morning. Speedy does it, please."

I stood, shook his outstretched hand, and headed out to meet up with Lincoln to find out if she'd been successful.

———

"Fuck" was the response when I asked her. We were in a small restaurant close to the Historical Centre, the best place to sit and be unobserved or overheard, the flow of tourists providing excellent and effective screening for anyone who actually sat down.

"Fuck good or fuck bad?" I joked, not sure if she was referring to the security work for the campaign or the work for our plan.

"Just regular fuck."

I eyed her closely. "Not getting what you mean."

"I can see why you're single, Screw-Top. The art of conversation isn't one you've mastered, is it? The ordinary give-and-take of information eludes you. Ordinary fuck. I'm tired. I've been on the prowl all day and have some results, but nothing outstanding. My shoulders are cramped from squeezing into tight corners. I've been nice and polite to a stream of lifeforms I would cheerfully have knifed. I haven't eaten, am hungry and thirsty, and will share details after food and drink. And frankly those turds at the HQ know about as much about security as the boot heel, in fact I now have to apologise to my boot heel. Bending over backwards not to appear threatening is one thing, wilfully ignoring basic security precautions is another. Just as well I quadrupled my fee given the nonsense that I have had to endure. Lanken save me from amateurs"

I'd been scalded by her opening words and barely heard the rest. She'd drawn a sharpened nail along an open wound, finding the deepest root of my fears and mangled hopes.

"Sorry Screw-Top, I know you can manage a conversation with casual expertise, and I am sure that you are single only because you are having such a hard time choosing amongst the lifeforms vying for your attention. I can recommend the Laurauin stew. They use actual Kjant onions from Laurauin, nothing home-grown."

I reminded myself that Lincoln did not know why I was living by myself and accepted the peace offering and the recommendation. We handed our orders in silence ... and ate in silence. Finally, over shots and a large jug of tangy blue foam to chase them down with, Lincoln described her day. "I started by going to see the target. I'd never been there before and only known about it by reputation, which is not exaggerated in the slightest.

I'm very impressed by the arrangements, discreet and comprehensive. Your plan's about as ridiculous as any I've heard, but I do think it's the only one with a chance. It'll still be as tight as a Colefax's bum in a mudslide. There's a location blur operating in the target chamber, high-spec and well-calibrated. Happily, they've been secure for so long that they haven't been keeping up with the market, and I was able to nail the coordinates before they caught my track.

"There was lots of discreet extra scrutiny as we exited, but I'd burned out the unit as soon as I had the details, so there was nothing for them to hook onto, though a lot of people are going to find that their recorders have malfunctioned. The space is wider than I'd expected, so I'll need to get the delivery into a very small radius to make sure there's time to operate. I spent hours practicing. The fine-tuning's tricky, but I expect to be ready for the show."

I offered a compliment and she flashed a quick smile of gratitude.

"That was the fun part. I then scouted locations. Lanken's Tears spare me from ever having to deal with property agents ever again. I imagined providing detailed specifications would speed up the process, "She shook her head and chuckled lightly. "I've seen filthy living spaces on ground floors in a section five kilometres from the square, having no functional wet rooms, that even Mud Wallowers would have found revolting. On the other hand, I was shown an unexpected jewel in the Lighthouse section, four spaces knocked into one and decorated in Steporvian New Age opulence ... which I did take. It'll nicely solve a pressing problem I'm having with another client. "

She took a large, noisy gulp of blue foam. "I did finally find a suitable space further out than ideal, on the limit of the range in fact, but a tank can be installed in the wet room quickly and the entrance can be fortified. I have a team working on that. The security team at the centre will track us quickly. I estimate we'll have 15 seconds before they take out the front door and 17 before they detonate the ceiling."

"How long will it take you to get out of the tank?"

"Five seconds," she replied. "I can't make it any quicker than that."

"How long to dress after you're out?"

"Another five seconds. The defence suit has layers that need to be sequenced correctly."

I nodded; my expression grim. "You're sure that you'll be ready to travel 10 seconds after returning from the centre?"

Lincoln replied in the affirmative.

"You're ready after 10 seconds and they're crashing through in 15, so that's a problem. That's too big a gap."

"Too big?"

"I need the energy from the door-entry for the drop, because if I use independent energy, we leave a trace. A five-second wait is too long to hold everything together. I need you out of the tank and dressed as the entrance is blown. That way, we're gone as as they enter, *without* leaving a trace. They'll find the route, which will take a good two minutes, and by then we'll be out of range."

"I can leave a trace for them which will speed up the arrival, they will hit the door exactly 10 seconds after the breach alarm goes."

"Won't it go when you enter the room?"

"No, that is one of the weak points they have allowed to develop. Lots of attention to getting out, not enough to getting in... Which brings me to the question that's become rather urgent, how do we get out?"

I grinned. I'd wondered if Lincoln would guess and felt a touch of pleasure that she hadn't. "We're taking the Rat Lines."

Lincoln mulled it over, then offered a huge smile. "Nicely done. How do we move through the Rat Lines without becoming goblin food?"

"I have a safe pass from the Chief Herder." One of the big

surprises that came with the job was the number of unofficial power centres I had to negotiate with to ensure work crews could work safely in the shit pots. There were big communities who lived there, and they all had to be placated. The goblins lived in the Rat Lines, a largely dilapidated and unused set of pipes that ran from nowhere to nowhere. They were a breeding ground for a large rodent that butchered up nicely. The rodent herders were goblins, whose origins no one knew or cared about. They claimed the Rat Lines as their own and ate anyone they found there. They preferred live food, so Involuntary Public Servant staff members were generally unmolested.

"That'll get us in and out, and it makes no difference for the distance," Lincoln advised. "Without an Involuntary Public Servant crew, we'll be considered available. What we need is a distraction."

"What kind?"

"Alcohol is the only thing that will pull them away. It needs to be a major spill or source. Lanken knows why, but they've never developed any brewing or distilling technology, and they have a mighty thirst. If we had time, I'd drop a shipment, but on short notice, it would attract too much attention."

"What if they could get into a BetteNotth warehouse?"

"That would be excellent, but unlikely unless you know something that I don't that you're going to share."

"I may know something. There's an obsolete vent access on the junction near a Rat Lines exit that I've submitted five reports about to the BetteNotth operations management, as well as the Public Service operations archive. I file the reports for cover, just in case it ever becomes a problem; it's been duly noted and reported. It isn't ours and is in a poor state of repair. I pick it up as part of the work-crew audits for various sections using the junction.

"BetteNotth won't repair it, because it'd be expensive to do so. The whole shaft would have to be renovated and the security threat is considered too small to balance the cost, because it doesn't directly access the warehouse. It emerges in front of the main loading dock, which is in operation constantly.

"Security wouldn't be ready for a swarm of goblins and they might be able to get to the vats before reinforcements arrive. If the goblins breach the vats, there's a good chance they'll simply let them fill up and pass out before sweeping them up. That would avoid casualties."

Lincoln nodded thoughtfully. " Why haven't the goblins used this already?"

"A poor state of repair isn't the same as broken. It isn't actually hanging open, but needs a nudge to do that, and I think we have that nudge. When you return to the tank, there'll be a displacement I was going to vent; instead, I could direct it at the hinges. It should be sufficient to snap them, and the grate will drop."

"Should?" Lincoln didn't survive by skating over mines; she inspected them carefully instead.

"I'll get an Involuntary Public Servant crew to spray the corridor as they pass by tomorrow. Two days later, they'll be ready to snap."

Lincoln frowned and drank the last of the blue foam.

"I think a little more bait would be good—an alcohol vapor leak coming from the vent would stir them up and give an edge to their appetite. It would also bring them closer to the vent so that when it fell, there'd be a sufficient group ready to swarm, and give us a chance to travel the distance without meeting too much opposition."

Lincoln pulled a cube from her pocket and called out a map of the location when I identified the vent junction and location. She then made a call, speaking an unrecognizable language, and organized the dropping of a vapor bomb for later that night. She also arranged for the security team to be distracted, and a hijacking that would take place outside the transit yard.

Lincoln got ready to leave. "Now, we have to be ready for everything to go wrong and deal with it on the spot." On that cheery note, she headed off in one direction and I left in the other.

———

The next two days were too long and too short. My HR handlers were demanding reports and updates hourly as the polls started to clarify United Platform for Citizen Respect gains. They were emerging as the third biggest block on the Standing Committee. This would mean that they'd have juicy sub-committee positions and be in a position to implement policy. This was now a serious issue across the Public Service, and I was being pulled into formal and informal meetings where attempts were being made to assess post-election possibilities.

We still had to maintain our numbers, which required my attention on department details. Pre-election jitters seemed to be running rampant. Rosby was working flat-out to keep problems minimal. The intense tribal identifications that the election normally drew to the surface had been enhanced by the prominence of the United Platform for Citizen Respect. Clearly, there was realignment on the way and the haves and have-nots were scrambling for positions, with everyone animated by ambiguity. Work, on the other hand, didn't energize anyone; it was barely a reason to gather into groups to plot, forecast, protest, air grievances, or whine.

At the United Platform for Citizen Respect HQ, preparations had reached a fever state. The desire to believe the polls and a desire not to be complacent mixed uneasily. Policy and strategy meetings pulled candidates away from campaigning, which inspired bouts of public activity to ensure that every potential voter was committed. I never got to complete any tasks, because I was moved to a more urgent one before being moved again. Everyone wanted to talk, and no one wanted to suggest anything or offer an actual forecast result.

I did get to learn an embarrassing level of detail about other volunteers' lives, domestic and professional, and was glad to learn that everyone was busy making a mess of their lives, too. I still had an edge on them, just not as much as I'd imagined.

Finally, and inevitably, the day arrived, announced by a knocking at the entrance to my space. When I looked, there was a box waiting for collection; it threw itself at the door every few seconds to announce its presence and urgency. I picked it up and my arms were gripped by a rip-claw charm. If I wasn't the person the parcel was intended for, I was going to lose my arms at the elbow. The charm took a blood sample and confirmed my iden- tify before dissolving. Inside, wrapped in a plain piece of drab gray cloth, was the Shoshone Circlet. It was disconcerting to see it out of its usual context. I looked closely; there was no sign that it wasn't the real deal, and for a second I had the fantasy that they'd stolen it so I wouldn't have to. That vanished when I noticed the corner of my health card showing underneath the cloth. Damn. I'd still have to manage my plan.

Folding the cloth over the copy, I put it in my work bag. Should I be terrified or excited? I headed for work, stopping at the voting box outside my unit, and after queuing for a few minutes, placed my vote. I did actually choose a United Platform for Citizen Respect candidate. There were running tallies and turnout numbers displayed on every available screen, but the real action wouldn't happen until much later in the evening, when the safe seats were out of the way, and the turnovers and marginal ones came into play. We were planning on using that as our cover, which meant I still had to get through the next hours without imploding.

This proved easier than expected. The demands for updates ceased; it was too late now. At work, the tension had largely drained from of everyone, and the actual event proved anti- climactic. A lull appeared as everyone eased themselves back into doing what they were supposed to have been doing ... in preparation to start doing it again. I did a tour, mostly to get a chance to see if the shaft cover had been sprayed. It had. The rest of the locations were in acceptable shape, so I filled the gap to the kick-off by completing reports, approving and declining requests, and cornering the group financial lead and getting my expenses signed off before they were booked to a new period.

Finally, the shift ended, and I picked up my work bag, waved at Rosby and nodded at Akion, who was standing at Rosby's desk. Akion nodded back and I ambled to the transit stop. After travelling to the square, I took a loop for two sweeps, keeping Lincoln's instructions in mind as I watched for anyone doing the same. The transit emptied twice before I disembarked and then took a flyer to the unit where Lincoln had rented space.

She greeted me at the door and seemed perfectly calm and assured. She was wearing a loose unadorned robe, which she'd shed when she entered the tank. We silently compared watch settings and moved into the wet room. On the ground rested the tank; it was slightly longer and wider than Lincoln, and a metre-and-a-half high, filled with distilled water. Lincoln would have no room to turn in it. It was just a doorway that she had to be able to get into and out of quickly. Our watches chimed and Lincoln dropped her robe. Naked, she stepped into the tank, then lay face-up before vanishing. Work had officially started.

12

LINCOLN WAS an Aquatic Ornamental and written into her was the ability to shift from one body of water to another. In their heyday, Aquatics would shift from one fountain to another across house grounds, synchronizing displays for the entertainment of their owners. It was base code for Aquatics, so it travelled with them no matter how they'd been bred. Ornamentals were among the few non-natural lifeforms who'd embraced natural reproduction; they wanted to preserve their looks.

Someone attempted to steal the Shoshone Circlet once a month on average. This meant the protection system was in constant use and could be observed by someone employed at the Mengchi Centre for the Promotion of Historical Knowledge. The system was simple and fatal; when the breach sounded, the room sealed shut and was flooded instantly with highly toxic water via an altered-state charm. There'd been a wide variety of liquids used, but water was finally established as carrying the most effective toxins.

The thief didn't drown, by the by. One string of toxins attached the clothing to the skin, another string removed the clothes and skin, and a third string illuminated every nerve in the flayed figure with horrifying pain, and the final toxin melted the body. The room was pumped out, the recovered clothes and skin analysed, and all biological family relatives and legal relatives rounded up and interrogated. At any sign of prior knowledge, they were executed and became Involuntary Public Servant staff.

For my plan, the key was the water. Lincoln could shift from one known location of water to another, and this would drop her directly into the chamber without having to go through the front door. Just ahead of her shifting, we'd sent a probe to the chamber to break the altered-state charm so Lincoln could shift from water to water.

Being naked, the first toxin string wouldn't activate. The charm would provide a barrier for the time she needed to grab the case with the Circlet and shift back to the freshwater tank.

That was the idea, but the only way to prove it would work was to do it.

I'd had enough time to think of ways that the plan could go wrong—from the probe not springing the charm and Lincoln landing in a dry room and unable to get back, to her dying in agony. I was sick with those thoughts when she reappeared in the tank and tossed the case with the Circlet before sinking again. I pushed the bottle with the anti-toxin into the tank and then concentrated on placing the case into a carry-all. The case seemed to resist my efforts, probably due to a secondary security charm.

I turned to look at Lincoln. She was stretched full out in the tank under the surface of the water and didn't appear to be breathing. The anti-toxin had clouded the water a little, but not enough to hide the multiple marks on her body. She appeared to have been jabbed repeatedly by a single-unit burner. I stood beside the tank with her work suit, ready, mentally running a countdown. She came out of the tank exactly on the mark, as the first assault on the entrance started, and pulled on the suit without a word. I was already wearing mine ready for the exit.

When the second assault came, the force reached the wet room as hoped. I opened the charm and it dropped us directly outside the entrance to the Rat Lines. I was about to say something when Lincoln grabbed the handles and pulled the drain covers open without any apparent effort, dropped in and started to run down the line. I swung the carry-all onto my back and followed. I had no idea if the goblins had taken the bait or not. Lincoln had said that it was a classic amateur mistake to set something up and then check if it had worked. That check would simply alert someone to the fact that it *was* a set-up and blow the plan.

It had to look natural and accidental. The goblins would take the bait, or not; you decided the risk and took it. This was easier to accept when it was being discussed in a safe location but running down the Rat Lines made the risk appear unbalanced and pressing. I heard movements in the shadows all around, rustling and scrabbling, and the occasional grunt and groan. A drop, of what I hoped was saliva and not a tear, landed below my left eye. Thanks to the multitude of micro drug doses running through my body, I didn't unravel on the spot. The writhing and screaming were all internal, and my body continued regardless.

The safe passages chips we wore wouldn't stop a goblin team from attacking, but they did stop other residents from taking action. The goblins were just the most prominent lifeform in the Rat Lines and enforced their dominance with the same efficiency as the Standing Committee did in the daylight above. The goblins, at least, ate you and that was that; others inhabited you while you retained full awareness, ebbing and flowing to ensure that you never achieved blessed numbness.

It was those lifeforms that observed us running the lines and studied the safe-passage chips in the hope they would wink out before we passed out of reach. The DarkSights in the face covering gave us enough vision to see where we were steadily running. Lincoln heard them first and raised an arm to alert me, and then I heard the footsteps as well. At this distance, it was impossible to be sure if the security team had followed or if it was a goblin team, not that it mattered a great deal. Both would be a fatal problem if they found us.

Lincoln had estimated that the security team would find us within minutes. They'd not know our destination, so they'd drop a troop into the Rat Lines and swamp us. The goblins were unknown; even if most of them swarmed into the warehouse, there'd still be some who wouldn't have been able to get in before the close-down. They'd be returning to the Rat Lines and they'd be looking for prey. The best outcome was that the goblins and the security team encountered each other; the worst was that they both encountered us.

Lincoln's fabulously unhelpful description rattled in my mind. "You roll the dice and you scratch your balls."

My balls were so itchy I thought a colony of biting insects were roaming around my scrotum. Still, I ran, following Lincoln's steady pace and trusting the medication in my blood to stop me from acting on fear and panic. That got harder as I felt, but didn't hear or see, a line of lifeforms sprint alongside me before careening into a passage on the left. We were making no noise as we moved, because the suits were silent movers, we were as noisy as shadows.

By my internal countdown, we were approaching the exit when the initial signs of a firefight became apparent. Like lightning, there were luminous flashes, followed with the rumbling sounds of heavily clashing weapons. A security team had encountered something, or somebody, who was happy for a confrontation. The struggle wouldn't remain small for long, because other security teams would quickly be drawn, as would other inhabitants of the Rat Lines. We'd have to cross a battle zone to get where we wanted.

Lincoln never faltered and continued at the same pace, heading for the exit with me close behind. There'd obviously been trouble, because I had to jump over a bundle of rags that once dressed a twitching body. We were on the fringes of the conflict; the bright flashes and strident sounds were more frequent and closer.

Then, we were in the cauldron, dark and quiet, a tangled mass of vibrations. In an underground fight, noise or light gave away your position, which was a bad thing; they were also an unavoidable by-product of weapons favoured by those likely to find themselves in such a skirmish—weapons designed to kill instantly, no wounding. A wounded opponent could still kill you.

The weapons were rigged with displacement units, which threw light and noise away from your location to a random one nearby. Of course, if you had a big enough fight going on, you might be illuminated by someone else's light and then become a visible target. For anyone trying to sneak across the battlefield without being noticed, the chances of *actually* being noticed were rather high ... and, as such, we were noticed.

We raced past a goblin team stripping security staff, leaving them ready for a pick-up crew. They started to fire on us right away, and Lincoln tossed a SoundBlaster at them. Bits of them splattered my suit. We'd announced our presence. The security teams would be converging at full speed. However, many goblins there were, there'd not be enough to slow the security forces sufficiently, so we had to make sure we made the exit before they did. This meant we could no longer travel around the perimeter of the conflict but had to step through it.

Lincoln had been explicit about this possibility. "We won't get to the exit unopposed. There's going to be blood work and you need to be ready. What do you prefer: blade or barrel?"

I just gaped, having no idea. The prospect of physical violence always terrified me.

"I think you're a blade," Lincoln stated, scanning my tense face. "A gun takes too much thinking, a blade is just reaction, and I think if you're put in the right corner, you'll start reacting. Give me your arm." She grimaced when she took it. "You could do with some strength exercises. It's a bit late now, but definitely go for it later. Open your fist and stretch your fingers. A Net Cutter for you, double-edged with a cutting point. Waving it in any direction will do damage."

Knife in hand, I resumed following Lincoln, but was caught off guard when someone swung in front of me and then swung their arm at me. I diverted the blow and the Net Cutter sliced through the limb without effort. The lifeform fell to the side. I felt no shock; I was too busy running and keeping Lincoln in sight. Glittery flickers fell into my field of vision and I swung my arm wildly at them, sprays of blood indicating contact. I felt like a prisoner in a foreign body, casually slicing lifeforms as I raced to the exit.

If I couldn't quickly establish a connection between my mind and my body, irreparable damage would be done. I was approaching the borderland of no return when I lost sight of Lincoln. She must have stepped through the exit, which also meant that it had to be in front and that I'd have to step through it, too. I did so and stopped running and fell to the ground.

Lincoln pulled back my hood and I vomited, screamed and shook—all at the same time. The vomit flowed like an acid volcano. I had no idea where it came from, given I'd not eaten for hours. Finally, it ceased. Vomit covered half my face and was clumped in my hair and on my suit. Blood threaded through the mess, but whether mine or someone else's wasn't important; the only important thing was Lincoln rubbing my back as she kneeled alongside.

Lincoln stopped rubbing and I heard her rummage in the carry-all that she'd lifted from my back. Standing, she poured a wash-and-revive mixture over me, cleaning vomit, blood and anything else off my suit, and calming me sufficiently to understand the current situation. There was a keyhole only I could piss through and if I failed, there was more than my stupid life to be lost. I had to die on my own specific terms, or I might as well have done nothing.

I rolled over and pushed myself into a standing position and regarded Lincoln, who looked like she'd been to a rowdy party where guests had spilled drink on her. Her hood was pushed back, and a mix of concern and calculation showed on her face. She was concerned about our timeline, because we hadn't included a stop here in the calculations.

The cauldron was readying to boil over. We needed to move from the exit to the stairs before it spilled. Lincoln walked to a wall and ran her hand over it, stopped and pushed; stairs fell from the roof. She was moving up them when I reached the base and had stepped outside before I was halfway up. The stairs started folding as I climbed, and when I emerged from the opening, we were standing on an empty second-floor retail unit with a large multi-paned window facing the street. Across the road was the United Platform for Citizen Respect HQ swarming with supporters who waved, cheered, and danced as count results flashed on screens outside the building. Every single person on the street was wearing a copy of the Shoshone Circlet. *'Reclaiming the Power'* was the tagline beneath a huge poster on the front of the headquarters. It showed the full name of the party—United Platform for Citizen Respect. The Shoshone Circlet hung from the "C".

"Very nice," declared Lincoln, standing at the window and scanning the street. "If I had doubts, they're crushed now. You have a future in marketing."

I walked over. It was dazzling yet confusing to see all those people wearing the Circlet. Suddenly, it had become the property of the enslaved instead of slave owners. Or maybe it was a cynical ploy to wash away history and give everyone a chance to wear a bauble. I talked to try and gain control of myself.

"Turns out that there's no trademark or registered image owner for the Shoshone Circlet. It's a Universal Heritage Product of Art, and no one can own it. Anyone can make a copy and sell it, provided the copy isn't made for criminal purposes ... no restrictions on political purposes. To be honest, I thought they'd pass on the idea as too radical; instead, they were only concerned about minimizing payments to me. I have to credit them. They saw heat in the idea right away, a universally recognizable image that's now become their brand. There are a lot of others wondering how they missed it and are flicking through gallery catalogues to find something for themselves."

Lincoln laughed, enjoying the multiple layers in the situation.

"Any sign of them?" I asked. She'd know best what to look for.

"Not yet. We're on schedule, so they should be—ah. We have contact. The rest should be visible momentarily."

Following her pointing finger, I saw a courier entering the headquarters.

"How did you manage the alert?" I asked while I waited for the drama to unfold.

Lincoln tapped her chest and an audio file played. "I want to register for a security bonus if this information proves useful. Some members of the United Platform for Citizen Respect party have created a plan to steal the Shoshone Circlet and display it at campaign headquarters after election polls close. It will be delivered by courier, so there'll be no direct connection. They'll claim they got a delivery and are as surprised as anyone. "

"That didn't sound like you." I was impressed with her vocal skills.

"It wasn't me. An old-time player helped me when I was on first footing. This was a chance to route something to him. How good is the copy?"

"Amazing. It'll take a lot of analysis to prove it's a copy, which is the defining proof that it's been created for criminal purposes. The only way it could be that good is if an Avian was involved, and that in itself is presumptive proof of criminal intent. The actual theft will close the case—say, is that them on the roof?"

"Right on time ... and time for us to go. There's more work to do."

As Lincoln and I headed for the stair door, the security team that had landed on the roof of the United Platform for Citizen Respect HQ was already moving into the building. They'd catch Zusak Sedge and Mr. Hennessey with the Avian-made copy of the Shoshone Circlet in their hot little hands.

[13]

WE DESCENDED to the basement parking level and got into an utterly ordinary, family-plus road vehicle, with Lincoln providing instructions to the drive unit. Quietly, we joined the river of traffic that flowed outside. Lincoln and I sat in the space at the back in fabulously comfortable seats, eating and drinking from the large picnic box on the floor between us. When we'd finished, I asked a question that had been nagging me. "Surely the security teams know the tipoff is a set-up? Won't they trace the call and pull the thread right back to you?"

Lincoln took a swig from her flask, placed it in the box, and reclined before answering. "They know it's a CP, so that's no matter. At least 40% of the calls they get are CPs and at least 80% of the calls that end with a bonus payment are CPs."

"CP?" I was confused.

"Combined Product. The person making the call is combining two items, information about an event that will cause a problem for someone, but be a benefit to someone else. The caller gets a bonus for the information, which is how they're paid for their services. When there's a change of top management, calls are investigated, and it's discovered that the caller found the information in an untraceable manner ... someone hacked their account and dropped the information in front of them. As responsible citizens, they reported the information to the relevant section, and as a reward for that, they get a payment. Now my turn, why create a duplicate that will be recovered? The security team will not need anything more that Sedge herself to act."

I sat back in the seat and thought briefly about what I would say< I was stunned that t had worked and was still a little unsteady from the flight across the Rat Lines. I had to be careful not to speak too freely now that I was on the threshold of the final act.

"When I was told to steal the Circlet my first plan was simply to make an attempt, there would be a news block on the details, but the attempt would hit the lines. That would give me enough time to get going before Zusak Sedge and Mr. Hennessey realised that I was not appearing with the Circlet. Then I was told that the key to getting the Claphain Jewel Box was having the Shoshone Circlet and suddenly I had to take the matter more seriously.

We needed to have the Circlet for ourselves and we had to show that it had not been stolen to prevent the war that would follow if it was revealed to be gone. The details of the theft would point to bottle born and that would have given Sedge everything she wanted. I needed a forest of Circlets to hide a copy in so no one would look to closely at it in the relief of recovering it. I also had to provide a bottle born thief to close the case.

The campaign provided the cover, the traces of Zusak Sedge and Mr. Hennessey would provide the motive and the thief. Everyone has a huge investment in believing what is in front of them. If we could get out alive, then we could *stay* alive."

I fell silent for a minute while I thought about the next step I would be taking.

"What was it like when you shifted?" I asked, changing the topic.

Lincoln scanned the area as she considered it. "Not what I

was expecting, not a bit. Shifting is a natural movement, the same as walking for you. I do it without thinking. A puddle on the ground will do if you have the experience. Not being stupid, the security system expects this as a point of entry. That's why various suspension liquids were used before they decided on water, which amplifies toxins much more efficiently than any other medium. There are underground labs that have been experimenting with dosages and dilutions for decades, and they've reached the same conclusions as the Centre team: mix the four together in the right proportions and they're very stable. To disrupt them, you need to release enough energy to kill any lifeform in the chamber at the same time. They key is in creating a delay, which has proven elusive.

"I'd never thought of my weathervane as a barrier until I had to seriously consider how to enter and exit the chamber. I pulled an egg from boiling water without thinking, until I looked at the smoking egg and made the connection. I had a way to delay the impact of the toxins—no idea if it would be enough, but still enough to start. So, I shifted and found out that the Centre team is very tricky indeed. The water is spiked with a powerful mindbender that slipped by the vane. I was in the ocean, in the middle of a multitude of colourful fish that moved with absolute beauty and grace. I wanted to join them.

"It was the toxins that saved me. When I peered below, I couldn't see the ocean floor, but my foot with a nasty burn; it was resting against the pedestal of the display case. A second burn on my shoulder pulled me halfway out of the illusion, enough for me to reach for the case, and concentrate on the shift. Everything intensified. The ocean became real and the burns started to multiply. I'd thought I wouldn't be able to shift with the case, that it would take too much effort.

Then the shoal parted and a big blue swan came into view, all eyes and grinning teeth. They were a fear of mine in my child-hood, as an FYI. Aquatics are their favourite food. As it closed in on me and dropped its massive jaw to take a big bite, terror prompted me to escape, which is when I shifted back to the tank."

Lincoln fell silent, and I didn't have anything to add. We sat in silence as transports moved through the convoluted route that Lincoln had designed. Finally, she spoke. "We're not being followed and there's been no forward observers either, so this looks clean. What's the plan when we get there?"

"There was a largely unused service entrance for the Red Halls. We'd be met by a information specialist, (I had been told politely that Book Worm was not how they referred to themselves) who will escort us to the library, which is where the NoWhere had been set up.

We walk in as nonchalantly as possible, look like we have official business, follow the information specialist, and when we get to the library ... I pretty much have no idea. Every NoWhere is unique; there's no pattern. If you have the key, I'm supposing we can find it. The only thing I'm sure about is that it's there. The library is camouflage, not in the original plans, and the space has remained empty for four renovations. However, the space was always listed as a library on all the plans and said library was set up months before the end, when storage and contents were moved in. When the searchers came through, they found a library where a library should be and, after examining those contents and storage carefully, left it alone."

"How did they miss it? I always thought they examined every microbe."

"They weren't looking for it, but for information, hidden or disguised records, trails that would take them somewhere or reveal what had been going on. The library was a relatively insecure location, open to a wide range of staff and showing no change in usage. There were more pressing areas that needed attention. Akion told me that a NoWhere was one of the possibilities they were actively investigating as part of the search.

When they screened for it, they found differentials that drew further analysis and finally pinpointed the location."

"Just to return to your plan, we're going to walk in, attract no notice, and make it up when we get there, right?"

"Ye-es."

Lincoln reclined in her seat, eyes closed. I looked out the window. We finally reached the park that surrounded the Red Halls, which was crammed with winding trails that brought you to breath-taking views and vistas. The plants were varied, native and off-world plants. Vegetable lifeforms clustered together in gardens of variegated grasses and flower banks. They were the Empress' pleasure gardens and had never been altered.

The proximity of the Red Halls was more than enough to keep citizens away. Tourist tours often scurried past. I'd walked every trail numerous times feeling peace in the whispering plant life. There was no security around the Red Halls and I'd frequently strolled up to and around them without any challenges. The wildly decorated main entrance, a single block of natural undersea stone carved into the wide-open mouth of a monstrous Killisa snake, was eye-fetching. Its tongue served as steps and venomous fangs hung over you as you entered. The Killisa was the only creature that produced no waste from feeding and never grew beyond the normal adult size of three metres. The operators of the Red Halls may have changed, but the message had not; what went in, didn't come back out.

The entrance we were headed for was much plainer, a simple arch in a wall with a wooden door. Ostentatious modesty was one of the marks of the Empire. The wood was from the burning forests of Loverni, harvested during the week between tree maturing and spontaneous combustion. Touching a tree could cause it to ignite. The door was slightly ajar and, as we approached, swung open in full to reveal a information specialist in the doorway, observing us with slowly blinking eyes.

The information specialist spoke softly. "Sir, I am Haddon. The honour of seeing you and serving you will shine for me and those who follow until the Final Day. You too, Lincoln Bluefish, friend of the One Who Saw. It is an honour to see you." Haddon stepped aside and we walked into the Red Halls, which were not actually red, but a drab ash-gray.

"The whole structure is called the Red Halls." Haddon led us along a narrow corridor. "The actual Red Halls are only part of the structure and are three floors above us. They were the throne room and reception room for the Empress, and are indeed red. The rest of the structure is not intended to be viewed by anyone, so colour is more muted."

When Lincoln had shifted in the chamber at the Centre, I was one degree removed; here, I was in the middle of it. I had to concentrate fully on the task at hand and push the weight of what I had planned off into the distance. Everything had become undone so fast that I was a log way behind processing it all. I could feel that it was coming for me and all I could hope was that I could exit before it caught up with me and prevented me from any action at all.

As we moved, I felt the weight of the charms woven into the fabric of the building. Some were so old they were just faint echoes, other were newer and they pressed in upon me. There was a powerful charm working to prevent anyone from keeping track of where they were going.

After an immeasurable length of time, we came to stairs ascending to what appeared to be a large alcove, with a door in the middle. Haddon extended a thin arm and touched the door, which shivered and opened. I was dumbstruck. This was a room straight out of my deepest dreams, and I wanted it. It was shaped like a large pie slice. Shelved walls arced around a generous but not cavernous space. Three balconies ran the length of the walls. Skylights threw soft, indirect light on everything—strong enough to read by, not so strong as to damage the contents.

Bookshelves, up to the second balcony, lined walls. In the centre were individual reading desks and chairs. My bum ached to sit in one, and I already had one in mind. I'd spread out a stack of volumes and sit there, get lost in them, and the rest of the universe could fuck itself. A soft touch from Lincoln brought me back to reality. "Sorry. Caught by a charm."

Haddon looked at me. "There are no charms in the library." They led the way past the shelves and across the centre, before finally halting midway down an aisle. "This is the location we've established as having the greatest probability of containing the NoWhere. There are two other locations, with slightly lesser probabilities. If this one proves false, we'll rerun calculations to establish the next location."

The information specialist withdrew and Lincoln and I were left to decide what to do next.

"You have the bag," Lincoln pointed out after a few seconds of serious staring.

I put it on the floor and removed the case. The blank head with the Circlet sitting on top appeared entirely undisturbed by the events and actions. Looking at it in the library, I was conscious of the enormity of what we'd done: stolen the Shoshone Circlet and walked into the Red Halls. I examined the case to determine how it could be opened. It appeared to have been moulded as a single piece—stand with head. I rapped it and glass shattered and fell to the ground.

"Stronger than you look," Lincoln quipped as she eyed the stunned look on my face and the way my arm remained frozen over the Circlet.

Drawing a quick breath, I reached for the Circlet and imagined it writhing under my touch and shrieking "thief, thief" like in storybooks. It didn't. It was slightly cold to the touch and gave no sense of residual power, which charms usually do. With the Circlet firmly in hand, I rose and, feeling self-conscious raised it above my head and waved it. No response.

"It has to be worn," Lincoln said quietly. "It was designed to be worn, so I'm guessing it needs to be worn now." She caught my expression and shook her head. "I won't put on a slave collar for *anyone*."

I placed the Circlet on my head, where it rested for a microsecond before suddenly expanding, slipping over my face, and tightening around my neck. Everyone had been wrong about the Shoshone Circlet. It wasn't a charm—it was alive and now it was *awake*.

[14]

THE LIBRARY WAS GONE, and I was standing at the foot of a stone ladder that led to a doorway carved to resemble the sun. I started to climb. At each rung, I could feel myself being assessed and scanned to ensure I had the correct key. The circle around my neck was warm and pulsed in response to the probing, silent questioning. At the top of the ladder, the doors were recessed; I stood in front, wondering what to do.

The doors were smooth and blank, and there was a line down the middle that indicated two doors. I put a hand on each, in case I could just push them open. That did nothing, so I tried pushing them up, down, down, up. Nothing happened. I examined the doors more carefully, in case I'd missed a keyhole or a code pad, anything that would provide a hint how to open them.

This was the most closely guarded location in the Empire. You couldn't find it unless you were wearing the Shoshone Circlet. Anyone wearing the Circlet would know what I now knew—that it was a living entity. This wasn't enough to gain entry into the space, as there was a second layer of security. Someone who got this far would have, should have, expected it.

A stray thought: in all of the Empress' images and portraits, including the one in the Mengchi Centre for the Promotion of

Historical Knowledge, which showed her wearing the imperial jewels, she'd never worn the Circlet. Lincoln had called it a slave collar and she was right. The Circlet demanded a host and the Empress would bow to no will but her own; when she'd come here, it would have been with another lifeform wearing the Circlet. She'd have had her own key and the combination would have opened the doors.

This was entirely useless to me, of course, because the Empress wasn't here to help open the doors. I turned to return and saw that the ladder had vanished. There was only one route back to the library and that was through the dim space in front.

The secret of the Circlet had been studied carefully for centuries but had never come to light. I had held the Circlet in my hands, and nothing happened, but when I put it on my head, something did. I was positive that in all of the tests conducted, wearing it had never been one of them. Someone had to wear it so that information circulated. The Empress and another entity stood here, but the Empress alone emerged on the other side, with the Circlet in her hand and the secret safe.

After handing the Claphain Jewel Box to a courtier at the end of a meeting, the Empress vanished. I could easily imagine a few missing details from that story. The courtier held the Jewel Box and the Circlet, the pair standing before the opening doors, the Empress then taking the box and killing the courtier. Upon departure, she carefully returned the Circlet to its usual location and exited in a waiting craft. Everything was in place for her return, except that she never did. Now I was here and had no idea how to open these doors and starving to death here wasn't an attractive alternative. I could step into the darkness—maybe it was an illusion and the ladder was still there. I stepped off the edge and found myself facing the doors again.

I focused on the situation, refusing to allow my attention to scuttle off on a tangent like a butter-bug scrambling from sudden bright light ... but a tangent came along regardless, and I thought about a fellow employee, a Natural, at Fogler & Twist. I barely recalled what she looked like, except for a huge, thick pair of glasses with aqua-blue frames that reflected light from ceiling stick-strips. As we drank tea, she'd started telling me about blood charms.

Blood charms were rare. The symbolism of blood was important, and the quantity didn't matter. A drop was enough ... wet work that content providers loved. Ripping out beating hearts, cutting throats, or opening veins to drain a lifeform was for shock-value, nothing more. All that was important was that a drop of blood was placed on the charm, and it had to be blood from the person holding the charm; this created the connection that activated the charm.

The Empress was an economical woman; slit a throat and you had a charm, as well as silence. Blood was still needed, just much less of it if memory functioned correctly. The problem was that I had nothing on me that I could prick myself with. I touched the Circlet on my neck without thinking. The surface felt smooth, but I found a little point beside the jewel, sharp enough to draw blood.

I pressed my pricked finger on the jewel and felt the connection course through my body as the Circlet took stock of its host. The doors opened and I saw rotted clothes on a skeleton gathered to one side. With the doors open and the host dead, the Circlet would return to hibernation mode, be safe to carry. The Empress could use it again as required.

I stepped through and they closed behind. Above was a circular high-vaulted ceiling with beams of hammered silver. To the sides were walls were painted with systems maps ... or so I thought. Upon closer inspection, I saw they were projections, views of the systems and planet clusters taken from impossible angles. What was unexpected: the projections were entirely up to date. A wide, jet-black stripe ran down one of the walls between the Sickle Quadrant and the Tellaborne system next to it, but I knew there was no such gap between them. Tellaborne

snaked up to the borders of the Sickle, so it might have been a
result of degradation in the charm over time.

The room was empty. No shelves or tables, no boxes, and no
Claphain Jewel Box waiting to be scooped up by yours truly. I
strolled around the perimeter. There was no disguised piece of
furniture. Nothing. The same for walking across the floor. The
ceiling wasn't a real possibility. Coming a long way, at great
effort, was the pay-off for treasure searches, but only successful
ones received publicity.

Wondering absently how time evolved here, I started down the
exit corridor, a gently sloping, curving tunnel with undecorated
walls that provided dim lighting. If *I* was deeply disappointed, I
could hardly imagine what Lincoln was feeling. Rehearsing what
I'd say to her, the words slipped away as I spoke them aloud.

An outline of doors appeared as the tunnel levelled. I walked
towards them and whatever lay on the other side ... and found a
small wooden box on the floor. It was plain, from the Screaming
Forest of Gilpin, a place in the Molyleafy system at the borders
of deep space. A small planet that could be a very big asteroid; it
had atmosphere, life and enough conflict. Someone, name
unknown, had landed on Gilpin and went to the Assembly
Building in the city of Xe, the leading force on the planet then.
No details of what happened at the Assembly ever emerged, but
that same day every lifeform and building in Xe were turned into
trees. The trees didn't scream, but visitors who stepped in, never
emerged—it was *their* screams that rattled branches.

One enterprising lifeform pushed 2,000 slaves into the forest
at the same time in one location. This overwhelmed the forest's
ability to consume everyone at once. A group was able to fell
trees and drag them from the forest limits before being pushed
back into the tree line. The wood from the trees scattered across
the systems, and the veins running through were very distinctive.

The box on the floor, even if it empty, would be worth
enough money to keep multiple generations spending recklessly,

without reaching the end of the hoard. Even without touching it, I knew it wasn't empty—*this* was the Claphain Jewel Box.

All that was missing was a large sparkly arrow with flickering lights pointing to the box. I suppressed a desire to scream. It would have been polite to let me "find" the damn thing in the room to the rear. This was a slap to the face. But subtlety wasn't the issue; ensuring results was what mattered.

Annoying as it was, I couldn't claim *not* to have found it. It was here and I was going to have to take it with me, regardless of whose plans I was following. Was there anything more aggravating than being a self-conscious pawn? Resting on one knee, I studied the wooden square of 30 centimetres with ruby-red veins trailing the surface and silvery lines in the grain. There were no visible joints or lid.

I saw nothing more upon closer inspection. I placed a hand on the wood, but it didn't respond, which was a relief. I lifted it; it was lighter than expected and I stood up, tucking it under an arm. The doors opened before I reached them to reveal another set of stairs and I followed them down to the library, where Lincoln stood waiting, her eyes on the box. I was happy to give it to her, because the veins pulsed within the wood, a very unpleasant and threatening feeling.

She took it without comment and placed it in the carry-all, and we strolled to where Haddon waited. In silence, Haddon escorted us to the entrance and closed the door behind. It was wonderful to be in daylight, to feel the light breeze and smell the plants. We'd done the impossible, the ridiculous really, and there was nothing left to say. I considered how to put the final stage of the plan into action as we left the Red Halls and entered the park ... and the attack took place.

The fire came from both sides of the path. Our attackers had a problem. They didn't want to damage the box, so they were aiming to disable us rather than kill us. Lincoln pushed me to the ground, and I lay there trying not to get in her way.

The attack had activated the defences in our uniforms, so the energy bolts hitting us were dissolving, but they'd not last long under this barrage. Lincoln was happy to apply force to kill everyone in the ambush. She removed two small silver balls from a pocket and threw them at the sources of fire; they exploded with no sound or flash. Bodies and parts of bodies spiralling into the air was a gruesome sight. Worse than that, though, was that they landed on us. Feverishly, I brushed aside a two-fingered hand, eyeball, and teeth.

Lincoln hadn't waited—when the bombs landed, she was on her feet, shooting into the chaos to ensure no one escaped. She motioned me to hurry, pointing at the Red Halls where the sounds of approaching staff and machinery emanated. I scrambled upright and sprinted after Lincoln, who abruptly vanished. I wasn't certain if she'd become invisible or had left the location, so I simply ran to where I'd last seen her. Harsh buzzing near my ears told me I was being targeted from behind.

I fell into bubble foam, which broke my fall quite nicely. Lincoln grasped my shoulder and pulled me to my feet. We were standing in a very dim room, so its size was hard to determine. Lincoln was smiling, proving again that having someone who knew what they were doing was vital if you wanted to do anything involving guns, bombs, ambushes, and security forces.

"I try to keep a couple of portable escape hatches with me," Lincoln advised before something exploded in the shadows. Off she raced, with me once again following.

Our pursuers got louder and louder. We scurried through a doorway and Lincoln stopped to bolt the door, which seemed a waste. A door was hardly going to stop whatever was behind us. Having a space warp would, though. The door displayed the typical pattern of a warp, a spiral design punched onto metal; the space on the other side shrank microns and then expanded them. A warp like that would have pulled in loose particles not shielded, like the following team and all their equipment.

They'd return with fresh crews and equipment, so there was a tiny window in which to act before we were tracked. I took the opportunity, loosened my false tooth with my tongue, and spat it into my hand. "I need you to do something for me."

Lincoln heard the urgency and stood very still.

"I need you to find my wife and daughter. They're in the Circle. This is a heartbeat and it'll guide you to them." I held out my hand. "Please put them on the 8:30 sailing of the Lacoon Cruiser tonight." I removed two first-class tickets from a deep pocket and held them out. They could live their lives in the open. It was a hopeless attempt at last-minute restitution, years in the making, and now being delivered by a stranger. "I'll lead the trackers away so you can get a head start. Please do this. It's the last thing I'll ever ask of you."

"Is this what you've been hiding all this time? The something you've been so careful not to talk about? Now you want to go off and be heroic, fuck you. Give them the tickets yourself and trust your friends."

The sounds from the other side made it clear we were out of time, so I spun and started to run. Lincoln could follow or do as I'd requested.

"Target acquired to the left!" An explosion followed.

I jumped, hoping that Lincoln had done as I asked. I landed at a street corner and ran for the retail unit around the corner, pushing open the door as trackers struck the ground behind. I raced into the changing room at the rear and dove through the mirror. It was just as well that I'd practiced this, so I didn't have to think. I was furious with Lincoln. She had no right to undermine me, to suggest that this was another crazy episode. Instead of being a true self-sacrifice, that it was a pathetic selfish act, a final slap at my wife and daughter. I was saying I'd rather be dead than with them.

It was true that this was the only way to secure their freedom. When I was dead, as in *fully* dead, the trail would go cold and they'd be able to walk in the sunshine. Guilt wasn't the main motive at play here, and shame and the unwillingness to meet their eyes and have them judge my weakness wasn't what was driving me. I was making the correct decision. Who was Lincoln to say it anyway? What did she know about the problems we had? Would *she* have done anything differently? No, she'd have made the same decision.

Thoughts raged and my body dashed and ducked as I leapt through a tunnel behind the mirror and pulled waiting chains that released a flood of acid steam. It wouldn't delay them for long, if at all, and that didn't matter. It showed I was being serious, not just a decoy. This was the real deal.

A triple-fork exit came into view. I took one and stepped on the dock at the marina. My boat was small and fast. It took off in a blink and I fell onto the seat. The plan had been developed four years previous, when I realized I'd have to leave a spectacular trail to cover the others. Having no idea which event would start the process, I concentrated on the route.

I'd run it regularly and updated it to account for changing circumstances. Though the various links changed as needed, they always ended at the same place. Suddenly, the boat caught fire, courtesy of an incendiary round fired by the pursuing team. This was a little ahead of schedule, but still within the bounds of the plan.

The boat split in two and I fell into the water, weights in my hands pulling me down fast, but not fast enough. A dart snagged my shoulder and I could feel tension in the attached line increase and slow me down. A quick release worked, and I dropped out of my suit as it was rapidly hauled up. I hit the sea bottom hard, the weights were calculated to push me through the water to generate some momentum when I landed on the doorway.

I passed the through the doorway feeling the ground once again beneath my feet. I walked between buildings, into the Celitrope Centre, the biggest personal living space development disaster in Mengchi. This was a substantial claim to make, but there was widespread agreement that the Celitrope Centre met the most rigorous standards for the title.

No one knew exactly how big it was as it was still growing, but the rate had slowed considerably, due to action by the Standing Committee to locate and deactivate the hottest of the growth cells. There were still a lot of cells, but expansion was considered acceptable compared to the cost of halting it.

The original design had been a mushroom with roots in the Cliffside, extending out before expanding into an enormous dome. This utilized abundant empty space over the water at Cliffside and provided a controlled traffic route into the city proper. The Celitrope Centre was designed to be a slum from the outset, so controlled access was a priority.

What hadn't been a priority was control over construction, which had been done as inexpensively as possible "using inno-vate methods which would deliver sustainable results in a reduced timescale". Self-replicating growth cells were used. Each had a limit, which should have delivered a completed, uniform construction. Unfortunately, all had been managed via multiple independent projects—rather than one master plan—with no communication between any.

The Celitrope Centre grew into the extraordinary beehive it was today, providing living space to a third of Mengchi lifeforms and contributing more than half of the city's civil security activ-ity. It was a boil on the bum of the city, but also a useful one, so no one did anything to fix it. It also seemed the most logical place for me to flee to, for the scale and diversity of illegal activity would provide excellent cover.

The immediate problem was surviving the journey from entry point to destination. Every part of the Celitrope Centre was controlled by an individual or a group—and all wanted payment for travels taken through it. There were continuing disputes regarding the control of different sections, so more than one set of owners could demand payment for travels across the same space. Market forces recognized an opportunity. Residents could pay into mutual funds, which covered certain Centre routes. The funds paid owners and kept a premium for administration. I was a member of 14 different one, so I wouldn't use any of those routes; I'd simply "freelance" my way.

I activated my Whisper Suit and vanished from view of all legal tracking devices, as well as 90% of the illegal ones used in the Celitrope Centre. For the remaining 10%, I'd use decoys. The Centre was full of lifeforms looking to make cash to buy a blaster or place to sleep unmolested. I'd built up a business of sorts, employing a rotating number to travel with me through the walkways. They'd walk alongside for a short while and then shoot off in different directions. While with me, they were covered by the Whisper Suit; when not, they'd return to regular visibility, trackers would follow them until they realised their mistake.

The decoys never robbed me because I had no money and I was willing to fight. The money was always waiting for them at the end of the chosen route. I'd done it often enough to establish rules, as well as my reliability, re payment. The signal had been sent when I'd passed through the mirror, so when I was on the walkway between buildings, the first group joined me.

The groups changed as we progressed, so by the time I was close to my destination, I'd had four of them ... before running into the Bricklayers. The Bricklayers weren't the biggest, most violent, or the best armed or connected in the Celitrope Centre —but they *were* the most territorial and they'd clearly taken over the area that included my destination.

My decoys scattered, fragmenting the Bricklayers' focus for an instant, which I used that to run, run, run. Having a single target, however, restored their focus and they hastened after me. I wore Running-Man boots so they'd never catch me; they'd simply box me in and find me. I needed to be out sight long enough to duck into my chosen location.

Information was useless until you needed it. I knew the layout of the three-unit area well enough to run it blindfolded. The Bricklayers wouldn't have yet generated that micro-knowledge (I hoped). To draw the Bricklayers into formation, I performed a reverse loop and hastily entered the necessary unit. Jumping up the stairs, I arrived at the space set up for the grand finale.

In the room with the best view overcrowded streets, I perched in a big comfortable chair and waited for the invasion. I reckoned the Bricklayers wouldn't pose a problem until I was well past caring about them, but the other trackers would be zeroing in on me now.

Taps on the walls around the windows was what I had been waiting for. Pulling a kit from a pocket, I checked all was in order. I needed to push a needle into my leg and the process would start, and no one would be able to stop it. I was ready for action when I heard entry holes being cut into the walls. Microphones and sound snoopers positioned over likely entry points were paying off. Preparation was everything. My plan was simple. Dying was easy, staying dead was not. I had to stay dead and be beyond the reach of those who knew how to wring information from an ex-corpse.

Once I saw the pursuers were close enough, I would use the kit and become infected. The kit would be visible in my hand which would warn them against coming too close. A team of Involuntary Public Servant equivalents would be sent in to seal my body in protective foam and carry me to a sky launch. We would be boosted into space and a sufficient distance from everything would vaporise. I would have become a dead end in every sense and my family would finally be safe.

Murky shapes appeared in the doorway, a couple of security agents in blur-motion uniforms; they remained stationary. A sword-like weapon flew past view and exploded before making contact. My suit absorbed the impact. The eye defenders I wore as part of the preparation for my death did just that—defended my eyes as blood and brains sprayed into the room from outside and splashed all over me. The impact from an explosion propelled me into a wall and my balls contacted the armrest of a chair after I'd awkwardly sailed into it, before falling and hitting my head on the floor.

In a daze, I heard serious fighting. Someone sprayed the room with energy bolts that sliced the chair above my upturned bum. Shouting preceded a wave grenade being tossed into the room, which tossed me about before hurling me at the opposite wall. There may have been voices or ringing in my ears before the silence, but eventually I came to the painful awareness of still being alive ... and having utterly failed.

"Trust your friends" is what Lincoln had said. I couldn't trust my enemies to follow a carefully planned trail to an undefended space to witness my death without fucking it up; instead, they'd managed to lose a firefight. By landing on outside walls, they'd loudly advertised their presence to the Bricklayers.

I lost the crucial witnesses to my final act, which were utterly necessary to convince my true pursuers that I was dead and unavailable for any post death-interrogation or modifications they might have planned. With that, the only trail that could lead them to my wife and daughter would end and the two would be free. I was alive, however, and my family was in the same danger they'd always been, and now I had no idea how to rescue them.

I pushed myself up on all fours and rested against a wall. The suit had absorbed enough of the impact to prevent broken bones and minimize bruising, but there was plenty left to make me fell sore all over. The kit wasn't damaged, so I put it back in my pocket ready for quick release if needed. The unit was a bloody mess, there were holes and burns on the walls and what was left of the furniture. The fighting had either finished or moved elsewhere, I guessed that iy had moved. Someone would return to here to see what was left, I had a bit of time to have the unit to myself. Stepping over the remains of various bodies, I went to the wet room which was not damaged, the action had been concentrated at the front.

I stepped into the shower unit. Hot spray cleaned the bloody mess off the suit, which I then removed so the interior could also be cleaned. Hanging it up to dry, I then started to work on my body. Twenty minutes under a med-repair spray and bruises were reduced to ugly shades of blue and green, and I could move without pain. Slipping into the now dry suit, I entered a code on the wall opposite. A panel swung open to reveal a shadowy opening and I continued downward in utter darkness.

Lifeforms needed to remove the organic waste they created, so they required drains—small drains that feed into bigger drains that opened into huge drains to bring that waste to processing centres like the one I was responsible for. I hadn't used the drains to get to the space because I'd wanted to be easy to track, without appearing to be so. Leaving was a different matter. This time I wanted to escape detection and that meant taking the shit expressway out of the Celitrope Centre.

I hit a stop and popped a light while I sorted out my Whisper Suit and started on the long walk to Lincoln's space. There'd be no hopping from place to place to expose me.

The drains were very active locations, full of crews doing innumerable tasks. None saw or registered me, and I simply walked for hours, deep in thought. When I reached the required intersection, I climbed a service ladder and moved along dome ducting and dropped into a public-toilet stall. Deactivating the suit, I checked my face in the mirror, drew a deep calming breath, and headed for Lincoln's space.

When I got there, I rang the bell and the door was opened by a young girl who stood in the entrance with a huge toothy grin. It was my daughter Petra who I had last seen 10 years before as a small baby in Asher's lap. I knew it was her because her eyes had not changed at all, black with flecks of gold in them. She spoke, "You have changed your hair, it's better"

I had my hair cut just the week before, how could Petra know that? The end of the universe started with me fainting.

15

FOURTEEN YEARS previously I was a single Firedrake, gainfully employed, bottle born citizen looking for a mate and not having much success. There were a couple of structural issues to be accounted for. Natural-Born and Bottle-Born didn't form life partnerships, not a legal rule, simply a fact. Social disapproval ran deep on both sides as well as more practical problems regarding children. The number of Natural/Bottle-Born casual relationships between free citizens of both groups, was the biggest single proportion of the entire relationship category, ranging from instant sex encounters to relationships that lasted more than nine months and less than a year. The number that lasted longer than a year was essentially zero, if there were any no-one was admitting to it.

I was looking for a life partner within the available pool of Bottle-Born free citizens. I had experience with Naturals; there was a difference between us that was exotic and erotic at first, and impossible to bridge over a longer period. Within the Bottle-Born, the divisions between the base groups were as profound as between Bottle-Born and Natural. I was a FireDrake base and carried remnants of that lifeform within me. This meant I didn't possess a natural compatibility with an Avian,

Aquatic, or a StoneBeater or any of the minor subgroups, just that preferences for like forms ran very deep.

The third biggest private-sector industry by revenue on Mengchi was the "introduction industry". It maintained there was a life partner for *everyone*. At 24 years old, with a stable job and a hunger for shared life I believed that. At 27 years old with a stable job, a hunger for shared life and three years of failure, I learned better.

I was who I was brewed to be I could not change that no matter how hard I tried. I tried really hard. I was not ugly, had no clearly unsavoury personal habits and I was looking to commit to a relationship. Everything that I should need to be successful in finding a mate. I must have read every piece of advice ever published on finding a mate in a competitive environment and tried to follow it. The last introduction had been a final throw for me.

"I'm so sorry, sir. Seti hasn't indicated she'd be interested in meeting with you. I'm also sorry to say that this organization won't be able to provide you with a compatible partner. Therefore, we're refunding your fee and closing your account. *Today*." Mrs Kenouly looked at me with sincere sympathy.

I wasn't surprised but frustrated that yet another meeting arrangement service was proving a dead end. By now, I knew it was entirely useless to argue, threaten to sue, cry, beg or return a few days later and try to join again. I was back on my own, in the most difficult market in Mengchi: trying to find a life partner. With a population of 250-million assorted lifeforms, this should be easier. Surely there was a large population of lifeforms looking for life partners.

Self-pity aside, there were great many things I could have done when I left the offices of the True and Only Meeting Services that rainy Wednesday afternoon—like stop using services intended for people who'd never find me interesting. As I left the office, I saw a very noticeable female FireDrake waiting outside. She had lush deep-red hair, that fiery red so difficult to produce. Her skin wasn't very pale; it had a dark tone that stopped her from being the ideal FireDrake. She was seated, so it was hard to determine how tall she was. The cut of her robes showed a happy curve to breasts and long legs. Her black eyes, set above a cute small nose and smiling mouth, regarded me in return.

She, in turn would have viewed a slim male FireDrake with dark-red hair, pale skin, sage-green eyes, a long nose and a mouth with a slight twist. I was wearing formal robes as I'd come straight from work; they showed that I didn't have a startling physique, but I didn't have a belly either. At two metres, I was slightly taller than the average FireDrake, which was one of the signature developments of my home farm. We nodded to each other, acknowledging each other's review, and I left. I did have little swirls of fantasy about the female FireDrake, but then I did with pretty much anyone I'd seen in the service.

Three days later, I got a call from an unknown number, which I answered anyway, part of my plan to be more open to the unexpected, and a female voice spoke. "Good morning Mr. Shakbout. We encountered each other a few days ago in the office of the True and Only. I was in the reception area as you were leaving, if you remember."

"I remember very well," I said tentatively. This could have been a call from the accounts department, softening me up before explaining that certain deductions were non-refundable.

"My name is Asher Arion and I was wondering if you would be free for a 45 this evening?"

In general, introduction services had different numbered forms for different levels of introductions. Form 45 was an initial no-commitment meeting based on a profile match-up. It was a low-key, non-threatening way to start and Thiegler was full of 45 Houses with tables spaced widely enough to offer privacy and enough exits to make leaving easy.

"I'd like that a lot." I'd done this often enough to have no expectations beyond inconsequential chat-chat. I had never been contacted directly by someone before; previously it had always been a notification from the service. I stifled the blatantly ridiculous hopes that blossomed instantly.

"Kantilever Kitchen at 7:45?" she asked cheerfully.

Smart. We could be done by nine and set up a second encounter with someone else that evening or head back to our respective spaces without feeling too much time had been wasted.

"Perfect."

"Perfect," she repeated and disconnected.

I felt better. Being called was always nice ... not to mention that visions of her lovely hair had flitted past my mind's eye several times over the past days.

I invested effort into getting ready. Yes, this was only a 45, but the fact that the agency had provided my profile after declining me made me think (hope) that there were more possibilities than usual.

Double-scrubbed, I sported sombre clothes (no pretension), befitting someone with a stable, well-paying job. No one ever called me handsome, but my features were all in the right places, and they were *naturally* mine. I aimed to be diplomatically early so that she could see me and decide if she still wanted to continue—standard 45 meeting courtesy. She was at the table waiting. I was delighted. Without hesitation, I approached the table with a big smile and a hand outstretched for that vital first physical contact. It was said that 85% of all 45 meetings finished at this point; physical contact was considered a hugely reliable sign of basic compatibility (Lanken's Tears, yes, I knew the numbers for introductions). Her touch was warm, firm and comfortable; I wanted more of it. Asher withdrew her hand without haste or delay.

"Thanks for coming," she said as I sat.

"Thanks for asking me." A slight silence followed and then I started on the second part of the introduction formalities.

"My home farm is Asher-Brooke Consolidated 67334, these

are my specifications" I laid an info cube on the table. This was crucial; the most minor variations in brewing could have significant consequences. It was always wise to establish basic compatibility before continuing.

Asher replied "My home farm is Asher-Brooke Consolidated 67375, these are my specifications." As both our farms were in the Asher-Brooke Consolidated 673 group we were brewed under compatible conditions and protocols. First hurdle cleared successfully.

This completed the ritual opening to a 45 and we could continue with the meeting itself.

Asher had seen my profile, so she started sharing. She worked as a content producer on the lines in different capacities: freelance, serial contract, and regular. She stopped as a regular due to creative differences with the accounting department, had a five-month stretch on the Whirling Wheel, and currently picked up freelance work. I was suitably impressed; working on the entertainment lines was a savagely competitive marketplace. Anyone who lasted longer than it took to get a one- segment content to the public was tough ... capable and accomplished.

I, on the other hand, was a corporate culture carrier, working in the internal services department for a medium-sized industrial conglomerate that had numerous off-world interests, making sure various operations could understand the other's requirements. It was enjoyable, hectic work, and I was waiting for a promotion to put me in Asher's salary bracket.

We swopped war stories without trying to outdo each other, some triumphant and some deprecating; all were laced with laughter. We hit the limit for the night, and I asked if Asher had ever seen the Blowout. When she shook her head, I asked if she'd like to. She did, we paid, and left.

We headed to the docks where my company had a warehouse and 15 docking slots. Taking transport to the docking slots, we caught a wire to a launch-view spot to view the extraordinary display of the Blowout, a ruptured disintegrating star. The vivid lights and unique dancing patterns of trapped planets was as entrancing as ever. Most Mengchi lifeforms could view the Blowout by looking up, but there was a dramatic difference from where we stood. Asher stared into the cosmic lightshow and then, suddenly, kissed me with exhilarating intensity.

———

Engaging and enjoyable, the sex at my place aroused an unexpected appetite for more. Having been publicly rated as "good" on a scale that moved from "excellent" to "ecstatic", I'd been self-consciously restrained during previous encounters. Asher was welcoming and willing to share what she liked. Delivering pleasure released me to want to do more and relax with what I received in return. There was no reason to think it was too good to be true.

We quickly slipped into a stable routine that had us spending more time with each other, usually overnight at my space. As we reached a three-month milestone, it was clear we were heading toward serious commitment, which would trigger payment to the introduction agency. If we established a life-partner contract, that would be another.

Asher told me she'd look after the payment, accepting my contribution with a sultry smile. A couple days later, she explained that she'd negotiated a severance from the agency and any future "developments" were between us. That was the moment I should have asked for more details. No agency had a process for negotiating a severance; their business model was based on fees that rolled in from every stage of an introduced relationship, from the 45 through the life contract, family, and divorce. All of which I knew, and if someone had asked, I'd have told them. No one asked me and I slid right over that knowledge without a pause.

Lying in the arms of my lover, I had what I ached for and what every Bottle-Born life ached for: family. We approached our twelve-month milestone, but Asher hadn't given any indication she wouldn't want to continue as a couple.

The critical week arrived, and Asher delivered a dinner invitation to a very pricey venue that took guests on a hovering trip over the city. Booking this was a positive sign, as was the fact that Asher was wearing the jewellery I'd bought her (two bracelets and a necklace, artisan-crafted). The appetizers were excellent, something to nibble until we got a cleared table, wine, and the main course. The advantage with the invitation was that it was *your* event; you got to speak first and could take as long as you wanted.

Asher talked about the project she was working on, an advertising string for a well-established brand developing into a small war. She wasn't bothered by the conflict; it was just part of the industry, but no one did it well. They bickered frequently and no one strove to carve a niche for themselves. The fighting served no purpose; it was just part of the process.

"I have goals, some achieved and some still waiting to be achieved. One of my major goals is to form a family and belong to a group that's more than a network. I want partnership and depth, trouble and joy ... waking up feeling okay and having someone think that that's fine. Not that this means energy has leaked and it's time to move on." Asher took a slow, deep breath as she scanned the room. "I don't know if I could tolerate living with the same person for a lifetime. The prospect seems reductive. How can I be creative if I'm always contained in the same, hmm, environment?"

She forked food into her mouth while I pondered whether she was inviting me to stay or go. Then she waved her fork, which I correctly assumed meant she had more to say.

"Naturals have families ... and are so damn snotty about them. They wave them in everyone's faces, as if we should celebrate the perfectly ordinary. There's nothing extraordinary about family and nothing extraordinary about *not* having families, either. It's a choice, not an imperative."

Asher paused for more fork waving while I stared at her in desperation. I had no idea what she was talking about, but the way she was saying it made me think I *should* know. The dreaded fork stopped and pointed directly at me. "Do you know what I hate? That bag of Ihagr spit, Ripple, who sits in meetings and talks about her perfect family, which makes *her* perfect. It's merely a rag to clean up her messes. Ripple with the perfect family ... while the rest of us eat her shit."

She'd not had a lot to drink, but she was getting angry and I had no idea what to say or do.

She placed a hand lightly over mine. "So, what do you have to say?"

I wished she'd stabbed me with the fork, but honesty was everything or something like that. "I want a family and I want it with you. I've no idea if it'll be perfect or if you'll realize that I'm not what you want. I want you and me ... and *more* than you and me." Not what I'd rehearsed. The words simply gushed forth.

Asher smiled fleetingly and kissed my hand. (Discreetly placed watchers noted this and nodded in satisfaction that all was progressing nicely.)

We had eighteen months to discover that living intimately with each other was hard work. Boundaries melted and reformed, and endless negotiation started and ended. The road to the end of everything began when Asher announced, "I want us to have a baby".

16

BOTTLE-BORN life forms had children all the time with genetic material from both parents, so they were both biological and legal parents. The process used to create the child was one of the fundamental barriers between Naturals and Bottle-Borns. We sported the differences in the way we described ourselves—and those differences stood at the root of our existence.

There was zero appetite to eradicate the differences vital to identity. Any Bottle-Born free citizen had the biology to have natural childbirth; there was no legal constraint on any natural lifeform from brewing a child. It wasn't done because we'd been created by alien hands as part of an industrial process. Creating a child was a way of domesticating and owning said process.

As Asher said talked about wanting a baby, it became clear that she was talking about the natural process, becoming pregnant and having a live birth. After the shock subsided, I was furious, confused, upset, horrified ... and speculative. She never raised the topic a second time. I didn't raise the topic myself for fear of what I might say that I couldn't *unsay*.

As the storm diminished, I found myself more and more in the grip of one single emotion: fear. I was afraid that a natural child wouldn't love me, be embarrassed, or feel distant from a creature so different from them. Could our shared life experiences be meaningful, given our radically different roots? Would I be a traitor to all other Bottle-Borns, turning my back on them in a most insulting fashion?

What I found out for the first (not last) time was that it was possible to tire of being afraid. Bone-weary with the weight of dreadful expectations, waiting for judgment from others, finally became—in a word—boring. Different ideas started percolating in my mind and a sundry of questions were spoken in the still of the night—such as, did I really care? It clearly mattered to Asher, but did I have an equal emotional investment in a different process for the same result? Who would know if I didn't tell them, not that it was anyone else's business anyway? Slowly I talked myself around finding every reason to make Asher happy. Stealing something from the Naturals that they considered to be theirs alone did have a powerful attraction, a little historical payback.

We were having lunch at a pick-and-sit, easy to get to from both work locations. Tellager, a natural colleague of Asher, approached us pushing a baby carriage. Asher introduced me and we exchanged pleasantries before turning to the smiling infant. He appeared content, but Tellager told us not to be fooled by appearances; the baby was a full-time tyrant. He asked Asher how she was doing on the current contract and they chatted a few more moments.

"Let's have a baby," I said as we watched Tellager wheel his son along the walkway. Tears trickled down her cheek and she rose, pulling me to my feet and wrapping her arms around me. Softly she told me how happy I'd made her.

The whole process of the pregnancy was both mundane and obscure. Asher became pregnant quickly and that was that. I noticed changes in her; she became a bit more unsettled and often asked if I was sure we were making the right decision. As soon as the pregnancy was confirmed Asher took me to the fertility clinic that her insurance had approved for use. It was a discreet building deep in a medical complex that served bottle born and natural patients. The medical staff at the clinic was all naturals, the patients were all bottle born, a detail that I paid no attention to until much too late, long after the damage had been done. No one expressed any surprise or curiosity regarding the fact that Asher was pregnant, they took the pregnancy for granted and therefore so did I. All successful frauds rely on the victim doing most of the heavy lifting, they take the bait and then do the rest by themselves. We went for weekly check-ups, I was reassured about the progress of the pregnancy and unobtrusively supported in my unexpected role.

There was a scare three months in, Asher had a severe fall at work and was badly bruised. The baby was fine; Asher spent two days at the clinic and returned in rather subdued form. She made some offhand remarks about the weight of history and the importance of duty and loyalty. They did not appear to tie to anything in particular and I just let the flow by as part of the consequences of pregnancy. I was conscious of being locked out of the process in a way that I would not have been if we had brewed our baby. I wondered how natural fathers coped with it, all the key decisions were being made by the body of another, hidden from view.

The day finally came, and, at Asher's demand, the birth took place in our own space. The clinic had offered space, but Asher stood firm. It was horrifying; no wonder Naturals made such a big deal about it (my most savage nightmares afterwards involved the process of one body bursting forth from another). Then she was there. Petra, our daughter. We had agreed, after several "discussions", to call her that and whose choice it had actually been was anyone's guess. Love enfolded my heart and soul as I touched her tiny, perfect hand. And Asher switched from looking like a set of spare parts to a happy woman to a glowing mother.

The clinic had sent over a staff member to see if all was going well. Asher refused to have them in the room for the birth or to touch Petra, which was all normal according to my information, so the medic simply scanned Petra with a hand-held device and announced that all was well and left.

The next seven days consisted of blurs—holding Asher, cuddling Petra, and understanding how life had changed. Petra cried, slept, fed, and smiled ... and changed colour. This seemed strange. There was no mention of it in any information I could find, nor was it listed as a symptom for any known illnesses or conditions. *Slight* changes were listed, but not changing from pale white-pink to bright orange, to red, to silver, and then back to pale white-pink. Asher wouldn't allow me to contact the clinic to ask and assured me it was entirely normal and natural. Given the breadth and depth of my ignorance I believed her.

On day eight, Asher got out of bed, washed and dressed, and announced herself ready for living, but not ready for work. She wanted to spend more time with Petra before any arrangements had to be made. The lifeform from the clinic who had been at our space for Petra's birth had given me details of a qualified nanny. Over the next weeks I realised the full extent of Tellager's comment, Petra was the absolute ruler of our lives. I felt like someone had sliced off the top of my head and poured in a mix of happiness and tiredness, filling up my entire body. I worked during the day and returned home to take over salve duties from Asher who slept while I was awake. I am sure we were both awake at times in this period, I would not swear to it. Three months after Petra was born, on a weekend, we were all together awake at the same time. Asher had the morning shift and I emerged from the bedroom and caught her request for breakfast as I crossed the living room to the kitchen.

Through the door, I heard the sounds of mother comforting daughter; I was overwhelmed with happiness. Grabbing the tray, I entered the room to find Asher sitting on the small couch with a low table in front. Petra was lying on her back, kicking her legs at Asher and smiling. I stepped around, picked up Petra and held her to my chest.

Petra snuggled in my arms, yawned, and fell asleep with a whisper of a sigh. I burst into flames and comprehended three things simultaneously. First, Petra was the source of the fire. Second, the flames felt comfortable and familiar (I was a Fire-Drake, after all). Third, Asher wasn't remotely surprised. Then the flames having subsided to a delicious heat beneath my skin, they had burned my life to ashes and I was left standing in a new reality that had no connection to any previous one.

Asher stood quickly and hastened to the door, listened, then beckoned me. I walked over;. Asher put a finger to her lips and motioned me out. Once I was in the common area, Asher closed the door and keyed a re-set for the space before walking off, clearly expecting I'd follow ... which I did.

Every space in Thiegler has a re-set facility, which deleted and recreated the space, so no trace of the former occupant remained. This was important if you didn't know what charm residues the previous occupants left behind. It also wiped out trails and traces for anyone trying to track the occupant, a staple of crime and thriller content on the lines. I followed Asher with nothing of my former life left, except the child I carried in my arms.

She halted at the entrance of a space a little way down, keyed in the code and entered. Petra and I followed. Still silent, Asher entered the kitchen, opened a cupboard, and pulled a tiny lever. A section of the wall opposite swung open. When she stepped into it, I followed her hearing the click as the door closed behind me.

———

Everything was mechanical, not charmed. A very dim light emanated from a source. The path was only wide enough for one person, so we walked in silent single file, which gave me far too much time to think. After walking in a straight line for what seemed a short forever, Asher stopped and raised her hand. I halted. Amber light flooded the tunnel from a nearly identical kitchen to the one we'd just left. It was a regular living space, nothing out of the ordinary. It appeared to be lived in, no one else was present at the time. Asher motioned to remain silent and led us out of the space and down out of the building.

There was a small square with a Labrossa tree in the centre and tables under the large spread of branches. Staff delivered drinks and snacks to lifeforms at the tables. It was quiet and ordinary . . . yet alien . . . and jarring.

Asher walked to a table away from the others. Drawing a calming breath, I gathered myself and joined her. Catering staff brought a sleeping seat for Petra and coffee and luscious cakes. After placing Petra carefully into one of the chairs, I took a sip of steaming coffee and began the confrontation calmly and amiably. "Please don't lie. I won't know if you are, but I think I deserve the truth."

"They're called Action Group 5." Asher fiddled with the cup as she spoke. "Their mission is to develop an autonomous energy-rich lifeform, one with access to a full range of energy that comes from their baseline and isn't constrained within the rules of a charm. The energy is free to be directed according to the will of the lifeform and can be used for any purpose. They've been trying to do this for over a thousand of years and are ready to continue for hundreds more—until they succeed or are overtaken by unforeseen events.

"There's a threat on the fringes of time and space that will become urgent. This threat is all-consuming, so there's no room for compromise. It'll either emerge or be locked out. I don't know more details and I only know this much because I'm an HPO like you."

"HPO like me?"

"High Potential Opportunity, the breeding program established to develop HPOs ... lifeforms with a *high potential* of producing offspring that generates an autonomous energy-rich lifeform."

"What? Like me? How like me?"

"You're part of the program," Asher said matter-of-factly, as if this were obvious and didn't require further explanation.

In the face of everything that had just happened I still had room to be shocked and stunned. Asher was claiming that I was part of this insane conspiracy story that she was telling me about. I did not doubt her, and I did not want to believe her, there was no part of my life to date that was not a lie, not part of a huge practical joke being played on me. "I came from a commercial bottle farm, part of the Asher-Brooke Consolidated complex. Are you saying that the third biggest industrial conglomerate in the systems is part of this Action Group?"

"I'm saying that you're part of the program. There's no need for the entire company to be part of the plan. You just need a cooperative Brew-Master willing to accept suitable payment for a minor adjustment to a lifeline. The results affect a group small enough to get lost in the ordinary margin of error if anything goes wrong. If you have a lot of time, you can set up hundreds of thousands of experiments, each one a one-off with that Brew-Master and the results, whatever they are, are data for the next round of experimentation. A few lines of code add to the lifeline instructions and they look innocuous enough, because they're a teeny part of a bigger plan."

She waited until a server stopped by with more coffee, waved him off curtly, and scanned my face as she thoughtfully sipped. "At private bottle farms, evaluated results are directly applied directly to measure outcome. Slowly, options are narrowed; over time, the path to producing HPO specimens becomes clearer. An unlimited budget of time makes everything possible ... if spent with care and attention. Every dead end a positive result, because it eliminates mere possibilities and provides clues re the next steps to pursue."

I had to know, "You—Bottle or Natural?"

Asher sighed softly. "I was born naturally to a Bottle-Born mother and a natural-born father. It's a known fact the best process has been to mix the two, so for generations there have been lifeforms who've had one of each as parents. Crossing base-lines doesn't work—the energy patterns are different and not compatible—so the lines are always within the original groups."

Curiosity started awakening—in droves. I wanted to know *everything*. An image flashed in my mind—me sinking my teeth into Asher's neck, her information-filled blood gushing and quenching my burning thirst. I wasn't angry, not at that moment, but detached and rational, an explorer in a new territory seeking to understand the geography.

"How did they know this would work?"

"Every Bottle-Born lifeform is a transplant, from one form to another. They adapt and fit together. Every Bottle-Born has sensitivity to energy, which no natural lifeform has, and it's this sensitivity that's the basis for the work. Developing and expanding it within a natural-born form increases the fit and the access to energy. Sometimes a lifeform can be too sensitive and dies from toxic poisoning emitted by charms. Sometimes they have no sensitivity at all. The variations excite them, because that implies a range, which can be explored and developed. A natural birth is necessary; processes rely on interactions between baby and mother that can't be replicated at a farm."

Asher appeared increasingly tired, as if giving information were draining her. My thought was that shock was wearing off and circumstances were beginning to press in on her. I, on the other hand, felt suddenly energized, rage was building and sending pulses through my body.

"You and me?"

She smiled faintly. "I knew I was an HPO from the get-go. I'd been told that I had a special part to pay in the mission and was trained for it. I was never allowed to be proud of this—it wasn't because of anything I'd done, but the work and sacrifices of others. I was a High Potential Opportunity, emphasis on *potential* and *opportunity*. This prevented divisions. And the rele-vant parents could be any female and male couple. Odds were better with an HPO pair, of course, but a lot of experience with the unexpected made everyone very humble.

"I had an utterly mainstream upbringing. My parents worked, I schooled, and the project was a minor part of our lives. I was never directed to do anything or go anywhere; I was simply aware of my responsibilities and they influenced my choices. On my eighteenth birthday, my 'body clock' woke me up and I looked for a partner. There were other HPOs out in the world, some aware and some not. I wasn't seeking either in particular."

She sipped tepid coffee and grimaced. "I visited every Thiegler meeting-arrangement service that had FireDrakes on their lists and sent details to my project contact. They ran checks and identified the HPOs on the lists. Lanken's Tears, there were a lot. Every now and then, I'd encounter someone in the same situation as myself and we'd have a sympathetic dinner where we compared scars and disasters. I was under no obligation to have a partner. I could have gone to a fertility clinic and been sorted ... or found a non-HPO partner. Being a willing participant is important to the project; it increases the odds of a successful outcome."

I clicked my tongue, not knowing what to say and waited patiently as she regarded tables, eyed Petra, sighed, and finally chose to speak again.

"I visited the True and Only Meeting Services because there was a hole in my schedule, and they were around the corner from a place where I'd finished a meeting. I saw you come out of the office looking defeated ... then you glanced at me and straightened your shoulders and left." Asher hesitated and scanned my face. "Are you sure you want no lies?"

Of course, I wanted them, comforting untruths that wouldn't slash me or grind the remaining shards of my heart. I could think of nothing I wanted more at that point than lies.

"No lies" My hunger said.

"I got your details from Mrs Kenouly. She told me you were no longer a client. I think she felt sorry for you and wanted to help. You came back as an HPO. All HPOs are developed with cues that support unforced attraction. If a spark is there, they'll amplify it. I could see you had a spark for me, and I had one for you. You were sweet and charming, and clearly falling for me, which was very flattering. I grew to really like you.

"The project ran numbers on us, as they did with everyone, and they became really excited. For the first time in my life, I was called into the project offices. Significant compatibility showed between us. We were moved into the 'possible' group. I was given an option to withdraw and wasn't pressured at all. While the odds were that I'd not be the relevant parent, they wanted to ensure I was aware that I *could* be.

"I never hesitated I was just filled with joy. The first step was easy. You were so hungry for a partner, I only needed to provide an opportunity, so when I kissed your hand, that informed project observers that all had successfully commenced. The second step was harder. Because 90% of potential partnerships failed at this step, there had to be a natural birth to make it successful. I saw your face when I asked looking like you had stepped out the entrance into the deeps of space instead of the common area you were expecting."

Asher hesitated; she seemed to be thinking about how to say what came next. I had frozen inside while I waited to discover just how big a fool I had been.

"I wanted to persuade you, to bring you round to the idea. Everything seemed so close. I was told step back and let you process everything in your own time and fashion. You never said anything, and I struggled *not* to demand an answer from you. Whenever we made love, I thought you'd say something. My body clock was ringing so loud, I was afraid I'd go deaf and not hear you. Finally, you spoke at the most unexpected moment. I wanted to throw you to the floor and fuck you then and there wringing every bit of juice out of you and into me so that I would have a baby. The Baby. I wanted to be the relevant parent; I wanted to be the one. The hero of the project, be the reason the universe was saved from destruction"

Asher smiled wryly. "The project was very happy. Each visit to the clinic gave positive results, still they had similar results before and it led to nothing. I was told then that I was in a direct line of births that had good results and the general expectation was that the relevant child would come from a line like mine. I was very happy; I was fulfilling the goal of my life and when I had a child I would be free to go off and live with you. Our child would join the project in turn and at some point, in the future the historical necessity would be achieved. I would have contributed to saving the universe. So, would you, you would understand everything when I explained it to you. We would be happy forever and ever. As the birth approached, I started to think differently. I did not want to be the relevant parent; I wanted to be a mother with you the father and our baby. When it came to it, I could not bear to have anyone from the project near me.

You were kind, loving, and completely lost. I saw Petra gobble you whole when you held her for the first time and that was when I finally cracked. My certainty began to fall away in big chunks like an ice cliff falling into the sea; Petra stopped being an idea and became a living child, an independent life-form that deserved to have her own future. Anyway, I was positive that I wasn't the relevant parent; there'd have been a sign before now.

"I didn't know for certain—that door hadn't yet closed. The project had emphasized that there was no timetable for a revelation, only time and observation. They did not think that there was any substantial likelihood of confirmation before six months based on their accumulated data so observations in this period would be light. I organized a tunnel via a series of shells, manual and mechanical labour from off-system providers. I never expected to use it, simply wanted the comfort of knowing it was there. Then, this morning, our three-month old child set you on fire and I made a decision for all of us.

Spontaneous fire is one of the major signals that the project looks for, there are others depending on the baseline. We were being lightly observed, they will still have caught the spark of power and be responding to it right now. That is why we had to leave instantly. We are being actively sought and need to keep moving or we will be trapped."

Asher looked like she'd reached the end of the road and wanted to remain where she was. I, however, was at the start of mine. It was a foundation fact accepted by all naturals that an autonomous energy rich life form was an extinction event for them; they had a Berg the ears now the Berg would have them in its teeth. Five hundred years ago, an autonomous energy-rich lifeform was discovered in the Ghtree system, a small cluster in an outer-spiral arm. It was quickly established as a fraud, which changed nothing. Naturals, fearing annihilation, started their own version first. It took only three days for the rest of the systems to realize the danger, quarantine Ghtree, kill and then incinerate every living creature in the system. It took 30 years of non-stop transportation to gather up all the ashes and dump them in some void in space.

Petra wasn't a fraud. This put the lives of all free bottle born citizens across the systems in mortal danger. The natural population would respond with overwhelming organized aggression and all the gains that we achieved since Radical Reason would be wiped out in a tsunami of blood. Energy was controlled in charms. Energy-rich lifeforms were turned into non-energy rich lifeforms, so they were on the same baseline as Naturals. Severed our heritage, the bottle born had to slot into a functioning space within the Natural world and we'd done so. Naturals never lost their primal fear, they could never imagine forgiveness for their original sin only revenge.

Slowly, Bottle-Born free citizens moved into the mainstream and took a share in managing and controlling the whole process.

It held down the rage, fear, frustration and desperate longing never given voice to. Slowly a new identity had emerged and solidified for the bottle born, we became ourselves. The weight of time had forced us to evolve whether we wanted to or not, cut off from our roots we sprouted branches instead and became something new. Slowly we had absorbed the details of our existence and accepted what we could not change.

The population of Bottle-Born free citizens had grown enormously during the interval, with equal growth in the dormant fear and anxiety of the Natural population. There could be no quarantine; there was no place that didn't rely on charm energy to survive. Bottle-Born lifeforms, at their deepest core, ached for the loss of that energy. We were a perpetually dry forest, waiting for the slightest spark, and I had a firestorm sleeping beside me. I didn't have any idea who Action Group 5 were or what their plans were, nor did I care. The casual way they were willing to sacrifice so many lives was breath-taking. There could be no doubt they knew exactly what the stakes were, they were not bothered by the. Truth to tell I did not really care about the abstract possibility of the death of millions, possibly billions of Bottle-Born lifeforms either. I was solely concerned by the fact that Action Group 5 were threatening my family.

The fact that I was an involuntary part of their project subject not simply a random product of the farming process but a made to order component for an unknown plan did not really come home to me until much later. Long dark years when I felt foreign fingers move my limbs and manipulate my emotions. I was designed to fall for Asher and to father Petra, were the emotions that raged inside me mine or the programmed responses of a puppet? Drugs helped; alcohol helped blunt the edges of the fears that cut me inside my head. Finally, it was one overwhelming emotion that pulled me out of the pit, rage was purely and wholly mine. It burned hot and cold, it always burned, and it helped me understand that I was a dupe, but I was not a slave.

"Listen. "I leaned forward and gripped Asher's arm and stared into her eyes, "This Action Group 5 is going to look for us. We have to move! We can't stay together; we'd be too visible. I'll go to the transport station. You take Petra and head for the Circle."

The Circle was a dumping ground for failed and unexpectedly successful experiments in Thiegler, a mass of lifeforms that couldn't find a niche anywhere else. Asher and Petra could hide for a very long time in that mess, long enough for me to determine how to move them to a safer, better life. For myself, I was going to locate this Action Group 5 and piss in their faces before I hacked them to pieces for, what they'd done to my family. I had an object for my rage and fear, I did not need anything else at that point.

I hopped to my feet and Asher did the same. She scooped up Petra and reached out to touch me, but then she whirled and walked away.

While walking for the station, I came across an arrest being conducted by a posse of Retrievers. Expressionless, they stood over an elderly lifeform on the ground.

17

TEN YEARS LATER, I found myself lying on a lumpy couch with a number of anxious faces looming over me. Lincoln smiled and winked before heading away and leaving me with Asher and Petra.

Asher looked worried and brushed my cheek. Petra sat on my legs and grinned. "Why did you fall over? We were worried. Mum said it was a reaction to stress. Are you stressed? I'm not, even if we had to leave home in a hurry. I like your hair. It's better than it was. Did *you* have to leave home in a hurry, too? Didn't anyone tell you to be ready? That's bad."

She stared curiously, waiting for answers. Asher pulled her off. "Daddy can't answer with you squeezing the air out of him. Give him a moment."

Petra nodded and dragged over a chair, sat and watched, still wanting answers.

"You know who I am?" was all I could manage.

Petra rolled her eyes, then scanned my face. "Of course, I know who you are. We've been Target Tracking for ages. Mum won't take me on any other Target Tracking's, but I always get to go on yours. Mum says it's really important that I know all about you, so that when we meet, we're not strangers. I couldn't talk to you when we are on Target Tracking ... because that might have spooked you and then we'd have to start all over again."

She glanced at her mother. "Mum says you're working for our future, that when we're together we'll have a different future to living in the Circle ... a lovely one with the three of us."

She smiled at me ready for the lovely future with the three of us to begin since now we were together and could talk to each other. She resembled Asher, except that she had my pale skin and twist to her mouth.

I wanted to hug her tightly and never stop, but I was terrified to actually do so. All my plans to save her were lost ... and I could only lose her again. I had no idea what to do.

"Dad looks like he could do with something to drink and eat. Would you ask Lincoln what she has, my pet?" Asher smiled prettily and Petra nodded, and headed off to do as requested.

Asher sat in the chair and looked at me in silence. Our last conversation ten years before had left too many unanswered questions. Petra, however, had given me hope about the question I hadn't asked. I considered how to ask it now.

Asher had placed my heart in her pocket, where it still was, bruised and battered. Where was Asher's heart, though? I knew she loved Petra, but what about me? She'd spoken of a future with me to Petra. Could it have been camouflaged to maintain peace?

"I ran because of you," she advised softly. "You walked in with that tray and you were so happy when you picked up Petra. You looked like a puzzle with all the pieces put together to create that final picture." She shrugged limply and offered a bittersweet smile. "I realized the hollowness of the project for what it is; we were tools, nothing more. Telling you everything was awful, never mind watching as I did so. I wanted to share something ... but I had to tell you what you needed to know first. Before I could, you took over and sent us away.

"When we saw you over the years, I'd stand beside you in a queue and will you to recognize me. Sometimes I was furious that you didn't. You should have seen though my disguise. There were times you looked so lost, I had to leave quickly before I gave myself away. Other times you looked so determined, so grim, I'd sent Petra off so she wouldn't see you looking like that."

"Asher—"

"Let me finish, please." She squeezed my hand reassuringly. "When Lincoln found us today, I knew who she was, and I knew you'd sent her. I was so happy ... until she explained the rest. She and I knew what you were doing. She didn't ask questions, just helped us pack and come here."

"You saw me? You stood beside me with Petra? How did you find me? "

I sat up, swinging my legs to the floor and a dizzy feeling swept over me. I had thought that I was under deep cover, taking all the care needed not to be found while I investigated the project that had blown up our lives. I had spent most of the last ten years quietly moving and checking, gathering information and trying to find them before they could find me. I had found that I was not alone, there were others seeking answers or revenge. There were networks that helped and supported, everyone bearing the risk that the other was a spy or a traitor.

They worked very hard and successfully to be not visible, to blend in enough to be simply not noticed. Asher was making a big claim that she had been able to recognize me in a crowd.

"Lincoln is furious with you, when she found me and Petra she was very angry with you. Apparently, you do not have the sense of a raft of plankton. You did not trust friends who trusted you, you were going off to be stupidly heroic. In all probability you would fail at that too since she was not there to make sure that you pulled the correct trigger. She stopped because Petra was getting worried about you. She said to tell you that she was not finished with you and as soon as you could stand there would be a sorting out. I was going to tell Petra something when we were on the cruiser and out of the system limits; instead you came back to us." Then she kissed me.

I admired the brazen way she brushed off my question, I was about to repeat it when the door opened and Hiral Lakeview came into the room, followed by Petra. I have no idea of the protocols for when you meet royalty, so I was stranded. Fortunately, Hiral did know what to do, putting the tray down on a low table she held out her hand and with a wide smile said "How nice to meet you Shakbout, Petra has told me a great deal about you." Petra nodded in agreement that she had in fact been leaking information as fast as she could. Looking at Hiral Lakeview in the flesh I could see the resemblance to Lincoln that I had never registered before, it explained a great deal about Lincoln as well. Lincoln called something about the coffee spout from the other room to which Hiral simply smiled and left the room.

The sudden assault was screaming loud, just as intended, a great way to knock you off balance. A hole appeared in the wall and two battle-suited figures entered—Zusak Sedge and Mr. Hennessey. Both had copies of the Shoshone Circlet on their arms, not very good ones, which I assumed was the point. Sedge pointed at Petra who'd been knocked to the floor, and Mr. Hennessey pulled a sack over her before lifting her over his shoulder. Mr. Hennessey turned to me and mouthed "see you later" and the pair exited.

Hiral and Lincoln burst into the room with heavy-pulse weapons in their hands and dangerous looks on their faces. Asher lifted herself up, rubbing her head to settle the impact of the noise bomb, while I managed to stand after two failed attempts. Hiral was the first to speak, "Who did this?" she asked.

"Zusak Sedge and a friend, Mr. Hennessey. He's a Scar Carrier. They've taken Petra. I have to find her" I said as my legs decided they would not support me quite yet and I fell back onto the couch.

"Sedge, I thought I had settled her the last time, well this time I will leave no room for doubt" as Hiral was speaking

Lincoln was looking at her mother as she suddenly realized just who she really was. For a fraction of a second I wished I had parents I could be surprised by.

"Which one took Petra?" Lincoln demanded. She'd recovered quickly.

"Hennessey stuffed her in a sack and left."

"A sack? Then they don't mean to harm her—the sack will mean safe delivery to whoever wants her. That will slow them down, because they'll have to be careful. They won't travel together but split up and aim to meet later. That gives us two targets to pursue."

"I'm going to be sick." My body was struggling to contain itself.

"Down to the left, second door," Hiral said, pointing, and I broke into a stumbling run to make it to the wet room before any mishaps occurred.

I just made it, pulled off my suit as I burst from every orifice; my organs have semi- liquefied, violently expelled from my body. If a tunneller jumped down my throat and exited from my arse, both ends would have been equally sore and raw.

When I stopped puking and shitting, I rested on all fours and waited for a warm and scented set of sprays to wash me, the suit, floor and walls, until everything was clean. Warm air quickly dried everything, and I was ready to climb into my suit and have a few words with Mr. Hennessey.

I returned to the room where I found the wall hole had been patched. All three were ready to inflict damage on whoever made the mistake of getting in their way. Asher looked very comfortable holding the pulse weapon; the blades in her belt looked custom-made. A connection finally fired in my tired brain, Petra had spoken of Target Tracking, Asher was a Recovery Agent, and they found and recovered fugitives for a fee. It was a very high turnover profession; the survival rate was slightly better than Brew-Masters. If she was doing the work for years as it appeared, then she was exceptionally tough. Rather late I realized that I really knew very little about Asher.

"Here, eat this and hold this." Hiral passed an energy slab and a track button. The slab was surprisingly delicious; usually they were like eating butter-coated rubber. "I make them myself," Hiral said proudly. "I like to know what goes into them before I eat any. By the way, I slipped a track into Petra's drink while we were chatting, so it won't be found during a frisk, and they won't risk a full scan, would take too long. It was just a precaution, given Petra's an energetic lady, I was concerned that she would decide to explore outside on her own. Now get going. We have business of our own and don't need any delays."

The three set their weapons to full-blast mode. Calm, concentrated expressions crossed their faces. I swallowed the button and headed for the door as the energy surge kicked in. I followed the track in front of me and heard the trio emerge behind. Mr. Hennessey wanted me to follow him so this race was going to be on his terms unless I could figure out some way of getting ahead of him. I started to run in the trace was indicating and tried to keep my imagination shut down.

———

The audio pinged and Lincoln's voice came through. I could hear the sound of heavy weapons in the background, followed by an explosion.

"Hey Screw-Top, how are you?"

"Fine thanks. Sounds like you're busy there."

"Turning things upside down and shaking them to see what falls out. I have to say it's proved to be very instructive so far. No sign of Sedge yet. It seems that as the teams were stepping into the room, our two vermin were scuttling out via the basement. There's a strong suggestion that they had some advance notice, since they were the only ones who left. The Circlet copy was seized in Sedge's office still in its delivery box and the recovery has cooled everyone down. Some bad news: they got the Jewel Box, as well as Petra, I think Sedge picked it up while everyone was watching Hennessey. "

"Fuck."

"Totally agree—sorry. Have to go. Just saw someone I really want to talk to jump out a window. Catch you later!" She was gone and I was left to rage at my stupidity.

Petra and the Jewel Box , both laid out nicely, ready for collection. There was only one group with the resources to hire Sedge and Hennessey, have knowledge about Lincoln, Petra and the Jewel Box , and the desire to leave Asher and myself alive to jam our faces into it. Action Group 5 had seized the moment with a flourish, setting me up to give them everything they wanted on a golden platter.

I got the message from Mr. Hennessey on a public comms channel, it was a plain picture of the front door of a living space with just enough detail to be able to search and identify the location. The detail that gripped my heart was the sack that was stretched out in front of the entrance. Mr. Hennessey was set on enjoying himself, it would take me precious time to get the location and then get to there. I was sure that it was not the final stop in our game..

I did a search on the picture. It was not far away, and I headed there on the run and raced up to the entrance. It was ordinary except for the fact that it was clearly open. No one left a living space open in Mengchi , it wiped out your insurance. I took the invitation and stepped through the entrance. I felt the tingle of the charm at the same time as I fell into the water. It was a large pool of crystal-clear water and at the bottom I could see the outline of a door and beside it a key. I hated swimming; a FireDrake thing. This confirmed the involvement of Action Group 5, Mr. Hennessey would never have had the time or resources for set up like this. I took a deep breath and pushed down to get the key.

It was far enough down for me to realize that I could get the key or the door but not both at the same time. More time carefully added to extend my journey. I put my hand on the key and realized it was stuck to the surface. I had to pull hard to free it which put a panic inducing strain on my lungs. I pulled it free and made the surface with no extra time. Trying to curse and breathe at the same time is difficult but not actually impossible. Holding the key I got ready for the dive and realized that the water had turned murky, I could no longer see to the bottom. I would have to dive and find the door.

The pressure of the water as I pushed down felt greatly increased from the previous dive, there seemed to be a resistance to my movements. I concentrated on seeing myself opening the door and escaping this watery pit. I touched the bottom and moved my hand around to find the outline of the door. I did so just as the limit of my lungs was being reached. With a finger on the keyhole to guide me I inserted the key and turned it. The door opened downward and the water rushed out pulling me along with it along a circular pipe. My lungs had passed their capacity and were forcing my mouth to open to take in something, water or air. I emerged from the pipe at some speed, flipped over so I was travelling upright and upside-down and trying to cram air into my lungs at the same time. I hit the wall with enough force to drive the breath from my body as I slid slowly down and stopped in a bed of damp comfortable moss looking at my back and legs still stuck to the wall.

My feet were much faster to understand than my brain. They moved sideways and I was off the wall, upright and running before I was conscious of the scratching of claws, grunting and snarling echoing from behind me. The rest of me caught up and I realized that Mr. Hennessey might want me to arrive alive to have his fun, but Action Group 5 wanted me dead now.

18

ACTION GROUP 5 were not the only group operating in the shadows across the systems and I was deep in the territory of one of them running for my life. I had crossed paths with The Parallelogram years before when Arran Sindar and I had broken into their library. The Parallelogram had some class of religious devotion to the Empress Ingea and they were fantastically well funded. What interested me was the fact that they also had a deep interest in Brewing and had the biggest collection of information in the systems on the topic. Access to this archive was by invitation only and the only lifeforms invited were also top-ranking members of The Parallelogram.

Arran wanted access to some of the secrets of The Parallelogram for reasons he never shared any more than I shared mine with him. He had managed to steal the identity of a suitable member and had patiently worked his way into getting an invitation to the library. There was a problem, what Arran wanted was not in the library and he needed a warm presence in the library to cover for him while he got on with his real work. We had encountered each other in an air vent where I was lying still trying not to attract the attention of a security patrol on the other side of the thin metal cover. A foot tapped me on the head followed by a comms cord. Having no choice, I plugged it in and Arran introduced himself. We chatted for the next two hours.. In the course of the conversation Arran probed me gently about the possibility of breaching The Parallelogram. I agreed to join him, and we spent the rest of the time settling some details.

Arran would bring me into the library inside the aura of his notetaker. Any security check would register two lifeforms, when Arran departed on his mission I would step out and two life-forms would remain in place in the library. It has no possibility of succeeding given that it was exactly the sort of plan that any self-respecting security organization would be planning against. Arran had a secret weapon. He was a lucky man, when it counted circumstances favoured him and he was sure that would do so this time. I was desperate enough to agree, absolutely no other way of getting in had appeared.

At the agreed time I met the notetaker, a two-meter-tall skin covered skeleton who wore a dark green full-length cloak and hood. Silently it lifted the cloak with one arm and ducking under it I entered the space. If I could have jumped back out instantly I would have done so, it stank. I could feel the stink settling on my skin and hair as I crouched to fit. The notetaker had an awkward gait and I was rattled in the space. I heard Arran's voice as he joined us, I could not distinguish the words. We walked for an unknown length of time before we started to climb a set of stairs. Then we stopped for the first security audit.

When I heard the sniffle of the guard hounds, I was suddenly grateful for the stink, it covered me completely making me invis-ible to their searching nostrils. Some more movements later and the notetaker opened the cloak and I fell out onto the floor of the most beautiful room I have ever seen. The walls and domed roof were all Airshire glass that shed comforting light while calming colours flowed around them. The floor was real, actual grown in the earth wood, polished and slightly ward to the touch. Individual reading desks with wooden privacy screens were grouped in a circular area in the centre, a stunning spiral of shelves packed with books, manuscripts, loose pages, maps, technical drawings and academic journals. An army of locators stick like bodies, tiny heads and extra-long arms and legs scurried all over the shelves getting and replacing documents requested by readers.

I sat at a desk and gave my list to the retriever who appeared as I sat. I buried myself in the documents and completely forgot about Arran until an armed response team burst into the room and the notetaker grabbed me by the collar and dragged me to the ground. Following the notetaker and keeping as low as possible I moved as quickly as I could towards a small gap in the shelves that I would swear had not been there before. I fell into a large tunnel and saw a body fall into it just ahead of me. That body landed on its feet, turned and waved me forward and started running. I followed it as I could hear a full-scale security alert rising above us. We reached a fork and we took the left-hand turn. The notetaker stopped, dropped the cloak to reveal that it was heavily armed. I heard the blast of bolts as I ran and finally, we reached and passed the boundary of The Parallelogram's location. Arran threw a charm down and we stepped out into a quiet alley off a busy street. Arran nodded to me and took off in one direction while went another. That is how we both earned permanent places on The Parallelogram's shit list and also that when Action Group 5 had dumped me there to be killed they had managed to be too clever for their own good.

Large predators are territorial, intrusions by another large predator into their hunting ground is serious and get a serious response. If The Parallelogram got the idea that I was an agent of Action Group 5 my current break-in along with my previous incursion would have a very different context. They would want to talk to me before they killed me. The problem I had was being taken alive, the standard approach was to kill any intruder and ask questions later. I had to convince them to capture me rather than kill me. Begging Lanken for a wisp of Arran's luck I tapped my comms unit and spoke.

"Cleanblood, cleanblood, extraction needed over" Silence, wait for three heartbeats and repeat. Cleanblood was an old Action Group 5 call sign that I knew they had abandoned after it got leaked into the wild. Action Group 5 would ignore it which was important; I did not want more of their attention. The Parallelogram probably knew that it was an abandoned call sign, but they would want to know why I was using it. The various groups were always probing each other, and someone would want to be sure about who I was. I was in the middle of repeating the call when I was netted from above, swept off my feet and up into a restraint pod. Immobilised in complete darkness I was emptied into a bare cell with no doors or windows. Fuck, this was a problem I did not have the time for. I needed to get to the central control room in the next minute or Petra might be lost forever. I needed to escalate the situation dramatically, have enough value to be pulled out of isolation into an impromptu interrogation.

All those hours spent imagining myself in difficult situations and how I would creatively get out of them were going to finally pay off. I knew it was not just idle dreaming no matter what that sliver of my mind told me. I put my left hand to my mouth and bit into the fleshy base of my thumb. It hurt a great deal, but I cracked the capsule I had implanted there. Instantly tendrils of blue and green smoke started to rise from my body and my breathing and heartbeat stopped. The response was everything I could have hoped for. The walls of the cell disappeared and a lifeform in a hazmat suit ran to me and stabbed me in the back of my hand with a needle attached to a small glass bottle. My lungs and hears started again, I let go of my hand and spat out some blood. I was wrapped in a blocking blanket, pushed into a wheelchair and taken at speed to the main control room where the shift commander was waiting.

Captured agents from any group have their own distinctive suicide protocols, this is done as a final Fuck You to whoever captured them, making clear that they have just lost a valuable asset. I had just mimicked the Action Group 5 protocol, much better proof than an obsolete call sign. I was pushed at speed along a number of blank corridors before we entered one that had windows on the right-hand side showing into offices where staff worked in cubicles. None looked up as we rushed past. The next corridor we turned int ended with a pair of security doors with an array of scanners mounted above them. We stopped in front of the doors while the scanners ran a check on us. I could feel the faint tickle of charms as the examination was carried out. I was sure that they had traces of me from the last time and they were being checked and organized for the shift commander. The doors opened and I was wheeled into the command room. The shift commander was standing beside her desk and looking directly at me. All of The Parallelogram's staff were naturals and she was a nice example. Standing two meters tall, with black hair, green eyes, high cheekbones, perfect nose and full lips she was a testament to carefully regulated breeding. Not even remotely the same thing as bottle breeding, I hasten to point out, absolutely no points of comparison I have been told more often than I could ever count.

The commander waved at me and I was pulled up out of the chair and the blocking blanket was removed. I farted. It was an appalling fart, I could tell from the damage it did on the way out. All the Naturals in the room dropped to the floor or slumped at their stations as the stench did its work. I now had ninety seconds to act. I stepped over the commander, thumbed the emergency button which isolated the command centre. It was very kind of her to have left her terminal open for me. I keyed in the tracker code into the terminal and located the final signal. Sent the coordinated to the transfer station across the room and then released a worm into the system. The Parallelogram had really nice equipment, the best I had ever come across and it was a shame to wreck it, still I did not want to have them following me or to be retaining any details about me at all in fact.

The transfer station was the way The Parallelogram send staff to a desired location and I stepped into it and found myself somewhere that I recognized at the smuggler's niche where Jovial had made his attempt on me. The worm must have kept the station active as the blast in the control room smashed pieces of equipment into the wall beside me.

This location made sense. Action Group 5 would have been very interested in someone with Jovial's skills and had used him to their advantage. Jovial was as slippery as they and would have known there was more going on than was being shared. He'd have tracked them here, which explained why Jovial jumped me here—because there was a power source he was drawing on, not a smuggler's niche but an interstellar portal. The rules were simple: more work needed more energy, and more energy needed a bigger charm. Whole buildings were set up as charms to provide enough energy for the required work. The big barrier was interstellar work, for which a system charm would provide coverage, but the charm had to be so big as to be wholly obvious. Breeding Stations were in interstellar space and of a suitable size. They were active transit points for all sorts of traffic, all of which carefully went unnoticed by the other. The portal in front was an entry point to this network and all I needed to do was activate it.

I stood in front of the portal and remembered that the last time I was here I had died after Jovial had launched his attack. The attack was not random; it had been triggered by the location. Jovial would not have been given an access code, he was a singular talent with biological charms using one to hack the access was just a theoretically impossible as the rest of his work. I was guessing that there was a key to the portal somewhere around the location that looked like an entirely natural part of the local flora and fauna. The problem was that there were no actually natural creatures or plants here in the shitpots. If they were when they strayed into the drains by accident staying here warped them after a short while and a couple of generation rendered, then something completely new. I was going to have search Jovial for what I needed.

I was sure that Jovial had been neutralised after the fight in the bottle farm he was still a tricky fucker and there was the possibility that he still had something in reserve. Muttering "Shit or bust" I reached for him and stepped into his memories. Using the sight of the location and the details I could see of the location as a filter I tried to steer directly to the relevant memories. There were a lot, I found out that Jovial had suspected that there was something useful here and had crafted a series of very small creatures to track visitors from the farm to the location. All of his spies were destroyed at the portal by the defences that were activated by whoever was using it. It was a broad spectrum defence, it simply eliminates anything that could be a threat.

Jovial identified that the defence had a threat threshold, any creature was eliminated, the simple plants that grew there were unmolested. I also discovered that nothing excited Jovial like a challenge, he set about developing a suitable plant life that would also be a camouflage for his probing. With my own limited knowledge of brewing I could appreciate just how extraordinary Jovial was, the work he did was astounding. A damp stain that covered the walls of the niche was actually various strains of a, barely, multi-cellular plant that had reached sufficient physical mass to act as a passive recorder of the actions of every lifeform that passed through the portal. I had my key now I just needed to turn it in the lock.

I stepped into the niche and taking a glove off my right hand placed it on the correct spot to get the information. Jovial had no idea whose physical body he would be using so the key was not encrypted. The code blossomed in my mind and I felt the cold power as the portal activated and I stepped through to the other side. I was standing in a wide corridor that six lifeforms could comfortably stroll side-by-side down, without brushing walls. The walls, floor and ceiling were mottled gray, with webs of barely visible cracks scattered randomly on every surface. The most visible feature was Mr. Hennessey pinned to the wall by a metal spear with a finely etched wooden handle half as long as the blade. The handle had a rope attached to it so the spear could be pulled out from the prey and used again. He was very dead, his head hanging, and his feet resting in a puddle of blood that had dripped down the wall. The weapon that had fired the spear was across the corridor from where he was pinned, probably set to fire when he'd emerged. Wholly mechanical, he'd not have had advance warning.

Petra and the Jewel Box were gone, so I assumed that they'd been taken by whoever had been waiting for the delivery. As there was no track to follow, one direction looked as good as the other. I started to run. The corridor continued with regular openings on the sides. I stayed in the main one, since I saw nothing to tempt me down any of the others. With my Running-Man shoes, I was fast, I ran for two hours, but saw nothing, just an unchanging corridor until I came across a piece of wood sticking out of a wall opposite the weapon that had fired it. I was back where I'd started. The difference: the body appeared to have been absorbed into the wall. This was a labyrinth ... a carnivorous labyrinth.

As I realized where I actually was, the muscles in my left thigh started to pulse and my right arm started to spasm. Every sentient lifeform in the systems knew about the carnivorous labyrinth; it ate everything that came into it, as it was designed to do. Touch any surface and you'd stick to it, pulled under the surface. Cut your hand off and bleed on the floor, and your feet sank under you even faster. With Running-Man shoes, you'd float above the surface; it would wait till you dropped from hunger, thirst, or exhaustion. This was the belt around the Sickle

Quadrant, the loop that kept whatever was on the inside from getting outside ... the lock on the prison.

The Sickle Quadrant was the Empress' Plan B. She'd been fleeing here when she was stopped, planning on opening the lock and unleashing the contents on the systems. If she couldn't have the Empire, then no one could. Most inhabitants of the systems assumed that the prisoners of the Sickle Quadrant were other lifeforms, designed for destruction and chaos, but still recognizable as lifeforms. They weren't; they were sentient biological weapons, self-directing diseases that consumed and re-grew their hosts for unknown lengths of time. No one knew how they travelled or interacted, or how they did anything beyond what was in the scattered note found in the Red Halls. That information had been enough to frighten everyone who'd read it, required reading for every elected politician and appointed bureaucrat above a set seniority level in every system.

There'd been plenty who saw opportunity, but none had ever been able to open the lock. Those too open with their thoughts had been dispatched to explore the labyrinth. Now, I was here and so was my daughter, and I had no clue how to find her. I could spend a dozen lifetimes chasing down every corridor and still have only searched a fraction. I kicked out so hard that I turned upside-down, suspended in the air, staring at the weapon that killed Mr. Hennessey. I noticed a fine thread hanging from the underside of the weapon. It fell to the floor.

Whoever had set up the weapon needed a path back to where they'd come from. A thread tied to a fixed point that unspooled as the weapon fell into place would serve that purpose.

I raced with the thread in soft grasp. Corridors and turns evolved into more corridors and more turns. I could have easily been running in one tight circle, but the thread kept me going. I turned a corner and found myself in a room I recognised with a sick feeling knowing just how far out of my depth I really was. I had seen images of this room virtually every day that I had worked at the Historical Centre, I had guided tours through a reproduction carefully spouting guestimates about the role of the room in the history of the systems. It was the throne room of the empire, the room Empress Ingea had used as her command centre. It was the heart of the war and the most famous missing room in history.

When the Quill Alliance forces breached the Red Halls, it was not just the Empress who was gone, the entire throne room was gone as well. The ornate desk made from granulated shiverwood that grew one tree at a time in the icy caverns of Despai. The oval conference table carved from the single largest gem ever pulled from the gravity well at the outer fringe of the systems. The twelve matching chairs made from the bones of the still unidentified energy bearing species that could not be successfully farmed and so were exterminated. Most of all was the throne itself where Ingea sat when she issued the orders for the destruction of Ranyor and the astounding strategic sweep that brought her to within a hairsbreadth of victory.

The throne was a mystery, there was no information about where it had come from, who made it or how they made it. There was speculation that the same artist who had created the picture that hung in the Historical Centre also created the throne. It was possible; it was an equal masterpiece of controlled magic. It was composed entirely of light, shimmering light that moved in hypnotic patters to compel awe and adoration of whoever was sitting in it. Petra was seated on it and I could feel the compulsion to bow and obey her engulf me.

Petra was wearing the same uniform that the Empress wore in the picture and on her head was a silver framework that held the firestones taken from the Jewel Box lying on the floor at her feet. Tied to the back of the chair with his head up so I could see the frozen ecstasy on his face above his slit throat was the Director of the Historical Centre. His blood had poured down the back of the chair and Petra was sitting in a pool of it. Petra saw me and I could feel the power inside her, amplified by the throne and the firestones, the force of her scream threw me out of the room and beyond the reach of the throne. "Daddy help me", the cry ignited the lifetime of held down rage that I had tried so hard to contain.

The Shoshone Circlet rippled and twist around my neck and I felt it ride my rage to fill every cell of my body. I stood up and blinked and my eyesight changed, I was seeing more than just the throne room now, I could see what was going on somewhere outside the room. Before the chair, a shape formed—a doorway like the entrance to the Red Halls. I could see through it, up a shiny path to a figure in the distance that appeared to be climbing down a ladder from the sun. There was no mistaking who was coming down that ladder, even at the distance I could recognize the figure from the image in the Historical Centre. Empress Ingea was returning to claim her Empire. She was going to slip into Petra like a stiletto and finish her long-delayed plans.

The voice was deep, clear. "This won't do." The only lifeform who could have spoken was me and it was not my voice, not anything like my voice. I was sure that my vocal cords could not have produced that voice. It was coming from the Circlet. The voice spoke again making sounds I am sure were a language, but I have no idea what they were. It was clear that it was a vocal charm, yet another impossibility for my list and a charm of terrifying power. My body was not intended to support the power that was flowing around it, I was dissolving in it like ice crystals in warm water. Then I was frozen, and the power coursed through me without touching me. The Circlet needed me to remain complete to serve its purposes.

A dragon filled the chamber and the Sickle Quadrant ... it filled the combined systems. Gold, black, and silver patterned scales held writing on each. Translucent wings spread across bone crossbeams that fractured the light and shed rainbows. A long ferocious head held a square jaw and flaring nostrils that emitted dense white smoke. A long tail ended with upright spikes and six squat legs displayed needle-sharp talons arching from the toes. It was so big there was no way I could have seen more than an incomprehensible detail, yet I could see it all and comprehend its appalling majesty. My brain refused to try and compute the problem and simply accepted what was in front of me. Dragons were the fever dream of FireDrakes.

"A dragon? Of all the fucking cli..." This was very much my own voice, I discovered that there was actually a limit to what I was willing to accept without a fight. I didn't complete the sentence because I noticed it hadn't seen me. The bright golden eyes, set in a ridge where the head joined the body, were focused elsewhere. I realized with a hammer blow of knowledge that there are predators in the far depths of space, far beyond the furthest reaches of puny explorations. And delicious morsels like myself should not attract their attention.

The dragon snorted, flicked its talons, knocked the silver framework onto the ground scattering the firestones. It disappeared, as did the doorway to wherever Empress Ingea had been hiding, waiting for faithful servants to call her home. The firestones by themselves weren't enough to bridge a gap; they needed power from an autonomous energy-rich being, so they'd set about creating one. Such patient dedication was as frightening as the Sickle Quadrant itself, but I'd pissed in their faces. An energy bolt hit me between the shoulder blades and flung me forward, the Running-Man shoes saved my balance, and I swung around to see what was attacking me.

I wasn't surprised to find Philbean, his hideous face contorted with rage and shock. He'd been chosen as the first servant to greet the Empress upon her return, to serve as the footstool that she'd stand on to survey the new domain. I'd closed the door to that ambition, and he was pretty upset— enough to forget how to win a fight. He merely wanted to smash me and hurled himself at me with that intention. Philbean was bigger, faster and much stronger than me, with sharp teeth and a powerful jaw; if he got close enough, he'd rip me to pieces.

Philbean slammed into me and we sailed across the chamber, slamming into the ground outside one of the entrances. His strong tail clutched my legs in a painful grip and his left arm pushed me down while his right hand yanked away his head-dress so he could close in with that jaw. His mistake was to leave my arms free. All I had to reach was the arm he was holding me with and slap the pack against it. The mechanism worked and I jammed a needle into his flesh, injecting the payload into his blood and bone. Philbean had enough time to look surprised before the takeover was complete, and he fell off me.

I righted myself with effort and went over to Petra, still tied and sporting a tiny smile. As I unbound her, she whispered into my ear. "I wasn't afraid, because I knew you'd come."

I didn't confess that I was afraid enough for the entire systems population; instead, I kissed her blood-smeared cheek. She hugged me tightly and I wanted to stay there in that warm embrace for eternity. There was more to do, and her mother would welcome a hug as well, so I ruffled her hair and smiled encouragingly. "I have to get the lifeform over there into this chair. Would you like to help?"

Petra nodded and slid an arm tightly around my waist as we walked over to Philbean. He'd curled up tightly, his tail pressed between his legs. He was surprisingly light for a large lifeform, a sign that the process was speedily advancing. We had no trouble lifting him and dragged him to the chair and, with a bit of effort, managed to place him in it with his tail hanging out behind. Carefully, I fastened him, making sure to put his head in the centre of the circle.

I picked up two firestones and pushed the others, along with the Jewel Box , between his feet. Philbean had to have used another portal to get here; there was no way that the Empress was going to enter via a sewer, so it had to be relatively easy to find. It was. Down the first entrance was a glowing carpet with swirling colours, the work of the same artist who'd created the picture in the Centre for the Promotion of Historical Knowledge. We stepped onto it ... and into a large, beautifully furnished apartment that had a dizzying view over Mengchi.

It was a fitting spot for an Empress to arrive and survey her subjects unannounced before revealing her presence and their future. I sent Petra off to find the wet room and get cleaned up and thought about revenge and justice. I rolled up the carpet and put it in the decomposer. It hurt to destroy such a beautiful work of art, but I needed to close the labyrinth door.

When I had (mistakenly) thought I could stop the pursuit of Asher and Petra with my death, I'd had a problem: how to remain dead beyond the reach of those who'd try to bring me back. It had to be clearly *me* who was dead, not a copy or a decoy. This was more difficult that it might seem—after thousands of years of bringing back the dead, or parts of the dead, increasingly smaller parts were required. Any tissue or blood from the deceased, sufficient enough to secure identification, could be used to recreate the whole body, which could then be "awoken".

In particular, all Bottle-Born lifeforms had to be constructed, so this quantity of tissue or blood contained had to ensure prior knowledge of the deceased was available to be explored. As far as I knew, this was more uncertain for natural-born lifeforms. The problem I faced was that I needed to be identified, which required tissue or blood to be positive; it would then give my pursuers everything they wanted. Unless I had to poison that tissue or blood so it was valid for identification, but no one would want to develop it in any way. My blood had to be both information and a threat.

Which lead to the only possible solution: a creature that came from the Screaming Forest. No one knew if it existed before the forest, or if it was part of the transformation process. A parasite that slowly travelled in the arteries of the trees, devouring their hosts until they burst open, spraying seeds all around. In each sticky seed lay a new parasite, ready to feast and grow. They possessed too much potential to be ignored. I had no idea what was done to eventually extract them from the forest, only that it was successful.

They were examined, cultured, altered, mixed, and bred until there was a weapon that could be pushed directly into a host; they'd multiply between heartbeats, so they were in every part of the host. As bones and organs, the host became much lighter than they'd originally been. My pursuers would have seen the package sticking in my arm and known it for what it was.

Extracting a sample at a carefully managed distance would be possible, identifying me would be easy, and replicating me would simply be a replication of the parasites as well. They'd seal me up and carry me to the edges of the systems and jettison me off into the depths of space to finally die.

That was the exquisite refinement added to the final mix: the host didn't die but lived with the agony of internal feasting that never killed. Death only came when another host entered range. The presence of a new donor caused the parasites to swarm and burst out of the host to take up residence elsewhere. In the depths of my guilt at deserting Asher and Petra, I'd thought I deserved the punishment of the unending life and agony I'd experience until, finally, I could no longer sustain the cloud and we all expired.

Philbean who had been ready to sacrifice my daughter was now waiting for someone to come so he could die, afraid that the next lifeform to come close would be the Empress, freed to enter the embrace of the cloud. I myself had always tried to avoid either revenge or justice; both were too cold, now I had embraced both and was glad to do so...

Petra arrived, looking lively, dressed in colourful robes. She looked clean and refreshed, and happy. We found a well-stocked kitchen and I organized a quick meal, which I ate while cleaning up. The wet room was on the same scale as the kitchen and I enjoyed the luxury. Collecting Petra, the two of us descended to the ground floor and made our way to the transport station. We went to the safe house Lincoln had recommended, because returning to her space was stupidly dangerous.

At the space, all was quiet, no warfare or combat to be seen or heard. I entered the code, had my eye scanned, and the door opened.

Strolling in, I spun and extended my arms. "Honey, we are officially *home*."

Dear reader,

We hope you enjoyed reading *Bottle Born Blues*. Please take a moment to leave a review, even if it's a short one. Your opinion is important to us.

Discover more books by Conor H. Carton at

https://www.nextchapter.pub/authors/conor-h-carton

Want to know when one of our books is free or discounted? Join the newsletter at

http://eepurl.com/bqqB3H

Best regards,

Conor H. Carton and the Next Chapter Team

ABOUT THE AUTHOR

Conor Carton has a lifelong ambition: to be the greatest space pirate cowboy outlaw wizard in the universe!

Writing is part of the rigorous mental and physical preparation he is undergoing to achieve this goal. In the meanwhile, he's an Irish middle-aged suburbanite who has been married to the same wonderfully understanding woman for decades and has a daughter he adores.

You might also like
Glad You're Born by Scott Michael Decker

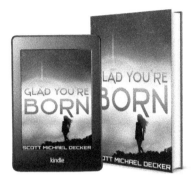

To read the first chapter for free, please head to:
https://www.nextchapter.pub/books/glad-youre-born

Bottle Born Blues
ISBN: 978-4-86752-667-5

Published by
Next Chapter
1-60-20 Minami-Otsuka
170-0005 Toshima-Ku, Tokyo
+818035793528

5th August 2021